HEIR TO
STONEMOOR

HEIR TO STONEMOOR

Kay Stephens

SEVERN
SH
HOUSE

This first world edition published in Great Britain 1995 by
SEVERN HOUSE PUBLISHERS LTD of
9–15 High Street, Sutton, Surrey SM1 1DF.
First published in the USA 1995 by
SEVERN HOUSE PUBLISHERS INC of
595 Madison Avenue, New York, NY 10022.

British Library Cataloguing in Publication Data
Stephens, Kay
  Heir to Stonemoor
  I. Title
  823.914 [F]

  ISBN 0-7278-4847-X

Typeset by Hewer Text Composition Services, Edinburgh.
Printed and bound in Great Britain by
Hartnolls Limited, Bodmin, Cornwall

Chapter One

"We have something to tell you, Tania."

Her father's words made her look up sharply from the table. Andre's grave expression destroyed her appetite, but she must not waste her portion of the roast lamb that was their week's meat ration.

Tania had been expecting trouble. Stonemoor House was big, but not so large that she could avoid hearing the arguments occurring repeatedly between Andre and her stepmother. She gazed towards Pamela now and steeled herself for the terrible news which seemed to be forecast in the awkwardness apparent in those normally direct blue eyes.

"We decided you must be the first to be told," her stepmother said huskily, and her eyes glossed over with unshed tears.

Somewhere deep inside her, Tania was weeping already, hurt by the irony that they should all be torn apart now – hadn't she put everything she had got into accepting her father's second marriage?

From the day of the ceremony Tania had willed herself to acknowledge how much Andre Malinowski needed Pamela. She had given her heart as well as her mind to welcoming the kindness and the concern

1

which that talented woman had shown unfailingly towards *her*.

The fact that they both were hesitating now seemed only to confirm that the news was grim. Tania glanced away from her father's serious grey eyes, and saw that Pamela's neat head of golden waves suddenly was bowed. She could endure this suspense no longer.

"Well?" she prompted.

The other two exchanged a look, she noticed the slight nod that her father gave, and his wife's deep inhalation that preceded her words.

"You're going to have a brother or sister, Tania love. I'm expecting a baby."

"Oh, I am thankful! That is so good." The girl sprang off her chair and ran to where they were seated near the head of the long table. No one heeded the mint sauce that she overturned on the polished mahogany as relief made her hasten to congratulate them.

She hugged Pamela first and read in her father's eyes the warm approval for which she would sacrifice a great deal. When it was his turn for a hug he smiled before kissing her.

"I am delighted that our news thrills you as much as it exhilarates the two of us, Tania. Since the day I asked Pamela to become my wife I have been praying that this should be granted."

"We shall be a real family, I think," Tania said, her voice strongly accented as always when emotions were stirred. She remained standing between them and grasped a shoulder on either side of her. "It is not good for there to be only one daughter or son. I hope that it will not matter too much that I am so

2

much older. But then, perhaps the new little person will have younger siblings one day . . .?"

Pamela grinned. "Let's get the first one here, shall we, before you go putting in requests for more. I'm new to this game, remember, and not exactly youthful." She had been thirty last birthday.

"But you *are*," Tania insisted, carried on by that immense relief. "You cannot have forgotten how you and I seem just like sisters."

Andre was beaming at them both, love evident in the width of his smile and the gleam of emotion in his grey eyes.

Pamela ran an affectionate hand over her step-daughter's long fair hair. "I couldn't be more pleased you're glad about our news, love. And you must remember always that no matter how many other children we might have, you'll remain a very special person. To both of us."

It was a glorious Sunday for January and when they had cleared away the remainder of the meal, which all three of them were too elated to appreciate, they set out to walk.

The sun felt warm, despite the wind gusting across the Yorkshire moors to bend the few trees on the horizon, as they tramped uphill towards Stoodley Pike. As their view of the stone obelisk, built to mark the end of the Napoleonic wars, grew more distinct, Tania unfastened the scarf that Pamela still insisted she must wear. They all had suffered attacks of the flu, one after the other, taking to their beds while no one was recovered sufficiently to have much energy for nursing. Pamela's mother Mildred had stayed over several nights, cosseting

3

and comforting, and reminding Tania yet again of her own beloved grandmother and those far distant days in Russia.

It was Pamela, though, who had continued the concern when Tania's cough had refused to respond to the doctor's medicine. It was Pamela, also, who had emphasized that a singer's voice was too valuable to be jeopardized by neglect.

"I know you think I'm fussing, but I shan't be satisfied until I stop hearing you clearing that throat."

The long walks in the country air had been Andre's idea, but it was her stepmother again who had ensured that Tania kept them up. She does love me, the girl had understood and had felt warmth permeate her whole being.

That Pamela often made the time for walking with her meant a lot to her stepdaughter. Unlike any other woman Tania had known, Pamela ran her own business. Her skill in renovating and decorating was evident throughout every room of Stonemoor House, but now the company that she had built up worked on public buildings as well as private houses.

Only since her father had remarried had Tania realized how fortunate they were that success in Pamela's career produced a special satisfaction that overflowed to embrace both Andre and his daughter. And now Tania could at last forget those arguments which, in recent weeks, had alarmed her. However vociferous the disturbance, it could be dismissed in the light of this wonderful news. United in looking forward to the child they were expecting, her father and his wife would continue to provide the security that had become life at Stonemoor.

"How soon will you stop working so hard?" Tania asked Pamela as she walked at her side, while they skirted a wood leading up from meadows. There seemed no reason now to disguise the fact that she had been aware of the source of the discord between Andre and his bride.

"I'm easing off already," Pamela told her, and sensed Andre observing her keenly. "But it's early days yet, and I do have a business to run. I haven't built Canning's up so successfully only to let it decline through neglect."

"But Ian helps, doesn't he, and he is very good. You've said so yourself."

Pamela smiled. "I'm not denying any of that. But that brother of mine's only – let me see . . . We're into 1949 now, aren't we? Then he'll soon be eighteen. Only about your age, love."

"But if he does a man's work— " Tania began.

Her father interrupted with a laugh. "That is not quite enough, my sweet. Before assuming authority a person must gain experience, and more than a little wisdom."

Tania groaned. "You would say that, naturally. Always, you are determined to keep young people down. Do you really believe that we remain as childen for such a very long time?"

Smiling rather ruefully, Andre regarded this tall, elegant daughter of his who looked much older than she was, with her long tresses tucked inside the collar of the fashionable New Look coat that Pamela had helped her to select.

"No. No. I am more aware than you think of the maturity that increases with each day. All the same, this world of ours is still a difficult place, no one should be overeager to face its realities."

Only this past week he had been outraged to read of the jailing in Hungary of Cardinal Mindszenty. It seemed from the show trial staged by the Communists there, that the sort of oppression experienced in his own native Russia was spreading.

Tania gave him a look. "When you speak in this way you make me think that you would have me become frivolous!"

He laughed and shook his head at her. "Not while you must still work hard to establish your career. But, singing aside, there is no harm in remaining carefree enough to enjoy life. As long as you can."

"I will remind you of that the next time you forbid me to appear with Ian's band," Tania retorted.

"Stop provoking each other, you two!" Pamela exclaimed. "You're as bad as she is, Andre. We're going to make a list of taboo subjects."

"What is taboo?" Tania asked, her accent thickening.

"Yes, what is it?" Andre echoed.

"Something that's unmentionable," Pamela told them, trying to keep a straight face.

"Sex, you mean? Is taboo another word for sex?" asked Tania with pretended innocence. "Taboo, taboo, taboo!"

"Now you sound all of five years old," Andre reproved her, but his grey eyes danced with amusement.

He was glad of silly moments of this kind. For too many years life had been serious, a grave struggle to accept that the cruellest loss must be endured.

Nothing would ever prevent him from looking back to the death of his Anichka, but thanks to his new wife there now was a future to consider, and for his beloved Tania, a mother substitute. There had been other losses though, earlier in his life, freedoms that had vanished. He must never overlook the harm that was done when choices were denied an entire nation.

"I know you were upset by Cardinal Mindszenty's sentence, that it reminded you of bad things in Russia," said Tania, serious now. "But there has been good news also. Only today we have heard that Norway is to join the North Atlantic pact."

Andre nodded and put an arm around his daughter's waist. "Ah, so. Perhaps we may anticipate a more lasting peace for your future."

"And for the little one's," Tania added. "When is the baby due?" she asked Pamela.

"Not for ages yet. Quite late in August."

"Poor you!" Tania exclaimed. "You will be huge through all the hottest months of the summer. I think you will feel exhausted."

"But long before then you will not be working," Andre observed.

Pamela gave him a look and disciplined the urge to argue. They had been so happy today, she must not spoil everything.

That night in bed, however, unable to sleep, the old debate resurrected. And now with Tania's endorsement of her father's wishes to supplement his appeal.

"You heard what Tania said," he reminded her quite sharply. "I'm not the only one who is concerned about you, and for the well-being of the child you carry. Can you not, if only to humour us, learn to delegate – let someone else shoulder the responsibility? Most of all, have someone other than yourself do the actual physical work."

"Oh, Andre – not again. I've promised to let up. I'm not going to abandon Canning's, though, how can I? You know what I'm like – I need my work."

"You have me now, and Tania, this massive house . . ." Andre wondered, not for the first time, if his resentment of the company she owned was partly on account of its name. Jim Canning had been her first husband. He was afraid this reluctance to relinquish control could indicate that Pamela was unwilling to consign him to the past.

"And doesn't everything about Stonemoor House remind you just occasionally of how I relish making a place look beautiful?"

"You know it does, all the time. But it is as a home that you created these lovely surroundings, I wish that you could be content simply to live here."

Here we go again, thought Pamela wearily. At times, she wished with all her heart that she could experience that contentment. She often admitted to herself that her own feelings seemed irrational. Andre was interesting company and his work as a classical violinist meant that he was here with her far more than many a husband might be.

"Content, Pamela . . ." he persisted.

"As Anichka would have been."

"Why do you say that? Comparisons are indeed odious, when have you ever heard me make them?"

"Not in so many words, I suppose. But you make them to yourself, and I *know*. You do not have to say that she would be content here. You have told me already, bit by bit, in details of your old life. Of the way that she devoted herself to you, and to your interests, travelling wherever you performed. I'm only sorry that I'm not like that. But this is the way I am – I can't deny my own ambitions." Pamela paused, sighing. "Even for you, my darling, even for you."

They had let the matter rest there, and Pamela was relieved. Now that she knew for certain that Tania had been aware of this contention she felt doubly guilty about her determination to continue working for as long as she was able. She needed to have Canning's on the firmest possible ground by the time this pregnancy obliged her to hand over the reins. No one, least of all Andre, seemed to understand that she was compelled to look ahead, several years ahead, and to ensure that nothing be allowed to jeopardize the business that she had built up since that dreadful time when Jim was killed.

It would be a further three years before she could even consider Ian as her potential successor. Ted Burrows was a reliable foreman, but she had no real desire to make him the manager. There was no alternative to keeping the running of the firm within her own hands.

The fact that she couldn't as yet visualize how that might be achieved did not trouble her unduly now. If being left a widow at the end of the war, with a business that had lapsed as her only interest, had not defeated her, these difficulties would not. Despite all that he said, Andre was a reasonable man, and would never permit their differences to cloud their love. Any more than she herself would. She had loved him so long when there seemed no hope, she'd not let anything spoil their life now that they had this good relationship.

Pamela met up with her brother at the steps of the hall they had all but finished renovating. Ian grinned, and ran up the stone stairs ahead of her. He knew nothing of the baby she was carrying, and she doubted whether knowing would have made him pause to assist with the large cans of paint that she had taken from her van. As a worker, she had proved herself the equal of most men.

In some ways, she regretted her need to keep the news of her condition from Ian. He was a likeable lad, this brother who always reminded her of the father they had lost while he was small. By contrast with her younger brother, Tom, Ian sometimes appeared quite cocky. His assurance, however, was not entirely assumed and was rooted in enough competence to mean that when he eventually matured he should become her able successor.

For the present, though, the status quo must be maintained, and that could only be so, if none of her workforce realized that her grasp of the firm would temporarily be relinquished.

Ted was there before them that morning, organizing the three casual labourers who had been brought in to help with these final stages of redecoration. The doors had been grained carefully by Pamela herself, and the men were now applying varnish.

She looked around the main hall in which they were standing, nodding approval now that the coloured walls were looking bright as well as clean.

"What do you think, Ian?"

"It's smashing. Every bit as good as that first hall we redecorated. And it's going to be finished to time, an' all. By, but it'll look grand for our concert."

"Tania said to tell you that she'll be here all right, for the dress rehearsal."

"Her dad's consented again then?"

Pamela grinned. "Grudgingly, as usual. Still, she's happy now. And Tania deserves a bit of her own way, she does work hard the rest of the time."

"Has she got that booking to sing with the orchestra in Leeds?"

"Oh, yes. Andre's delighted. Especially because she refused to use their relationship to influence them. She even adopted a different surname for the audition."

"Really? But it isn't as if his violin solos could tell anyone anything about the standard of her voice."

"Even so. I gather she enjoyed revealing who she was as soon as they confirmed that she'd made the grade."

"He's playing with the same orchestra, isn't he?"

"But on a different night. I'm going to be spending a lot of time driving around to concert halls to support them both." She couldn't help feeling thankful that by the time she became heavily pregnant the concert season would be over until the following winter.

Ian had been getting ready to work while they talked, Pamela was glad that he never gave her a moment's anxiety concerning his dedication, these days. Those occasions when he had taken advantage of being her brother were behind them now. When the time came, he would make the kind of boss who would lead by example.

She liked to think that she herself had always done just that. Certainly, there had been little past evidence of workers complaining that she expected more of them than she herself would tackle. Which was just as well: there could be enough resentment generated through having a woman for their boss. And there was nothing she could do to alter that fact.

Today, Pamela's role was one she enjoyed. The supervisory angle was a part, but mainly she was here to decorate the stage that was a feature of this central hall. The popular band with which Ian played the saxophone was one of many performers for whom this stage provided a platform. A cheerful background had been requested and, conferring with the owners, Pamela had persuaded them to accept her idea of giving the back wall a scene reminiscent of a Claude Monet painting.

Her youngest brother Tom, now doing artwork for one of the Yorkshire magazines, had helped to get her thoughts down on to paper. Armed with his watercolour sketch of meadows, a suggestion of full-leafed trees, and an expanse of dappled sky, she was eager to begin.

As always while she worked, Pamela's mind seemed divided. On one plane she was concentrating on the paint being applied, but still there was room for other thoughts. Today, she was relishing the anticipation of the baby who would be theirs later this year. No child ever could have been more wanted. After being widowed she had recognized that Jim's death seemed

12

even more cruel for appearing to remove the hope of having children.

Throughout the years before her friendship with Andre developed into love, she had been devastated by the power and the depth of her maternal instincts. At times like the birth of a son to her cousin Charles who had married Dorothy her greatest friend, she had hated herself for the inability to be wholeheartedly happy for them. And now, at long last, she was to have the child who would make her feel complete, a whole woman, fully a person. Perhaps best of all, though, would be making Andre a father again.

He was a good father to Tania, had done well with the girl, especially in his persistence that had brought her over from Russia. Ensuring her escape to England must have been all the harder after witnessing the murder of Tania's mother during his own struggle to reach freedom.

Pamela sometimes wished that she could happily give up this work that had mattered so much to her ever since the war ended. The discussions between them, which all too often turned to arguments, hurt her quite severely. But she felt hurt even more by Andre's refusal to see that she had put so much into this business that it had become a part of *her*, and not something she could bring herself to relinquish.

Sensing somebody approaching to stand a little behind her, Pamela turned and smiled when she saw Ted Burrows.

"Problems?" she asked while still applying a light cerulean blue high on the wall in front of her.

"No, for once, everything's OK. Hope you don't

mind, but I'm just fascinated wi' what you're doing. It isn't so oft' that we're asked to do owt of this sort, is it?"

Pamela laughed. "This is the first time I've tackled anything described even vaguely as a picture. But if it turns out owt like this sketch our Tom's done for me, it'll be all right. Have you seen what he's painted?"

Ted turned to examine the sketch which Pamela had pinned to her stepladder. "You're certainly a family of craftsmen, aren't you? I hope your mother's justly proud?"

"You've met Mildred Baker, you'll know how she feels because of the way the three of us have come on. Not that she says much to any of us about that, mind you! It's more likely to be a harangue on what she thinks we might be missing than much in the form of congratulations."

Ted grinned. "Aye, I dare say."

"Although I have to admit, she's confessed to being relieved about me," Pamela continued. "Since I married Andre. She was never prepared to accept that a successful business compensated for all the shortcomings in my life afore that."

"And did it?" Ted enquired. "Did it compensate?"

"What do you think, Ted? 'Course not. There's nowt to beat a good marriage, is there?" And family, she added silently, aware that this foreman of hers would be pleased for her when he eventually learned her news.

Keeping her condition secret from her workers was growing more difficult. Right from the start, Pamela

14

had known that she was pregnant, had felt somehow different. The sickness plaguing her every morning had begun at a very early stage, and now it seemed to appear at intervals throughout each day.

At home she tried to play down how unwell she was feeling. She could see no sense in providing her husband with further ammunition for his opposition to her working. Although she suspected that Andre was watching her for signs of distress, she had no intention of acknowledging that his concern might be well-founded.

With her mother, there had been no chance of concealing anything. Mildred, bless her, had known about the pregnancy even before it was confirmed by Dr Philipson. She also seemed to recognize how taxing it was proving. Only once had Mildred advised that Pamela should stop working in such a physical job; she had learned over the years that repeating her advice was a waste of breath.

Mildred Baker sympathized with her daughter more than Pamela realized. She had always admired the grit that had gone into building up the firm and, whatever her own instincts now, could appreciate that Pamela must feel towards Canning's as anyone would towards a child they had nurtured. Mildred also consoled herself now with the thought that the arrival of that flesh and blood child would cause her daughter to reassess her priorities.

Looking back, Pamela was pleased as well as relieved that Mildred had, for the time being, agreed to keep the fact of her condition from the rest of the family. Having matured during years when women tended not to flaunt their pregnancy, Mildred could

15

understand that working with a load of men provided potential for embarrassment.

There were days now, though, when Pamela almost regretted having kept the matter secret. Feeling lousy was never helped by humping around great cans of paint, and as for the smell of the paint itself . . . All too frequently, just removing the lid from a tin was enough to send her rushing to the nearest lavatory.

In between bouts of sickness, however, she still enjoyed her job, and by now had earned the right to be choosy about the tasks she herself took on. Painting that back wall of the stage was one that she relished more than anything she had tackled in weeks. She had loved experimenting with techniques ever since the early days when renovating Stonemoor House had demanded so much research and a degree of trial and error.

The owners of the hall were invited to inspect the stage when it was finished, and when their representative exclaimed in genuine surprise over how well it had turned out Pamela was delighted.

"I must admit I gave myself a pleasant surprise, an' all, as soon as I'd applied that last brushful of paint! I've never claimed to be an artist, but I do seem to have progressed beyond slapping on a couple of new coats or a layer of varnish."

"You have indeed. I'm so impressed with this landscape panel that you've set me wondering if you might oblige us with completing another."

"Oh, aye – where's that precisely?" The entire building was virtually redecorated now. Pamela could not think of any wall that would benefit from further attention.

"I'll show you, if you like, if you've got a minute."

Together, they went out into the foyer and Pamela was conducted slowly up the wide staircase.

"It's just up here that I were thinking of. Where there's this bend in the stairs. That blank wall facing you would look fair grand with a mural."

"Well, all right, but what sort of thing do you have in mind?"

"Eh, I don't know. Happen summat to do with the theatre, do you think? We've got that room up here where we serve refreshments in the interval, you know. It might be nice to give our audiences summat to keep 'em in mind of the show they've been watching."

"Degas did some beautiful backstage scenes, do you think something of that sort?"

"Sounds grand to me."

"I'll see what I can come up with. I'll get my youngest brother to help, he provided the sketch for the stage."

By the end of that week Tom had produced a simplified representation of one of Pamela's favourite Degas pictures. She was looking forward to transferring it onto the wall, but also more than a little intimidated by the prospect. She had never tackled painting human figures, had no idea if she had it in her to do so.

Yet again, as soon as Pamela began on the actual work she became enthralled. Freely admitting to cheating slightly, she had encouraged Tom to depict the dancers in positions where their features weren't fully revealed. But she was planning to have a go at

17

one face, initially. She could always paint out the detail if her interpretation didn't work.

For several days she concentrated on the background, a typical Degas view behind the scenes with plenty of red velvet curtaining. Conveying the shading and texture of the velvet was a challenge, but Pamela was very pleased eventually when Ian paused to inspect and seemed quite impressed.

"Now I'm coming to the interesting bit!" Pamela exclaimed. "As you know, I've never done people before."

Blessing Degas for living in an era of long skirts, she outlined the forms, then began to experiment with mixing shades to obtain a realistic skin colour. While she and Tom were working on the design they had laughed as they contrived to have hands concealed in order to make her work easier.

I don't know if I'm even any good at arms, Pamela thought now, thank goodness I didn't make this any more difficult for myself!

The task was very exacting, she was feeling quite exhausted, but she continued steadily, determined that day to have the one figure to a stage where she might judge whether or not it was all right.

One by one, the men finished for the night and called to her as they left the hall. Down below in the foyer she heard Ian and Ted Burrows chatting as they also prepared to leave.

I'm going to have to call it a day, Pamela decided reluctantly, I'm tired out and Andre will be complaining when I arrive home late. As the outer door closed after her brother and the foreman she finished applying the paint remaining in her brush.

Maybe this was going to turn out reasonably well, considering that she didn't profess to be an artist. This woman here looked nicely proportioned, even graceful. Wondering if she had got the flesh tones right, Pamela stepped back to take in the overall effect. Not bad at all – the red velvet curtain seemed to lend a glow to skin of arm and neck. Trying to visualize how the finished painting might look, Pamela took a few more backward paces.

One heel of the old shoes she wore for work slipped off the top step. Overbalancing, Pamela felt herself falling, reached out for the handrail, and missed. Head first and on her back, she plunged down the first few stairs below the landing, and hurtled into the wall corner giving her temple an almighty whack. The corner had checked her fall, though; this time she managed to grasp the rail. She hauled herself round until she was no longer on her back with her head below the rest of her body.

I'm not really hurt, Pamela assured herself. Could have been a lot worse. I've got to be careful now, though, get my breath back.

But the shock, if not the actual fall, had made her feel sick. She would have to get to that downstairs cloakroom quickly.

Struggling to her feet, Pamela clung to the handrail. Her head was aching already and she felt dizzy. She placed one foot on the next stair down.

Her shoe heel had loosened, the moment she put weight on that foot the heel broke away, her ankle turned over and she plummeted down the staircase.

But I never faint, Pamela thought, as she came round on the cold floor of the foyer. Regaining full

19

consciousness, she realized that she hurt in so many places that fainting should have been no surprise. And she still felt appallingly sick.

She tried to stand, discovered that one ankle was sprained, and the other leg . . . Oh, no, she thought, staring at the jagged bone protruding from a wound on her shin: that's what a compound fracture looks like then, and felt a wild desire to laugh. But she was alone in the building, and must not give way to hysteria. Inspecting her leg seemed to have taken her mind off the nausea, the urgent need to vomit was abating. She suspected that this state might prove impermanent, she needed to get help while she remained capable of doing so.

There was a telephone somewhere near the main entrance, all she had to do was drag herself across the floor and then, somehow, to her feet. The distance felt like half a mile and, with every inch that she hauled herself along by aching arms, Pamela discovered yet another bruise.

I've got to get there, she realized. Nobody else can help me. She felt quite tearful now, ready for giving up. But beside the telephone was a chair, the sight of it encouraged her while she cringed with pain and continued the slow, slithering process. Eventually, she was able to grasp either side of the seat with a hand, and succeeded in pulling herself upright. Grasping the back of the chair she forced the twisted ankle to support her until she manoeuvred on to the edge of the chair and reached up to lift the receiver.

It was as she dialled for an ambulance and began explaining what had happened that Pamela noticed the pain deep inside her. Among all the other hurts

20

and sensations she recognized something new and alarming. Between her legs she felt a warm trickle beginning. She watched, appalled, as the narrow trail of blood descended her torn stocking.

"God, not that!" she screamed. "Not my baby!"

Chapter Two

Andre was holding her hand. Her head was aching fiercely, as was just about every part of her. One leg felt heavy but not so painful as she recalled, the other ankle throbbed. Remembering the internal pain, Pamela opened her eyes, her dread agonizing.

"Andre, did I . . .? Did we . . .?" She swallowed, unable to form the awful words.

"My poor love," he murmured huskily, the grey eyes were misting in that strong, squarish face which today looked haggard.

"We lost it then?" she said dejectedly.

"Not yet, no. They say you may not lose the baby." He tried to smile. "It is you yourself who are causing me the greatest concern. You are injured in so many places."

"But the baby – you are sure? It is still there?"

"Yes, my darling. You bled a little, but it is still there. As I say, they think – hope that you may keep it."

"Then everything's all right."

"Not exactly – your leg has a . . ."

". . . Compound fracture, that's what they call it, isn't it? I could tell when I saw the bone."

22

"Don't. You must not even think about that terrible accident."

She had been almost unconscious when the ambulance arrived to pick her up, but the crew had told him what they had found when Pamela had struggled to the door of the hall to admit them.

Those ambulancemen had been so concerned that they called back at the hospital shortly before Andre arrived here. They had explained about her injuries and their fears for the baby before another call sent them running out to their vehicle. During the wearying hours since then the doctors had told him more, about the examination that had revealed the precarious state of the foetus, and that the operation to set Pamela's leg must be carried out immediately.

So far, it seemed that she had survived that operation remarkably well. The risk they had been obliged to take in order to prevent Pamela from being lamed had not further harmed the baby. But they would need to be patient. Even if all went according to plan she would be hospitalized for some time: on account of the fracture and other injuries and the shock, but also because only by ensuring total rest could they do their best to avert a miscarriage.

Gently, Andre explained this to her.

Pamela nodded, surprising him with the degree of her acceptance, and also alarming him. He had never known her to be so acquiescent.

"I'll do anything and everything they say, Andre. So long as we don't lose this child."

He wanted to tell her that there would be other babies, that she must not become obsessed, needed to say that all he wished was that *she* should recover. Somehow, though, he could say nothing more. And, still affected by the anaesthetic, Pamela seemed too drowsy to comprehend anything beyond the fact that he was with her, and as yet she still had their baby.

Mildred Baker came bustling in on the following day, flopped down on to the bedside chair and gave her daughter a sharp look.

"They tell me you're still hanging on, that you're still holding on to the bairn. I hope you realize what a scare you've given us all!"

"Hello, Mum. It's good to see you. Sorry if you've had a fright, you weren't the only one."

Mildred smiled, and her tone softened. "Aye, I dare say. I know you didn't do it on purpose, love. I just wish . . . well, that you'd have taken more care of yourself. The work you do is no sort of a job for a woman, especially when she's expecting."

"You've been talking to Andre."

"Naturally. He came himself to tell us what had happened, he knows how I hate that telephone, and he wanted to see that I didn't get too upset. But I *am* upset, how could I help but be? So are the lads. They send their love, by the way, our Tom and Ian."

"That's nice, thank them both for me, won't you?"

"How are you feeling really, love, are you a bit better today?"

"I think so, thanks. Since they put the plaster on my leg it doesn't seem to hurt as much. But there's that many bruises up and down that I can't lie comfortable at all. Still, the pain in

24

my inside went away, that was what bothered me most."

"I hope that some good is going to come out of this, that you'll happen see sense now, let somebody else get on wi' running Canning's."

"Well, I'll certainly have to talk to Ted Burrows about taking over the reins while I'm here."

"Not only as long as you're in here, I hope. Nay, Pamela love, if you get away with this being just a warning of what might have happened, you want to count yourself lucky. I know how much yon firm matters to you, but you've been desperate for a long time to have this youngster, haven't you?"

Pamela sighed. "Aye, Mum, I know. You don't have to remind me. But I keep trying to explain, most of all to Andre – Canning's has been like a child to me an' all. I had to nurture it, build it up, learn ways of making it succeed. How can I abandon it?"

"Like any lass that gives up interesting work to look after a family, I suppose. You're not the first faced with that decision."

Rain was obscuring nearby buildings, obliterating distant hills. Her future seemed even less clear. "I'll see. I just don't know. I thought I had it all worked out. Because of the kind of job it is, I was going to take the baby with me. It'd be no trouble. There's often nobody in the houses I'm redecorating. Nobody to disturb."

"Except for that good husband of yours who's worrying himself sick about your ideas."

"Andre might come round."

"Oh, aye?" Mildred glanced out through the

25

window. "Good Lord, is that a pig soaring past the church tower? And on such a rotten day?"

Pamela laughed, reached out and gave her mother's hand a squeeze. "I could have done with you on my side, you know! But, since you're not, I have to admit I expected you to agree with Andre. And I can't resent anything you're saying, Mum. I've known all along that my ambitions are a bit too radical for lots of folk."

"I only want you to be happy, love, that's all really. I know you're different from us, that you've been determined to get on; that you've had to be since Jim were killed. I've allus respected you for making a go of it like you have. I suppose if you hadn't got a bit of fight in you, you'd have given in long since. Happen me and your Andre are going to have to understand that you're still tenacious."

Pamela was relieved to hear the compliment. Her mother's misgivings had reinforced everything that Andre had said, perturbing her until she'd needed to remind herself that Mildred was only concerned for her.

"Charlie and Dorothy send their love, she'll be in to see you in a day or two. When you've picked up a bit."

"That's nice. How is Dot?"

Her friend was pregnant again, three months ahead of Pamela herself. They had talked of how good it would be to have babies almost the same age. I *can't* lose mine, Pamela thought yet again.

Tania arrived while Mildred was still there. Watching them embrace, Pamela smiled, although rather ruefully. What had her own mother got that she

26

herself was lacking? She'd have given a great deal to have Tania hug her so unreservedly from the day they met.

Today, however, the girl was being particularly sweet. She did lean over and give Pamela a kiss, and she'd brought a bouquet of fragrant narcissi.

"They're beautiful, Tania, thank you ever so much. I've always loved spring flowers."

"My father sends his love, he'll be in later to see you. He has a rehearsal today, did he remind you?"

Pamela shook her head. "I don't think he did, but I can't be sure. So much has happened."

Tania sat on the edge of the bed, and gazed anxiously at her stepmother. "How are you today? When we rang through this morning they told us that you still have the baby."

"That's right, love. And I'm not feeling as sore. I'm hoping it won't be so long before they say I can rest just as well at home."

"You must tell them that you have two people there waiting to take care of you."

Pamela beamed. "That's nice to know. But you both have to attend rehearsals, and you have your singing classes."

"Even so, we shall both give you a lot of our time when you do come home to Stonemoor. And I have been thinking – you will need to have a new interest. You will miss your work quite terribly."

"I think Pamela will be content just to rest," Mildred said gently.

Her daughter shook her head. "I dare say Tania's

27

nearer the mark. I've never been used to doing nowt all day, have I?"

"We were talking last evening," Tania continued. "Father was telling me how you enjoyed learning about the period when the house was built, that you read a great many books. If you wanted to study while you have the time, I should be happy to get the books you need."

"I'll have to have a think. It does seem a shame if I let this spare time go to waste."

"You love that old clock the Misses Norton gave to you both, I wondered if perhaps you had done anything about learning its history?"

"That's a splendid idea, Tania. And you don't need to go buying books, you know. There's a perfectly good library at Belle Vue. Tell your Dad it's near t'People's Park, he'll take you there."

The books were the first thing she saw after Andre had driven her up to Stonemoor House where sunlight was gleaming on its walls of Yorkshire stone. Pamela smiled and thanked both Andre and his daughter for the trouble they had taken in choosing two volumes which provided information about antique clocks and a third on the furnishing of eighteenth and nineteenth-century homes.

Pamela did not tell them that she felt too disheartened to care very much about studying anything. The hospital doctors had been unanimous in warning her not take up her work again. The surgeon had explained that he had inserted a metal plate in her leg, and she would be wise to avoid any risk of further injury. What was worse, the consultant who had helped to avert a miscarriage advised that she should forget all ideas of returning to such an active occupation.

"You must not entertain it during these next few months or I won't answer for the infant's well-being. And if you wish to contemplate a larger family, you'd better resign yourself to an easier life."

Andre had been present while she was being discharged, so there was no way that Pamela could conceal their warnings. Not that she would have done other than comply, at least until after the baby was born.

As soon as she had adapted to being at home and was up and dressed during some part of every day, Pamela asked Ted Burrows to call.

Ted seemed to have acquired more self-assurance during her enforced absence from work. The moment he was shown into the sitting room she noticed that he appeared unmoved by their surroundings, whereas she had been ready to help him feel at ease in a place which she knew to be very different from his own home. When renovating Stonemoor House for Andre, she had done her utmost to restore the elegance of its early nineteenth-century origins. And since then they had chosen together antique furniture and gilt-framed mirrors to enhance its feeling of space and light. The result was far more impressive than the homes in which ordinary folk like herself had grown up.

Today, however, before Pamela had got beyond the enquiry about his wife and family with which she had followed their greeting, Ted was relating how well he and the men were coping without her.

29

"But for that wall painting you were working on, the job at that hall is completed. We've made a good start on that big house we're doing right through. Proper champion, it's looking an' all— "

"So Ian was telling me," Pamela interrupted, she didn't like the feeling that she was already out of touch with what was going on.

"Aye – well, the lad's keen, I'll say that for him. Takes a lot of interest in all that's happening. A bit too much interest, at times."

"Really? In what way?" She didn't mean to have Ted Burrows coming down hard on her brother. There was no sense in stifling the lad's enthusiasm.

"Oh – you know – allus wanting to know what's going on. Other folks' jobs, when he should be minding his own."

"He's been keen to learn right from the start. We don't want anyone curbing his interest too much, do we?"

"Not so long as it stops short of interfering. He's still got a lot of learning to do, needs to bear that in mind."

"Anyway, Ted, I've been looking ahead, naturally. Being laid low like this is a nuisance, but it isn't insuperable. I'm going to rely on you a lot, during the next few months."

"I don't think you'll find much wrong with the way I've deputized for you up to now, Mrs Malinowski. The chap as owns the place where we're working at present said only t'other day how suited he were."

"Good. Glad to hear it. Well, Ted, I'm appointing you assistant manager, I shall inform our permanent employees of this. You yourself can tell any casual labour you take on."

"*Assistant?*" Ted murmured, frowning. "I was thinking more of – well, I am managing the firm for you now, aren't I?"

Pamela kept her smile steady despite her inward unease which might have produced a frown as grim as his. "Not quite, not all aspects of the business, I'm afraid. I shall still manage those, you will find. I was hoping you would look on this promotion philosophically, as a step in the right direction. It goes without saying that this – this progress will be acknowledged in your wage packet."

"I see."

"I trust that you'll find that satisfactory, Ted. We've always worked well together, I want that to continue."

"Aye. You need it to, don't you? Now you can't get about."

Pamela made her smile reassuring. "Ah, but I shall not be immobilized much longer. I shall soon be helping you to keep an eye on things. And as for that mural, I've somebody in mind for completing the job. I'll be in touch with the owners of the hall tomorrow."

They talked for a few more minutes so that Pamela could refresh her memory on new jobs still to be begun, and the number of men who would be needed to complete them. As Ted was about to leave she thanked him for coming.

"That seems to be quite satisfactory," she added.

"It'll have to be, won't it?" he responded, still disappointed. She'd tried twice to make him say he

31

was satisfied, but he'd held out against her. *Assistant* manager, indeed! He'd earned more than that.

Whatever Ted Burrows' opinion of the position, her brother Ian found the man's promotion hard to swallow. Pamela had invited both him and Tom to the house that evening, and she was saddened by Ian's reaction to the news.

"I wish you hadn't done that, you know, Pamela. He's swell-headed enough, as it is. Allus telling me what to do, when I don't need telling."

"But I've got to have somebody in charge while I'm stuck at home like this. Someone has to take responsibility."

"You could give me more. You know – more responsibility. I've been with you a long time, haven't I? And I've learned a lot."

"I know, Ian love, I'm pleased with the way you've taken to decorating. You've picked up most of the techniques you'll need. But you're barely eighteen. You need more years on your back afore folk will take orders from you and so on."

Ian straightened strong shoulders, his sherry-brown eyes glittered. "Some of the chaps ask me stuff now. They don't all like going to him."

And that could create problems! thought Pamela. "Even so, there's more to running a business than knowing how the work's done. Just try and be content for a while, eh?"

"Well – if Ted's going to be assistant manager, that leaves us without a foreman. You could make me foreman— "

"Not so fast, love. I've only promoted Ted today. Just give me a while – I need to have a good think."

Pamela had sensed Tom watching and listening throughout their discussion. She had noticed his glance flicking between herself and Ian, had read occasionally in his expressive eyes a certain amusement regarding his brother's ambition. Now she had a proposition to put to Tom and she wasn't at all sure how he would respond.

"You know that sketch you did for me from the Degas, Tom," she began. "I suppose you'll know that I wasn't able to complete the painting from it. I've been wondering if you'd like to have a go yourself . . ."

His youthful cheeks glowed. "Me? But I've never done owt of that sort, have I? I can't paint on walls."

"Are you sure? You could have a try. Ian could go with you, demonstrate mixing the kind of paints we use, and applying them. I could tell you which sort of brushes . . ."

Pamela could see Ian was interested in becoming involved in something different like this. Tom, however, was looking anxious.

"Using our sort of paint, you don't have to worry about little mistakes and so on," she reassured him. "You can always paint them out, it's easy enough to cover 'em up."

"Well . . ."

He wouldn't have been their Tom if he hadn't hesitated. "Ian'd take you to have a look at what's still to be done, wouldn't you, Ian?"

It was agreed that Tom would at least go and see that wall. Pamela immediately felt better. Handling the business from home was more difficult, but she was beginning to believe that it was nowhere near so impossible as she had feared.

Once the next few weeks were over and she could get around more easily, she would be able to visit the men wherever they were working, keep an eye on the jobs in hand, and on relations between the individual members of her work force. If Ted Burrows came round to accepting his status, she doubted that Ian would be content without being made foreman. But a foreman at eighteen . . .? She couldn't think that would go down at all well with the rest of the team.

It was early summer before Pamela was fit to visit the men on site. On her way there she called in at the hall where young Tom had completed the wall painting which she had begun. He had taken a photograph of the finished picture but, being indoors and shot on his black and white camera, the photo hadn't revealed the mural's quality.

Inspecting the painting for herself, Pamela was well pleased with the result, and complimented Tom when she telephoned to thank him.

"As a matter of fact, you've made a better job of it than I ever would have myself! Seeing your work has convinced me I'm no artist."

Going back to that hall had been traumatic. As soon as the caretaker showed Pamela into the foyer the helplessness she'd felt while struggling to get across the floor to summon help came surging back to her. When she began limping up the stairs, she found herself clinging to the handrail, terrified of falling.

Only when she began examining the painting itself was she able to push memories of that dreadful day to the back of her mind.

Glad to leave the place, Pamela drove straight to the house where the men were working. Even there she soon discovered plenty to remind her how many changes had been forced upon her. And that most of them were no more acceptable to her team than they were to herself.

Ian and the apprentice who had been taken on shortly before her accident were in one room, sanding down the walls in preparation for hanging wallpaper.

Their voices were raised with all the youthful arrogance that accompanies a grudge against authority, and reached Pamela long before she pushed open the door.

"We don't have to stand for it, you know," Ian was saying. "I've been with Canning's longer than Burrows, any road."

"But would your sister do that – tell him off for putting on us?"

"'Course she would. He's supposed to be learning us the trade, isn't he? Not making mugs of us all the time."

"But, like Mr Burrows said, I've got to start somewhere."

"Suit yourself," said Ian contemptuously. "But you want to think on – let him browbeat you now, and he'll allus do it. Look at the way he treats me, these days. I haven't had owt interesting to do for ages."

"Haven't you, Ian?" his sister said sharply from

35

the doorway. "And I wonder why that is – have you maybe got on the wrong side of Ted Burrows? I wouldn't be surprised, if you often go sounding off like this without caring who might hear."

Ian had flushed, but his eyes still showed his indifference.

The apprentice seemed acutely embarrassed. "Mrs Malinowski," he murmured awkwardly, shifting from one foot to the other.

"For your information, Ian here does not get preferential treatment of any sort, and nor will you. What's more, now I know what's in the wind, I'll be having a word with Mr Burrows. If the pair of you are too daft to know which side your bread's buttered, we'll have to find a way of making you understand."

"But I wasn't really complaining," the lad began miserably.

"Good. Then you'll be content to finish what you've been told to do, and without grumbling. Parts of the job are boring, but they still have to be done. Learning to accept that is just as vital as anything else we can teach you."

Pamela watched the apprentice turn to work on the wall again before facing her brother. "Ian, I want a word with you."

"I'm sparing you a telling off in front of that lad," she said as soon as she had led Ian to another room and closed the door behind them. "Not that I'm sure you deserve sparing anything. I won't have you undermining Ted Burrows, do you understand? Ted's got a difficult enough task while I'm out of action, without you adding to his problems."

"Happen he has," Ian protested. "But you don't know how he picks on me."

"All right, tell me – what's he doing that's so dreadful?"

"Well – you know – like I was saying back there. He's treating me as if I were an apprentice an' all. It's allus either stripping down woodwork or sanding walls, never owt interesting."

"Oh, what a shame! You poor little love!" Pamela said sarcastically. "Grow up, Ian, for heaven's sake. Be glad you're in work, and that it's not all that uncongenial. To hear you, anybody'd think you'd been sent down the mines. You know you've done lots of interesting work in the past, and you will again."

"I don't know that, not now that he's in charge. He's got it in for me."

"I can't really believe that, unless you've given him cause. Think about what I've said, love. If you're continually resentful, and let Ted see that, you're only going to incur his annoyance. And you certainly won't be impressing me as a potential foreman."

Pamela hadn't liked discovering how discontented Ian seemed, but in a way she had relished speaking to him about his attitude. For those few minutes she had felt that she still had a role to play in Canning's, a role that no one else could fulfil in quite the same way.

The fact that Ian evidently took her words to heart made her feel even better. A couple of days afterwards she had occasion to see Ted Burrows again, and was pleasantly surprised by his account of recent events.

"Your Ian seems to be really buckling to, suddenly.

He's been giving that young lad a hand, demonstrating the best method of applying undercoat, and you know how thankless that can be. I've told him I shall expect him to show how we set about giving woodwork a fine gloss."

Pamela grinned. "All the rubbing down between coats, you mean?"

"Aye. Often enough, I get interrupted when I'm doing owt of the sort, there's allus one of the other chaps coming to me with a query. I've told Ian I shall expect the two of them to concentrate, and to show me a perfect job when they've done. And do you know – I believe they're going to do just that."

"I wouldn't be surprised," said Pamela, wishing she could be present to see Ian and the lad at work, but feeling thankful that her brother was once more responding well.

Now that she was fit enough to go out and about more, Pamela quite frequently found herself visiting the house where her men were working. Apart from feeling frustrated that she herself must not pick up a paintbrush or hang a roll of wallpaper, she was happier. This contact with the company she had built up meant so much to her.

Andre, however, had been noting how often his wife was away from Stonemoor House, and also how tired she always seemed after spending just a few hours on her feet. She was very evidently pregnant now, and he became quite alarmed about how exhausted she got.

When the inevitable reproach came one evening

as they relaxed near the windows of the sitting room, Pamela was shaken.

"But I'm not doing any actual work, Andre," she protested. "And somebody has to keep an eye on things."

"You have a perfectly good assistant manager, my darling," he reminded her gently. "You are paying him well, are you not? You should not be forever following him about, checking his efficiency."

"I'm not, I— "

"You are what?" Andre asked lightly. "Attempting to convince yourself that you are indispensable?"

"No, no, I've never thought— " Pamela broke off, shrugged, and gave a rueful smile. "Yes, you're right, of course. But Canning's is mine, can you blame me?" She realized how repetitive she was becoming.

"Blame?" It was his turn to shrug. But then he sighed. "As I have said before, I only wish that you were more content here. In our home. Awaiting our child. Can you not give your mind to *us*?"

Afraid that she might have made Andre feel she was neglecting him, Pamela tried very hard to become more involved in their home life. But most of the work was done by Mrs Singer, the deaf and dumb lady who had been Andre's daily housekeeper since long before he and Pamela were married. She liked Mrs Singer too well to take everything out of her hands, but she did offer her shorter working hours in order to do more planning of their meals and the actual cooking.

Tania as well as her father seemed happier with this arrangement and Pamela began to think that sacrificing her own satisfaction might have been worthwhile. Privately, she promised herself that she would review the situation once the baby was here and she had established a new routine. They were into June now and the projected date for the birth seemed to be approaching so quickly that she felt she might tolerate these present limitations.

Andre's practising of the violin continued daily, even though the concert season was over until the autumn. Pamela had wondered if he would feel some of the deprivation that she herself experienced when less involved in active work, but he seemed quite serene.

He had been pleased by the ending of the Russian blockade of Berlin, which he declared a sign that the Russian authorities meant every word of their agreement to attend a fresh meeting of the Big Four foreign ministers.

"It is just possible that they are coming to understand that the world today will not permit Communist efforts to squeeze out the Western powers."

By the end of the month, however, Pamela was becoming uneasy because President Truman was struggling to calm the anti-Communist hysteria which seemed to be spreading through the United States. If that happens over here, she thought, I only hope that folk will understand that Andre *is* opposed to Communist ideals. The Russians seemed to be making themselves so unpopular that people were unlikely to make distinctions between those of differing ideological beliefs.

While Pamela and Andre were keeping an eye on international affairs, Tania was becoming excited about less serious matters. When the newspapers were full of the appearance at Wimbledon of Gussie Moran in her lace-trimmed panties, Tania delightedly cut out the pictures. These were displayed in her bedroom next to photographs of Rita Hayworth and Aly Khan whose wedding she thought very romantic.

"I hope she is not becoming frivolous," Andre confided to his wife.

Pamela smiled. "She's young, that's all. I'm sure you don't need to worry. I suppose she is bound to find such things exciting compared with the life from which you rescued her."

Sensing that Tania was keeping her mind open to all kinds of influences, Pamela was happy to go along with her suggestion made early in July. The girl said one evening how much she wanted to see Princess Elizabeth who was visiting Halifax that month.

"We never had a royal family in Russia during my lifetime," she reminded them. "I need to appreciate all that it means to have a monarch. And she is the heir to her father's throne, is she not?"

Andre promised to take them into Halifax on the day. Since their honeymoon, he had driven the car that he had given his wife, and was doing so increasingly now that Pamela felt encumbered by pregnancy.

"Where will be the best place to see the Princess?" asked Tania. "We must have a good vantage point."

"According to the itinerary, she's to attend a large assembly of schoolchildren, in the open air. So long as it's a fine day, we'll stand somewhere outside the ground where they'll be waiting for her."

"Can't we go inside there?" Tania demanded,

41

determined that no one should have a better view than they.

Andre laughed. "I would imagine places there are reserved already. But you may, in fact, have a closer view of the Princess from the footpath as she approaches the entrance."

When the day came they found a good position at the roadside near the sports ground where masses of scholars had assembled.

"I hope this is not going to prove too overtiring for you, Pamela?" Andre enquired. She had appeared almost as eager as Tania to be present, but she did still suffer from pain in that leg and because of the baby often seemed weary.

"Eh, I'll be fine, love," Pamela assured him. She had glanced about when they arrived and was reassured that she might go to lean against the wall a few paces behind them if she should feel unwell.

Listening to the warm Yorkshire voices all around them, Pamela wondered how Andre and Tania really felt in this land so different from their own, and in a part of the country where even fellow Englishmen sometimes declared the dialect difficult to comprehend.

Only when she had been moved away from here to serve in the WAAF during the war, had she herself realized how strong were the accents of some Yorkshire folk. On airfields in the south of England she had mixed for the first time with girls from all over the country, and from all classes. That experience was good for me, Pamela reflected. She had gained the confidence to do something with her life.

A sudden rustle of anticipation was running through

the surrounding crowd. People began craning forward as the cavalcade of cars bearing civic dignitaries and their Royal guest moved slowly into sight.

"She is here, she is here!" Tania exclaimed.

Andre turned towards Pamela with an indulgent smile. "I would swear that this daughter of mine has become a small girl again!"

"I heard that, you know," Tania remarked, but the Royal car was much nearer now, she was leaning forward to see more clearly.

The Princess was smiling as she glanced from side to side and acknowledged the enthusiastic crowds. How young she looks, Pamela thought, young and yet touchingly dignified.

Princess Elizabeth was some eight years younger than herself, already a mother, and present in the very heart of the nation's anxious concern for the health of King George VI. She's good at smiling, Pamela observed, and wished that she herself might have as much composure when faced with problems. But then the Princess would have been trained to behave well, her mother had always appeared interested and charming, even throughout the blitz on London.

And my mother taught me a lot too, Pamela acknowledged silently. Mildred Baker had brought up the three of them on next to nothing, uncomplainingly, and alone since their father's factory accident.

The cars had moved on now, and the Princess was being welcomed over the loudspeaker system within the sports ground behind them.

"You have seen her now, shall we go back to the car?" Andre, who was worried about Pamela, suggested to his daughter.

"Not yet. We cannot," Tania protested earnestly. "We can hear what they are saying out here. And she may come this way again on the return journey."

"And she might not," Pamela warned her. "It will depend where they are taking her afterwards."

There was an address by their Royal visitor, to which the crowd listened as attentively as those privileged to be able to see the events taking place. But the singing by the massed scholars was the thing that stirred the three of them most greatly. Pamela felt a lump rising in her throat when the youngsters began their first number. When they launched into 'Land of Hope and Glory' she noticed that both Andre and his daughter seemed choked with emotion.

Aye, well it's a great country still, in lots of ways, Pamela thought. And was fervently thankful that Andre had chosen it as home.

The crowd was thinning when she saw him. Immaculate in his police sergeant's uniform as he paused to speak to one of his constables, it was Roger Jenkins, the old friend who had meant so much to her, once. These days, just catching sight of him made her uncomfortable, even though she no longer blamed him for the situation that had compelled her to avoid him for over a year. She didn't like the way that thinking about Roger and Leslie Rivers made her realize how prejudiced she could be.

Still shaken by seeing Roger, Pamela was unprepared for the first pain, only a twinge, but somehow she *knew*. This was a good four weeks ahead of time, but that was no surprise. There had been all that trouble in the early months.

"I think we'd better call in at my mother's while

44

we're in Halifax," she said calmly. It was too soon yet for dashing to the General Hospital, but she had no intention of letting Andre drive her out to the wilds of Cragg Vale if this was more than a false alarm.

By the time they had travelled the mile or so to Mildred Baker's, Pamela was questioning the wisdom of her own decision not to go to hospital. Those pains were fierce and occurring frequently.

Chapter Three

"What's the matter, love? You're not so well, are you?"

As soon as she looked more carefully at her daughter, Mildred interrupted Tania's excited account of how they had seen Princess Elizabeth. "Did you wince just now, Pamela? You're very pale."

"I've just got a bit of a pain, it'll soon pass off."

At the word pain Andre rushed to his wife's side. "It is not . . .?" he began anxiously. "Not already?"

"Actually, I think it could be," Pamela admitted, trying to smile although another contraction was making her cringe.

"You should have said," he reproached her. "I would have taken you to the hospital immediately."

"We had better take her there now, Father," said Tania.

"Hang on a minute, both of you," Pamela insisted. "You're a couple of loves for being so concerned, but it is a first baby, remember. It's unlikely to arrive that quickly. What do you say, Mum?"

Mildred, who was steering her daughter towards the nearest chair shook her head. "I don't know what to think. There's allus the exception that proves the rule. And you did have that bit of bother early on.

46

Any road, you just sit quiet for a minute or two, we'll see what happens."

The next pain came after an even shorter interval. Mildred frowned and glanced towards her son-in-law.

"It might be as well to get Pamela to the General now. They'll have more of an idea how long it's going to take."

"You have none of your things with you!" Tania exclaimed. "Shall I take the bus back to Stonemoor and collect them for you?" She had enjoyed helping her stepmother gather together clothes for the new baby and the items that Pamela herself would require in hospital.

"I'll come with you, Tania love," Mildred volunteered. "That'll be more useful than all of us hanging round at the hospital, waiting."

"I can't imagine why this is all happening so quick," Pamela said as Andre settled her into the car again. "They tell you the pains build up very gradual, like, especially with your first. I do hope everything's going to be all right."

"I am certain it will be," Andre asserted, although in truth he himself was filled with apprehension. God, but he would never bear it if they should lose this child, or if Pamela herself . . .! Having his first wife killed in front of him surely had been enough? There could not, *must not* be any further traumas.

Despite the twinges assailing her inside, Pamela was able to direct him over the shortest route to the General Hospital. This was just as well for they were walking along the corridor towards the maternity ward when she felt the sudden rush of her waters breaking.

47

From that moment the nurses took charge. She was taken from Andre and hurried into the ward then told to undress and don a white gown.

"It looks like we've just got you here in the nick of time!" a capable looking midwife exclaimed. "There's many a lass in here who's been struggling day long that'll envy you."

"But why is it coming so fast?" Pamela demanded breathlessly. "And about a month too soon?"

The midwife smiled. "Eh, lass, if I could tell you what governs the length of time a bairn takes, they'd be paying me a fortune! Some are slow coming into the world, others arrive in a bit of rush."

"Even the first?" She still did not feel reassured that all might be well.

"When you've lived as long as I have, you'll know there's nothing certain in this world. I've seen doctors confounded more times than I can count. They think they've studied all t'possibilities, then something occurs that they didn't predict."

Pamela smiled, encouraged now by this large, cheerful woman who seemed to exude competence. "I'll just have to be thankful that we got here in time then."

"You will that! And thankful afterwards, for what I dare say will be an easy birth."

If this is easy, thought Pamela some while later, I'm glad I didn't have to put up with anything worse. The pains were indescribably severe, so intense that she felt the babe might be expelled with a force that would tear her apart. She was beginning to feel so alarmed that she could not concentrate on all she had been told about using her breathing in co-operating to help the birth.

"I'm not doing this right at all, am I?" she said in one of her more lucid moments.

"You're doing champion," she was assured. "It won't be so long now. All you've got to remember is to pant when I tell you, and to push – push like you never thought you'd have to."

Pushing and crying out, and pushing yet again, Pamela finally was interrupted by the midwife's triumphant words. "That's it, Mrs Malinowski, you've done it now. And you've got a lovely boy . . ."

A boy, the son who would make Andre so very proud. If she'd been able to choose, she would have chosen a son. The little lad had cried as the midwife delivered him, and now was crying again as she held him for Pamela to see.

"We'll have you cleaned up in no time, and the baby as well," one of the nurses was saying. "Then your husband can come in. Only for a few minutes, mind. You need to rest, you'll be tired out."

Pamela felt she was beyond tiredness, utterly drained. She couldn't begin to think how women endured a long labour. Hers had been short, but even so the most exhausting experience of her life.

She was all but asleep when she heard Andre's voice beside her.

"Thank you, my darling, thank you," he said huskily. "He is beautiful, you have made me completely happy. Happily complete."

She opened her eyes and gazed into his dear, familiar face which now wore a quite unfamiliar glow of utter delight.

* * *

49

Pamela had slept for a few hours when her own mother and Tania were allowed in to see her. They had met Andre in one of the hospital corridors and had been persuaded by him that his wife needed rest before seeing further visitors.

The three of them had driven into the centre of Halifax where they had toasted the baby's future with tea while he tried to answer all their questions about his son.

Since driving them back to the hospital Andre had been into the ward to see Pamela, but had curtailed his visit in order to allow the other two to go in.

Seeing her daughter's wan face and shadowed eyes, Mildred had smiled sympathetically as they approached the bed.

"By, but it's taken it out of you, love, hasn't it? Still, you're on the right side of it all now, and with a smashing young son. Your Andre's that proud! But I dare say he'll have told you that himself."

"More than once," said Pamela. "But it's nice to know how pleased he is. And we're so lucky – the baby's a decent weight, even though he came so soon. They're not having to put him in an incubator, so long as his breathing and that continue to be all right."

"That's good, love. How much did he weigh?"

"Five pounds, thirteen ounces."

At that moment a nurse came towards them carrying the infant.

"Now you can see for yourselves!" Pamela exclaimed, holding out her arms for the child. "Just have a look, Mum. He reminds me of our Tom when he was born, although he has Andre's mouth and chin already."

Mildred smilingly agreed after studying her grandson. Tania had been hanging back slightly, she beamed when Pamela and her mother both urged her to come closer.

"He is very little, I think," said the girl, her voice hushed. She was feeling quite awed. This was the first baby she had seen so soon after its birth, and the fact that he was her half-brother was difficult to comprehend.

"If you sit in that chair, I'll let you hold him," her stepmother told her. "While he's quiet. I shouldn't be surprised if he's trying his lungs again before so long."

Tania was looking apprehensive when the child was placed in her arms, but Mildred smiled approvingly as the girl made certain that the baby's head was carefully supported.

"Have you decided on a name for him yet?" Mildred enquired after she had found another chair and brought it to the bedside.

"Not finally, not with him coming so sudden, like. We've talked of Mihail Dmitry – Dmitry was Andre's father's name, wasn't it, Tania?"

The girl nodded. "It has been a family name for generations. But if you call him Mihail will he be Michael to people in England?"

"I suppose so. Happen when he grows up he'll want to have a name that's more usual over here, but he'll always know he's been given these reminders of being Russian. We'll be glad to know that, an' all."

The baby continued to sleep peacefully and Tania

51

eventually handed him to Mildred who nodded to herself contentedly.

"Eh, he's fair grand, bless him, whatever you settle on for a name. It's champion being a grandma, you know. Makes you look to the future with fresh eyes."

And eyes that are moist, her daughter observed, smiling to herself about the film of emotion glistening against blue irises. Mildred Baker claimed never to go in for much sentiment, but she was moved by important occasions.

"I think that he is adorable," Tania asserted. "When you come home to Stonemoor I shall help you to care for him."

"You want to watch out, making rash promises like that. I might hold you to them. Especially by the time I've got used to having him around and I'm eager to be working again."

"Working!" Mildred snapped, all tenderness evaporating. "You're surely not intending to go out to work? You'll have your hands full with this wee mite. I've never heard such nonsense."

At that moment Andre came striding back into the ward. Seeing her father, Tania sensed that she must prevent contention arising between him and his wife, and instantly changed the subject.

"Pamela has been telling us that you have yet to make up your minds about the baby's name. Are you really not certain?"

Andre looked towards Pamela, and then to his mother-in-law and the infant she was holding.

"I wish him to be Mihail Dmitry, but I am just so very happy that I shall insist that Pamela must have the final word."

"Two words – Mihail Dmitry," she responded firmly.

Sitting beside her father as he drove out to Stonemoor House, after leaving Mildred at her own home, Tania was pensive. She had not realized how tiny new babies were, how adorable. Mihail had felt so fragile in her arms, yet at the same time warm enough to make her acutely aware that he was very much alive, a person.

Her own adult future had seemed so ill-defined until now that she had scarcely contemplated the very real possibility that she one day would marry and have children. The plans occupying her head had centred around success in her singing career and the difficulties created by trying to combine the popular music that she loved with the classics which she knew she ought to be perfecting.

It seemed suddenly that the whole of life was a matter of making choices. Today, she had begun to understand more about the way her stepmother felt torn; it was quite possible to wish for a family of one's own and also the kind of work that would be satisfying.

"How soon will it be before Pamela brings the baby home?" she asked. She knew that babies developed swiftly and did not wish to miss any part of Mihail's progress.

Her father shrugged. "I really do not know, my dear. Everything happened so suddenly that I was more concerned to have them both come through safely than to ask about that kind of thing."

"Well, I hope it will not be long. I shall love to show him around our home."

Andre laughed. "I suspect he might be a little young to appreciate his surroundings."

"Well, you know what I mean . . ."

Andre did know, and was delighted that his daughter seemed as thrilled as he himself to have this new member of their family.

On the day two weeks later when he brought his wife and son to Stonemoor House, Tania was at the door to welcome them. She had noticed during visits to the hospital that Mihail appeared less red and wrinkled than shortly after his birth. Today, he looked as though he also had gained enough weight to make up for his premature arrival.

Pamela confirmed this as soon as his carrycot had been placed in the sitting room well away from any draughts. "The nurses believe he's just as strong as a full-term infant now."

The presence of a baby instantly changed the focus of the household, and Mihail acquired yet another admirer as soon as Mrs Singer saw him. The housekeeper had never had children of her own, but her love of them immediately became apparent.

Over the years, Pamela had often felt saddened that the warm-hearted housekeeper could not speak, but with pen and paper always to hand they had succeeded in communicating their mutual respect. '*Me and my hubby would have given owt to have a bairn like him,*' Mrs Singer wrote now, in a rare willingness to confide something about herself. '*I hope you're not going to mind if I make a fuss of him.*'

Pamela smiled. "In a few weeks time, Mrs Singer, I shall be only too glad if somebody wants to take him over for a bit. I have a feeling that I'm going to find the days speeding by with his lordship, here, demanding attention!"

It was Tania, however, who took over Mihail on that first day, wandering into the sitting room to kneel beside his carrycot whenever she supposed that he could be feeling neglected.

Pamela was rather amused by this, and touched. She had always been afraid that Tania might be jealous of the newcomer. Discovering that the girl was so fascinated by the baby generated great relief.

"You've brought Tania up very carefully," she told Andre when they were in bed that night. "She has accepted Mihail as if she fully understands that there is more than room for both of them in our hearts."

Tania's interest in the baby continued as she first was allowed to assist with his bath, then later to bath him on her own. The smallness of his fingers and toes enchanted her, and she became quite obsessed with her belief that Mihail smiled especially for her.

"Pamela says it is only wind," she told her father one evening when he came into the room while she was cuddling the infant in his warm towel. "But I know it is because he recognizes me already. I am going to sing old Russian lullabies to him, the ones my grandmother sang. Did you know Pamela has asked me to try and settle him tonight?"

Andre smiled indulgently. "I did not know, but I am sure she will appreciate a few minutes' peace. I shall come up when you have him in his cot. I always must say good-night to my son."

Tania was pleased for her father that he was so

delighted to have a son, *of course she was*; but it was from that night that her own happiness seemed gradually to become eroded.

She was content enough to hand over to Andre after she had laid Mihail in his cot and sung him an old Russian lullaby. The baby's eyes had closed already, and he was breathing serenely. Smiling affectionately towards the infant, she spoke to her father.

"There – I have succeeded. I was afraid he would cry and refuse to settle without his mummy. But you see – he does know me, and trusts me to look after him."

"Or is well-fed and ready for sleep!" Andre teased. "I realize that you enjoy pretending you would make a fine mother, but that is simple enough when you may hand the baby back to his real parent."

Without understanding the reason, Tania felt rather hurt. It wasn't like her father to diminish her in any way, especially when she had spent so many months making the effort to help their life at Stonemoor to continue happily. Perturbed by these emotions and trying to rationalize her reaction to Andre's words, Tania needed to get away. She hastened past and along the landing towards her own room.

She could still hear him speaking to his son, could see in her mind's eye the now familiar way in which her father rested his arms on the side of the cot and gazed fondly down.

"That is good, young Mihail, sleep well. You will need all the strength you may gain in these early years, all the growth. Of mind as well as body, my son. I have such plans for you. We both have."

Tania closed the door of her room, yet still the

voice penetrated. "I have waited so long to have a boy, no one knows how long. Whatever you become, you always will be so very special."

Tania shivered, found a cardigan, flung it around her shoulders, and clutched the garment to her. It was the height of summer, a stifling night, and she felt chilled through to her bones.

I am not special any longer, she thought. She immediately condemned the idea as unjustified, but was unable to dismiss it. All at once her capability when handling the baby seemed spoiled. Minutes ago, she had felt satisfied by having coped without advice from anyone. But her father was right, the few tasks she had completed were too small to be worthy of even her own satisfaction. Worse than that, she now was beginning to suspect that her eagerness to help with the baby could have been no more than a quite pathetic attempt to show that she still had a function here.

I *do* love Mihail, though, she reflected. I want to do things for him. He is fascinating. I almost wish that he were mine.

But Mihail was not hers, he was not even fully her brother. He really belonged only to her father and Pamela.

When Andre passed her room he called Tania to join them downstairs. Pamela was standing near the sitting room fireplace when they entered, and she was frowning. She did not really wish me to put her baby to bed, Tania thought, no matter how capably I did so.

As soon as Pamela spoke the cause of her frown was apparent, and it drove all other concerns from her stepdaughter's head.

"Did you hear the phone?" she asked them. "That was our Tom. He says my mother's very poorly. She's had a cough for ages, now they've had to have the doctor and he says it's pleurisy."

"Pleuri . . . what is that? Something connected with the lungs?" asked Andre, concerned.

"Aye – some kind of inflamation. It's very painful, Tom says. She's in bed with it, and that's not like my mother."

"I am sorry. Who is caring for her? That sister of hers perhaps?"

"My Aunt Elsie? Shouldn't think so, she's worse than useless. Not that she can help it, mind. She's never been well herself."

"But who is caring for her?" Tania enquired. She loved Mildred Baker, could not bear to think of her being ill and having only those two young fellows to tend her.

"Tom says him and Ian are managing between them, but I don't know . . . I just wish I could go over there, or have her here perhaps."

Andre was shaking his head. "That would be unwise. You yourself are not fully recovered from the birth. And we must think of Mihail. Is this illness infectious? We must not put either of you at risk."

"I don't know how it starts, I'm sure," Pamela replied, running her fingers through her golden hair as she tried to think. "Maybe I could pop in there to see her tomorrow, get something organized for her."

"No," Andre contradicted. "You shall not go there."

"*I* will," Tania asserted swiftly. "I will go to Mildred, and I shall remain there until she is well again."

"Eh love, that's a grand thing to offer!" Pamela exclaimed, smiling, her blue eyes alight with relief. "Are you sure?"

Tania nodded emphatically. "We have always got on so well together, your mother and I. I am the one who is free to nurse her. Oh, I have singing classes, I know, but I shall not neglect them. I can just as easily travel from Halifax. The important thing is that I shall be there each night, and will be able to organize everything."

"You have greatly pleased Pamela by making this offer," Andre told her an hour later as he drove over to Halifax, "And you have pleased me also, you must remember that."

Oh, I will, Tania thought as she got out of the car. But she could not help wondering if either Pamela or Andre would miss her at all.

Ian opened the door to her, and the relief in his sherry-brown eyes would have been sufficient even if Tania herself were not already certain that she was doing the right thing.

"This is super of you, Tania," he said. "When our Pam rang back to say you were coming I could hardly believe it."

"Well – here I am. And you may take this case up to my old room where I stayed that other time. I shall go and see the invalid."

Propped up against her pillows, her breathing laboured and her eyes darkly-circled, Mildred looked unnervingly unlike her normal self. Tania rushed towards the large old-fashioned bed, and gently hugged the woman to her.

"You will get well now," she told her firmly. "I am here to look after you. I shall see that you take your medicine, and I will cook you delicious meals. Much better than those two sons of yours."

Mildred tried to laugh as the girl stepped back slightly, but then she coughed, and felt up the sleeve of her winceyette nightgown for a handkerchief.

"Eh, bless you, Tania love, it's that good to have you here! I knew our Pamela couldn't come, but I'm sure you're just as capable."

"I am, I am." She stopped then, and hesitated, she had been about to relate how ably she had cared for her half-brother only that evening. Suddenly, however, she did not wish to talk of him. "With me here, you need not worry about a thing. Soon you will be well again, but until you truly are very fit I shall stay here."

Mildred was tired, and once Tania had made the bed more comfortable by shaking up her pillows and smoothing the rumpled sheets, she drifted off to sleep.

Her breathing sounded even worse in the quiet room and Tania was reluctant to leave her. Only when Ian appeared in the doorway was she persuaded to go out on to the narrow landing.

"She'll be OK for a bit," he assured Tania. "The doctor thinks that stuff he's given her will stop her getting any worse. And if she wakens in the night it'll be all right to give her another dose."

"I will come downstairs and see what needs attention there, in that case," said Tania. "I suppose you two men will have left lots of dirty dishes, and pans that should have been washed."

Ian grinned as he started down the stairs. "Actually there's nowt like that needs doing. When Pamela rang to say you were coming tonight me and our Tom got cracking on t'washing-up. There is some ironing, though. Mum hasn't felt up to doing that this week."

Tom had been out when Tania arrived, but she gathered he had simply gone to the next-door house to tell their old neighbour of the help that would be arriving.

"I could see the relief on her face," he confided to Tania now. "She's a willing old girl, but she's turned eighty and not really up to looking after poorly folk."

Tania smiled. "So long as I am here, no one else need be troubled. And I shall only go out for my classes. The rest of the time I shall be in charge here."

"In charge?" Tom teased with a grin. "Does that mean you'll be issuing us with orders?"

She laughed, thinking back to the occasions when she had enjoyed Tom's company as well his brother's. Getting to know her stepmother's family had made such a difference to her enjoyment of life in the West Riding. "I am not so sure about you, but I do know Ian is unlikely to accept too many orders!"

"Right," Ian said. "So long as you understand that, we'll all get along famously. And, seriously, we're ever so grateful to you for stepping in to help."

Looking around the homely, rather old-fashioned living room which always felt so welcoming, Tania noticed crumbs on the carpet and hearth rug, but

61

someone had dusted the heavy furniture. She smiled to herself. Was Ian the one who had been determined to make the place look better for her?

Several times in the night, Mildred's protracted coughing brought Tania into the room to tend to her. Administering medicine or turning the crumpled pillows to make her more comfortable, Tania found she was feeling surprisingly contented. Never in her life before had she felt that someone depended upon her. She herself had faith that the doctor would heal this dear friend of hers, and somehow she had acquired enough belief in her own ability to feel that she could cope.

As the days passed and Mildred's breathing became somewhat easier, enabling them all to sleep more soundly, Tania began to enjoy her stay in the little terraced home. Both young men were personable, good fun as well. With a few months' experience on the design team of his magazine, Tom had become more assertive. His work brought him in contact with many interesting people from several walks of life, and had broadened his outlook until he seemed more the intellectual than his older brother.

Ian, however, was the one who had always been Tania's friend. She could see him now, as he'd been at their first meeting at Stonemoor House, gazing up at her. She had sensed then that something special was drawing them to each other. And she had never forgotten how Ian had kept in touch with her at the time when, before Andre's second marriage, Andre had been obliged to leave her at Stonemoor while he returned to Russia. Then there were the occasions when she sang with the band in which Ian played the saxophone. She relished such events still, for providing a lightness often missing from her more serious professional engagements.

Strangely, they talked only rarely now of the concerts in which they were to appear. Singing with the band was just a part of her life, accepted as agreeable, providing fun, but now they were also interested in other topics.

Ian was becoming fascinated by current affairs to a degree where Tania wondered if he might one day take an active part in politics, if only at a local level. She loved to listen when he spoke of national or international events, enlightening her by illustrating how they affected day to day life in an environment such as theirs.

Ian had been following the strike of dockers which had lasted for three weeks of July, and expected her to be interested that the Transport and General Workers Union had banned Communists and Fascists from office.

Tania, who had reacted to growing up under a Communist regime in Russia by blocking out all political thoughts after escaping, was surprising herself with how seriously she considered such matters.

She also began taking an interest in the business world, and heard Ian out concerning the way in which Tate & Lyle were opposing nationalization of the sugar industry.

"There ought to be more folk like Lord Lyle," he asserted. "Even though we keep having our rations cut, we don't want independent companies to finish."

Tania could appreciate that State interference

would be unwelcome to someone like Ian who worked in a company as small as Canning's. On a different level, she could not help but be amused by the Mr Cube figure created as part of Tate & Lyle's campaign.

"Each time that I see a pack of sugar," she said, "I shall remember all that you have told me about the firm. You are quite right, I think, to be against this nationalization."

Ian was delighted that she seemed so ready to accept his beliefs. He had been attracted to Tania from the start, but nevertheless had wondered if she could be a little young for her age. These increasingly serious conversations were reassuring him that, despite their very different backgrounds, they often were like-minded. And if he had ever doubted her commitment to the things that mattered, her devotion to his mother had driven away every last misgiving.

With the girl's care, Mildred was improving daily. Eventually, she was allowed out of bed in the afternoons, and before very long was getting up in time for the midday meal that Tania prepared.

Now that Mildred was so much better Pamela and Andre visited her. Seeing how her grandson had grown during those early weeks helped Mildred to overcome some of the depression accompanying her illness.

"You will soon be able to go out walking with Pamela and the baby when they call," Tania told her with a smile. "You must get well quickly now, or you will be missing a great deal of his development."

Whilst saying all this, Tania was aware that she

herself was missing many of the changes occurring as her half-brother progressed. When Mihail was born she had been determined to savour every minute sign of his development, but now she felt almost glad to be missing some of them. In fairness to her father and Pamela, she admitted privately that they both had greeted her lovingly, hugging her while they spoke of how pleased they were with the way she was caring for Mildred Baker.

They also, however, had failed to conceal their preoccupation with Mihail. Once they had ascertained that Pamela's mother was greatly improved, every other sentence became devoted to the infant.

Watching and listening, Tania sensed that the three of them were a family, complete without her. And she felt shaken. She did not believe that she was jealous, but she did feel that she had become superfluous. After they had taken the baby home she caught herself looking out of the window towards the row of similar grey stone terraced houses and feeling glad to be here. She was so perturbed about returning to Stonemoor House that she began seeking reasons to prolong her stay in Halifax.

Following another of their visits Tania decided the time had come when she must think out what she really wished concerning her own future. Even someone with little imagination could have pictured the way that life at Stonemoor House would develop. The entire household would be geared to provide Mihail with every advantage. Her father had astonished her today by insisting that he intended putting down his son's name for one of the major public schools.

Tania had been rather amused to note that Pamela

had not agreed with this intention, but *she* knew her father, he would have his way. At one time, Tania would have fully understood Andre's reasons for wishing Mihail to have a private education. With their history, it seemed quite reasonable now to mistrust anything organized by the state. But here in England a good education was becoming available to all. It was beginning to seem to her that her father's devotion to the boy's future was obsessive.

Ian came into the living room that evening while Tania was sitting at the table, elbows resting on the chenille cover while she stared pensively at nothing.

"What's wrong?" he asked immediately. "Not Mum . . .?" He had been so shattered to find she could be ill that he would be some while adjusting to the idea that he need no longer be alarmed on her behalf.

Tania shook her head and tried to smile. "Nothing to do with her, she really is a great deal better, you know."

"Then what's up, love? You're looking as miserable as sin!"

Again, she shook her head, but Ian was too concerned to leave the matter alone. He crossed the room, took her hands and drew her to her feet. "I'm your best friend, aren't I? You can tell me, Tania, whatever it is that's bothering you."

"You will think me very childish, and a spoiled child at that."

"Never. I'm too fond of you to think anything of the kind. And I do want to help."

Sighing, Tania leaned her head against him. "It

is perhaps that I am being foolish, I do not know. Only – well, when I think of the way it will be at home, I feel that I may not belong there as I have in the past."

"Because of young Mihail? That's understandable, love. He'll be needing that much attention they'll be bound to be wrapped up in him."

"Yes. That is how it seems, you expressed that very well. But I don't want to feel like this. I *am* glad he's there, you know."

"There's been times years ago when I hated our Tom. Times when he seemed to get everything he wanted. But you shouldn't let this upset you, lass. You're grown up, will soon have a life of your own."

Tania gave him a look. It was strange that Ian should be speaking this way, so often recently she had longed for her own life, her own home even, someone who belonged only to her. Was it possible that Ian not only realized what she was feeling, but was experiencing very similar emotions? Might they one day offer each other a solution – a lovely means of creating a happier life? Together.

Chapter Four

Tania replaced the receiver and looked across the room to where Ian was sitting. They were the only ones in the house. Tom had taken his mother to the cinema to see *The Red Shoes*. This was Mildred's first evening outing since being ill with pleurisy. At first, Tania also had looked forward to seeing Moira Shearer dancing in such a romantic picture, but her dreams of sitting there with Ian had been ruined when he said he was staying at home. The telephone call just now had confirmed how right she had been to suppose that her stay in Halifax was all but ended. And now she had missed an ideal opportunity to begin establishing a stronger bond than friendship between them.

"That was my father," she told him. "He wants me to go home tomorrow." For a moment or two she had been delighted to hear Andre emphasizing that Stonemoor House was where she belonged. Only then she had recalled the differences that her young half-brother's presence would always make there. She must not keep looking back. She must do something about this yearning to have a place of her own, with a person to whom she mattered more than anyone in the world.

"I shall miss you, I shall miss you so much."

Sounding quite husky, Ian startled her. Suddenly, he came hastening towards her across the tiny room. He gathered her into his arms, crushing her to him until her breasts were hurting. And then he was kissing her, fiercely, his lips stirring over her own. He might have been willing her to remain with him, to become a part of his life.

Tania sighed, offered kiss for kiss, feveredly, anguished by the sudden knowledge that tomorrow they would be apart. All those days, all the days which had extended into weeks, almost to a month, had passed – and now there would be no further opportunities. Never once until now had they embraced like this, never had she felt such passion compelling her to gaze into his sherry-brown eyes.

Ian groaned, tensing as he held her. "I need you, Tania," he murmured, sounding surprised by the intensity of his longing.

"And I you, and I you, my Ian." She had known he was nice-looking, but had not realized how attractive his strong shoulders seemed.

"One day," he said, his mouth still close to her own, "one day, if we feel like we do now, we might get married."

"I always will feel like this, I will always want you."

Ian smiled, kissed her again, more gently. "I certainly can't think I'll ever want anybody else."

He had admired Tania for years: since that first day they were introduced, she had entranced him. But the prospect of Tania ever becoming his had seemed sheer fantasy. If she hadn't come to look after his mother, he might never have felt how *right* living in the same house could feel. He might never have believed his hopes were realistic.

His talk of marriage had surprised her, but only into understanding that if Ian was ready to commit himself to her she would be thrilled.

"We do not have to wait," she told him, eagerly. "We could belong together soon, Ian. We could have our own little home."

"That'd be super!" he exclaimed, hugging her to him again, pressing at her, wanting her to recognize his need, to know that he had realized tonight that all his yearning was focused on her. In a place of their own there would be no one to question what they did together.

He led her to the settee, drew her down with him to its well-worn cushions, and held her close, kissing her again, parting her teeth with his probing tongue.

Tania relaxed into his arms, grew aware that he was caressing one breast, and his touch was awakening a new urgency within her. She sensed somehow that this massive attraction brought with it the means of creating all the completeness for which she was longing.

Pulses that she had never suspected she possessed were generated just by having Ian near, a glorious compulsion which elated, but also made her very slightly afraid. Innocent, she might be, but a fool she was not, her mother Anichka had instilled a certain practical wisdom. Somewhere beyond sensation, Tania was conscious of her own responsibility. This young man of hers was healthy and he was powerful, she could relish the extent of his need, but she must remain conscious that she should be the one to restrain it.

"Let's go up to your room." Ian sounded desperate. "Tonight's the only chance we have."

"We must not," Tania told him. "I do not want our love to be underhand. We only have to wait— "

His laugh was harsh, startling. "But I can't wait! I'm – I'm just full of— " Ian paused, adopted the word which she had used. "Of love for you. Please, Tania . . ."

The 'please' almost confounded her. It wasn't like Ian to beg for anything. And there could be no mistaking the strength of the desire that was making him stir against her as they lay there.

Gently, tenderly, she kissed him on the mouth. "You must not think that it is because I do not want to," she said in her quaint English. "You will see how swiftly I wish us to marry."

And they were committed to each other now, she reflected. With kisses and caresses they would endure, until they finally were married. Her dream then would have come alive. And with Ian!

They talked for hours that night, before the others came in from the cinema and afterwards. Tania was certain that her father would agree to their marrying. "He knows you already, and likes you," she said. "It is not as though I were wishing to marry a stranger."

She would ask Andre the minute that he had driven her home. When he had agreed to the wedding she would feel quite differently about life at Stonemoor, would see it as just a prelude to her greater happiness. To her beginning to be her true self.

"As soon as he gives his consent, we'll tell my mother," said Ian, looking forward to living with

Tania, to having a constant release for this dynamic urge that promised sheer ecstasy. "She'll be really delighted, she thinks of you like one of the family now, doesn't she?"

Despite her affection for Ian and his mother, Tania was surprised to feel quite elated after she had set out with her father along Burnley Road, and left behind all those dark stone buildings. Out here, there was so much space, meadows and woods with an occasional glimpse of the river and the canal which flowed through the steep-sided valley. Perhaps she and Ian might find a house in the country.

Andre was feeling proud of his young daughter as he drove her home to Stonemoor. He had chatted for a time with Mildred Baker and was pleased by the evident improvement in her health, but even more so by her unstinting praise of Tania.

"You are a good girl," he told her as they got out of the car. "It fills my heart to see how unselfishly you cared for Pamela's mother."

"They are a lovely family," said Tania, smiling as she faced him while noticing how the walls of Stonemoor House appeared to glow in the sunlight. "They make you want to be with them."

Pamela gave her an immense hug the moment that they met just inside the front door. "I can't tell you how thankful I am for all you've done. I felt so torn when I couldn't go dashing off to help out."

Tania smiled into her stepmother's blue eyes. "I was happy to be there. At least – once your mother began improving, I was. They all seem like my own family, you know."

Determined to do everything right, Tania entered

72

the sitting room and crossed swiftly to the open window, beyond which she could see Mihail sleeping in his pram, in its usual place for a cloudless day.

"He looks to have grown while I have been away, even since you called to see us. I shall have to spend lots of time getting to know him all over again. I hope you will let me get him ready for bed tonight, Pamela?"

"Of course. I'll be glad to have you take over for a bit. Just so long as you're not overtired after all the work you've been doing."

"Tired? Not in the slightest. I've been too happy to feel tired."

"Pamela and I have been talking while you were away, my sweet," Andre began. "We have decided that it is time that you were given rather more space here. We thought one of the larger bedrooms should be yours. If you wish to come with me now you may choose whichever you prefer . . ."

Tania hesitated, her heart beginning to race. Her intention of tackling her father immediately about marrying Ian, had been deferred when she realized that she would be more likely to have her own way, if she took care to prepare an atmosphere that would be receptive to her ideas. Now she suddenly was confronted with having to explain why she would not require a larger room here.

"Very well," she agreed, and remembered to add a thank you before hurrying ahead of her father out of the room. Whatever she must say (and at this moment she had no notion of what that should be) stringing together the words would be far easier if she did not have Pamela's reaction to consider as well.

"We have always talked frankly to each other, have we not, Father," she began as they reached the landing. "I wish you to listen to me now. Shall we go into my old room?"

"You are happy in here, no? That is what you are telling me . . .?" He was smiling, eager to show his understanding as he stood just within her room and gazed all around. "Then there is no difficulty, little one. This room will remain yours, forever."

Tania was trying to smile back, but had become preoccupied with attempting to voice the true cause of her feelings. Choosing a life partner was a large step, its seriousness was beginning to strike her quite forcefully. But the very weight of her decision was producing a powerful urgency that seemed at odds with all this hesitation.

"I had thought I would always be completely happy here," she said, not entirely with regard for the truth. "I have been so glad to see how marriage to Pamela has given you so much joy."

"It has indeed, my dear, and as you know that has increased now that we have a son as well as— "

"Quite." She had to cut him short before she let slip any hint that Mihail's arrival might have affected her own attitude. "And seeing the three of you has made me think about my own future."

Andre was frowning already, Tania understood that she was not being so careful as she might over choosing her words.

"Now, do not look so worried, I am not about to abandon my singing or anything. But I do need to have a life of my own. A life where family – *love* are the prime ingredients."

"You have that here, Tania, and always will have."

She sighed. "Oh, I know that is what you wish to provide, you and Pamela also. But can you not see – I want to create all that for myself now, in my own home. With someone I love."

"And so you will, in time. When you meet— "

"I have met him. You know him also, have known him longer even than I have. Ian is the one I want to be with, to share a home wi— "

"*Ian?*" Andre interrupted. He was astounded. The boy was no older than this bit of a girl who was shattering him. Where on this earth did these children suppose they would find a parent who might consent to such nonsense?

Tania tried to speak lightly. "You are in love with his sister, you cannot be surprised that I find Ian is the man I love."

Andre made an effort. "Tania, Tania, you are much too young to even think of committing yourself to someone for life. And he is just as immature."

When she spoke again her accent made her strangely dignified. "You do not know Ian as I do. He had to grow up early because of having no father alive. He has been working for years, has he not?"

She has considered this thoroughly, Andre thought, and was afraid that he was losing her already. He could only hope that she was not about to confound him with all the answers.

"Working, yes – but have you given any thought to what he might be earning? You need to go into all that, my dear, love does not provide the wherewithal."

"I wish that you would credit me with a little intelligence!"

Being opposed was making her angry now, more angry than she recalled feeling for many a month. "Ian and I are aware that we shall need to be practical. But when I sing they pay me well. His job could not be more safe – in fact, once Pamela pays him according to the true amount of work he does, Ian will have a good income."

Andre flinched, already hurt by Tania's wish to get away, he wondered how she could be so wrong about his wife. "How dare you criticize Pamela! She has always been a good sister to Ian. And a good mother to you. You have no right to judge her conduct of business matters. Matters of which you understand nothing."

"I am not, I am not. I have no wish to criticize. But do you not see? Ian and I have thought about everything. Because the only thing we really want is to be together."

"I am sorry, no. I cannot – *will not* give my consent. You are both too young, far too imma-ture." He felt quite light-headed with stress induced by the shock. "*If* you both feel the same way when you are twenty-one you may raise the subject again."

"But that is three years, Father, three! Do you really care so little about me that you would condemn me to three years of misery?"

"You are being melodramatic, and it will serve you badly, I fear. If you take the trouble to consider, you will realize that this reaction only demonstrates how much time you need in order to mature."

76

It was his last word, and Tania understood that no further pleas would have the slightest effect upon his decision. She felt choked by furious tears, so distressed that she did not know where she might find comfort. Briefly, instinct told her Pamela could sympathize. Ian was her brother, after all, the young man she entrusted with her work. Pamela was fond of him, would want his happiness.

Pamela, however, also regarded Ian in much the same way as Andre thought of them both. Hadn't she heard her speaking of how young he was? She knew well enough that this was behind his lack of promotion. The truth was that only Ian himself would really understand.

Tania left her father standing, still perturbed, in the doorway while she ran hurtling down the stairs to the telephone.

"He will not even listen," she gabbled into the receiver. "He has no idea what it is like to be in love, and to be kept apart like this. I am missing you terribly now, how will I even survive till the end of the week?"

Hearing the commotion and Tania's overstrung voice, Pamela had come to the door of the sitting room. After a few moments' silence, her stepdaughter was continuing, tearfully now, sounding hysterical.

"We shall have to speak to Mildred together. She will be on our side. She is too kind to treat us so cruelly. And you said – she does like me. We could even live with her for a while. Anything will be better than this. It is so intolerable here . . ."

Andre was coming slowly down the stairs. He seemed to have aged by ten years during the few minutes since he had brought his daughter home so joyfully. Pamela gave him a look.

"What *is* going on? Why on earth is Tania screeching down the phone like that? And what's my mother got to do with anything? I don't want her bothering with any of this, you know. She's only just getting over that pleurisy."

"I know, I know," said Andre gently, trying to smile reassuringly. "It is all rather confused, I am afraid – a misunderstanding perhaps. Those two children seem to imagine they are in love."

"Imagine!" Tania shrieked from out in the hall. "Imagine! Did you hear that, Ian?" she enquired into the telephone. "That is what my father thinks, that is how bigoted he is."

Pamela drew Andre further into the room and closed the door behind them.

"Ian? Our Ian – is that really who she's talking to?"

"Yes, yes. We shall be obliged to leave her to have her say, I think. Let her get this out of her system. She must not marry him, of course."

Must not? Pamela thought. Is my brother not good enough then to marry a Malinowski? But the reaction was a defensive instinct, entirely unjustifiable when she paused to consider Andre's attitude towards her family. Andre had spoken only on account of Ian's age – and she herself knew as well as anyone how immature the lad still was.

"Well, certainly not for some long while," Pamela agreed at last. "They can't know their own minds, and they both need to concentrate on their work if they're to make anything of their lives."

78

From beyond the closed door, Tania's voice continued, but more calmly now with an occasional giggle which reassured Andre that his daughter was recovering from her outburst.

"She sounds better already," he remarked. "I feel sure that so long as we do not forbid her seeing Ian the attraction will wane."

"Don't count on that, love," said his wife. "Ian's a grand-looking young chap. Even though he is my brother, I can see why any lass would fancy him."

Andre shrugged. "I have nothing against him, naturally. So long as he has behaved as he should."

Once again, Pamela felt her hackles beginning to rise. She willed herself to avoid a heated argument. "We had a strict upbringing," she told him quietly. "Our Ian knows where to draw the line." Although, she added silently, your Tania can be a bit of a provocative madam at times.

The rest of the day continued uneasily, but Tania did keep her promise to get the baby ready for bed.

Pamela, who recognized the effort to win approval, joined her in the nursery when Mihail was in his cot.

"Hello," said Tania dully over her shoulder. "I suppose he will have told you everything."

"That you and Ian want to marry, yes, your father has. That's one reason why I wanted you and me to have a bit of a chat."

"You will not put me off, you know. I want Ian and he wants me – and we need all the things that you have – a home, a child— "

"Yes, love, I'm sure. But there's time enough."

Tania groaned. "I should never have even hoped for a minute that you would understand. Especially after *he* had spoken to you. He is positively antiquated in his outlook."

"Your father isn't, not really. But, Tania love – you've so much living to do, you oughtn't to be eager to tie yourself down with responsibilities so soon."

"We are willing to work, more than ever determined to make a go of our careers. We would save together to furnish our home."

She had seen a little house, long before even beginning to think seriously of having a home of her own. On the edge of the moors, but beside the main road through into Lancashire, a stone-built cottage with a tiny garden, it seemed to have been empty for months. To be crying out for someone to take it, to fill it with loving voices.

That same evening Ian approached his mother with the suggestion that he and Tania should become engaged. The agitated telephone call had reminded him that they both *were* young, he was for more likely to obtain Mildred's consent if he began diplomatically with mention of an engagement. Once she became used to the fact that he and Tania were committed to each other, the subject of wedding arrangements would be easier to introduce.

Even with such circumspection, his idea met with astonishment and no small degree of disapproval.

"Engaged? At your age? Nay, Ian lad, you can't have thought what you'd be taking on."

"But, Mum – you like Tania, you're very fond of her."

"Aye, I am that. But that doesn't stop me seeing

that she's no more ready for settling down than you are."

"But we are, Mum, we are – really ready. She's a lovely lass and— "

"I know all that," Mildred interrupted. "But so far as I can see, you've neither of you got any experience. You're young enough to have lots of girlfriends, before you end up with a home of your own and bairns coming along."

"Tania's the only girl I want. And I only said engaged— "

"Aye – well, I don't hold with long engagements, never have. They only put ideas into a couple's heads. All that planning for when they're married. Stands to reason it sets 'em thinking that they ought to be able to carry on before they're wed as if she already had a gold band on her finger. You know what I mean."

"But it won't be like that. I think too much of Tania to— "

"Oh, Ian, grow up! I was your age once, you know. When a pretty lass and a young chap are thrown together a lot, they're bound to want to do more than hold hands."

"You can't see it, can you?" Ian persisted heatedly. "That's the very reason why we do want to get wed."

"Ah – now we're coming to the truth, are we? It isn't really an engagement that's going to satisfy you, any road, is it? It's marriage, you're on about. And I'm afraid that simply isn't on the cards. Not afore you've a few more years on your back."

Ian continued to press Mildred to give her approval, at least to his engagement to Tania, but she remained adamant. With frequent references to the need for being sensible, and her advice on the wisdom of looking around before he tied himself down, she left Ian with no space to manoeuvre.

He had arranged to take Tania to see *The Red Shoes* one evening and, not wanting to spoil the film for her, waited until he was driving her home afterwards to recount all that Mildred had said.

"I'm afraid it does look as if we're going to have to wait, if we can't get anybody to agree," he added. "We'll just have to put our minds to it, and show 'em that we mean what we say, and we will get married, no matter how long they make us delay."

"We could elope," Tania suggested. She had been reading about a pair of lovers who ran away to marry when their union was opposed. She would love to make that kind of gesture to prove how serious she was about Ian.

"You don't mean that," he said, frowning. "Ordinary folk like us don't go in for eloping."

"They do if they are keen enough on each other," she reminded him. She was not happy about his accepting the prospect of waiting.

Ian shook his head. "No, that wouldn't seem right somehow." Ever since he had been the best man for Andre when Pamela got married he had dreamed of being surrounded by his family and friends whenever he came to make a similar commitment.

He saw how dejected Tania appeared, and gave her shoulders a squeeze. "Don't look like that. It isn't the end of the world. You'll see – they'll come round. Happen we've only got to hang for a bit, it needn't be a matter of waiting till we're twenty-one."

But the house I want will have sold years before that, Tania thought miserably. And I have set my heart on living there.

On the following day Tania passed that house again on her way to audition for a concert performance in Manchester. Her father was driving her there, a situation which she found disturbing, however unavoidable. Living in Cragg Vale as they did, although close to the Lancashire border, they were not on a route used by the Manchester buses. The journey promised to be uncomfortable. Ever since Andre had forbidden her marriage, she had taken elaborate steps to avoid animated conversation with him. Today, she professed to be studying the score of the piece she was to sing, but she was in fact feigning concentration whilst indulging in the dreams which seemed now to be the only means of sustaining her life.

Seeing 'her' house, however, cheered Tania; especially when the 'For Sale' notice witnessed to its still being on the market. She glanced from the car, smiling to herself as she pictured Ian bringing her flowers grown in its garden. Through a side gate she caught a glimpse of a lawn at the rear. She could visualize children playing there, hers and Ian's, and a line where she would dry their clothes. She would need to persuade Mrs Singer to teach her how to do the washing.

When she was caring for Ian's mother that was the one task they had refused to let her tackle. While Mildred was ill in bed Ian's Aunt Elsie had come to do the weekly wash. From the fuss that the elderly lady had made, it had seemed a daunting operation.

In her own home, though, with Ian there all the time, everything would be completely different. Even the most mundane jobs would be fun. She would cook for him, and while they were saving hard would even clean. She would have such a tiny house all bright and shining in a matter of minutes.

"You are looking more cheerful at last," Andre observed, and startled her from her reverie. "No doubt you have recognized that having to wait before marrying will benefit you eventually. You and Ian will appreciate each other all the more for being patient."

"If you say so." Tania did not mean to relent. In fact, she was sorry now that the pleasure induced by seeing the house had made her overlook her own determination to make her dissatisfaction evident.

"You should do well today," her father continued cheerfully. "I've heard you practising, even if you didn't invite my opinion." He had been hurt by Tania's suddenly ceasing to employ him as her musical mentor. He had loved the occasions when she had consulted him on phrasing or requested his judgement of other aspects of her singing.

In some ways, nevertheless, he had understood. There had been times (especially since taking up the violin again after the long period of neglect before coming to England) when he himself had been unwilling to have anyone assess his playing.

"Are you anxious about this audition? Is that why you are so quiet, my sweet?" he enquired, glancing sideways as he sat at the wheel.

Tania shrugged. When she spoke her accent sounded strong, the English quite stilted. "I need to do well, of course. Now that I am thinking seriously about the future, I must earn good fees. But I know the piece, do I not?" She had sung it through for Ian, and he had seemed quite moved, even despite his preferring popular music.

"And how is that jazz band performing? You have not spoken of them for some time."

"Classical musicians are not the only ones who play mainly in season, you know," she reminded him stiffly. "Actually, they are rehearsing now. I am to sing with them, naturally."

Andre withheld his instinctive comment on *that*. Relations with this daughter of his already were sufficiently frayed. This was not the time for discouraging her enthusiasm for contemporary songs.

As he had feared she might, Tania asked him to keep away from the rehearsal room where she was auditioning. Leaving her there after arranging a time to return, Andre felt restless. He found a space for parking the car and began walking.

Manchester had become special to him, reviving as it did with every visit, memories of the night when he had asked Pamela to marry him. He had returned to the concert platform and was elated already when they met up after the performance. She had enthused about his playing, he supposed, although all he remembered now was that he had known, beyond doubt, that he must spend the rest of his life with her.

She had been driving the little van that she used for her work and they had stopped high on the moors which had become to him so expressive of the freedom engendered by coming to Yorkshire. In no time at all they had reached a mutual understanding of their need of a new life together. That night he had taken Pamela home to Stonemoor, and had loved her with all the passion which had intensified over the months of being contained.

But he was not wrong, was he, to be denying a similar expression of love to Tania and the young man she fancied? They *were* too young – too young for knowing their minds when desires were hammering so vociferously. And too young also for the serious business of making a home, of making that home lasting. His Tania had seen enough trouble in their native Russia, had grown solemn beyond her years through witnessing too many injustices, too much suffering.

Andre loathed the need for denying her anything. Her past deprivations had earned her some enjoyment now, lightness to temper ambition, and a delaying of the grave matters which became an inevitable part of adult living.

"Just enjoy life, my little one, make that sufficient," he murmured under his breath. And prayed that somehow his thoughts might reach her, that she might understand and become content.

During the journey back to Stonemoor House Andre began to believe that Tania might be prepared to do just that. She had come rushing out to the car which he had drawn to a halt near the stage door.

"I have done it!" she exclaimed, beaming. "They said I was so good that they had no doubts about choosing me to sing with them."

"Very good, my sweet. I am very pleased. Were there many other contenders?"

"Masses and masses of them, I was afraid that I did not have a chance. Most of the other girls were very glamorous too."

"But you also can look sophisticated, especially on stage." Watching and listening as she performed, he often felt his throat aching with pride, and experienced a certain disbelief that this was his child.

"They are to pay me more than I have ever earned," Tania continued, sounding excited.

"I should hope that they are, you need some proof that you are improving each time you appear."

His daughter nodded, but she was much more interested in what such large fees might accomplish for her. If no one relented and permitted her to marry Ian, she must begin to shape her own future. She would have to save for that house alone. There was no way that she was going to let it be sold to anyone else.

Chapter Five

Mihail was christened on the last Sunday in September at St Paul's church in Halifax where his parents had married.

Tania had been delighted when asked to become his godmother, and her pleasure increased as soon as she heard that Pamela's brothers Ian and Tom were the other godparents. She chose her outfit for the day most carefully because Mildred Baker would be there. It had to be something smart yet fairly simple because she was determined to impress as being down-to-earth and sensible. A suit in a quite heavy cloth, practical for a northern autumn, its best feature was the shade, a blue that seemed to add colour to her grey eyes.

Pamela, who had been pregnant when clothing coupons finished last March, was celebrating her regained figure and the end of rationing in a pearly-grey lightweight coat which had a gored skirt reaching well below her calves. Her matching hat was of velvet with a pink trimming to link with the dress glimpsed at the neck. For once, it was Tania's turn to wondered if her stepmother would be warm enough in the chill West Riding.

Tania was relieved when Mildred greeted her just as lovingly as in the past, giving her a hug as well as a kiss when they met outside the church. She saw Ian smile, evidently he was as pleased as Tania herself that his mother's refusal to let them marry did not indicate any general unease about their friendship.

Perhaps if we are patient she will relent in a few months' time, thought Tania as she followed the others into the church.

In the back pew Dorothy and Charles were waiting. It was going to be a true family occasion. Pamela's old friend Dorothy was married to Mildred Baker's nephew. They had two children, Jim now a toddler and Janet who, just a few weeks older than Mihail, was about to be christened along with him.

Tania had met Dorothy and Charles only occasionally, but their little boy had attached himself to her from the start, and came tottering unsteadily towards her now.

One day, I'll have a boy like that, she thought, and realized that her own half-brother would seem more interesting within the next year or two. A great surge of what she supposed must be the mothering instinct came rushing through her, making the prospect of waiting to have her own family seem all the more intolerable. But Ian was at her side now, bending to tease young Jim. Smiling up at her, he winked.

"You love kids, don't you? It won't be so long before it's our turn if I've owt to do with it," he whispered. "There'll be a way."

Just as they were all gathering around the font at the west end of the church, the heavy door opened to admit two elderly sisters. Sophie and Hilda Norton, the previous owners of Stonemoor House, were invited today because of their continued interest in Pamela and Andre.

Twittering agitatedly on account of their taxi arriving late, they seemed to Tania to resemble a pair of restless starlings. But the sisters soon responded to the solemn atmosphere and quieted as they smiled about at everyone when the vicar began to speak.

As the service came to an end Tania grew more than ever certain that she somehow would win Mildred round. Being with Ian always increased her awareness of how much she needed to belong with him completely; surrounded like this by family and children, she felt as though she would never endure even one more year on her own. If only she could obtain his mother's agreement to the marriage, persuading her own father would be easier. And how could Pamela fail to support them if Mildred Baker had consented?

Tania dropped to her knees in the wooden pew, and prayed fervently for help. She was the one who was the more sure of the way their future must be shaped. She, therefore, must make things happen.

The Norton sisters were joining them at Stonemoor for a buffet meal. Andre was arranging for them to travel with Dorothy and Charles when Tania intervened to suggest an alternative.

"The Misses Norton will be happier with you and Pamela. That is if you can fit them in along with the carrycot? I am quite happy to follow in one of the other cars."

Taking good care to be in Ian's vehicle rather than with his cousin Charles, Tania got into the back seat with Mildred.

"How are you feeling?" she enquired. "Fully recovered now from the after-effects of that pleurisy, I hope?"

"Eh, Tania love, I'm champion, thanks. And that's largely due to the good care you took of me, you know. I shan't forget."

"It was no trouble, really."

"You're a grand lass." Mildred paused, smiling at her. "You mustn't ever think I'm not fully aware of that. I hope you understand it's only because I believe you're both too young for settling down that I've had to say no. It's nowt to do with you yourself, nothing personal, like."

Tania was thankful that Mildred herself had raised the matter. Smiling back at her, she nodded. "I do understand, I really do. I only hope that as time goes on we shall be able to convince you that we are mature enough for marriage."

"Aye – well, two or three years'll pass quicker than you expect, then we'll have to see, won't we?"

Mildred's response hadn't been half so promising as Tania hoped, but she reminded herself that this was the day when she was to make everyone see how adult her attitude had become. She neither pestered Ian's mother to change her mind, nor behaved as if disappointment was making her gloomy. All the way out to Stonemoor she chatted about the christening service, her half-brother's steady development and, quite briefly, about her impending concert.

"Well done," said Ian, a hand on her shoulder as they went into the house. "You've discovered that Mum doesn't react well to folk going on and on when they're after summat. Just don't lay it on too thick,

91

will you – all this small talk, I mean. It was starting to sound a bit unnatural."

Tania turned her head away to conceal how hurt she was. She had put all that she had got into sustaining the good relationship with his mother. Ian might have appeared grateful. Deep within her subconscious, a fresh anxiety began to trouble her. Was he beginning to have doubts now? Would he still be as eager to marry her at the end of the three years that everyone kept mentioning?

Still determined to reveal nothing of her own unease, Tania threw herself into helping to entertain their guests. Mrs Singer and Pamela had prepared the buffet meal, but Tania now appeared at her father's side, offering plates while he supplied drinks, freeing her stepmother to show off the baby and chat to everyone.

Seeing the Misses Norton inspecting the longcase clock some while later Tania went over to them.

"It still works beautifully, as you see!" she exclaimed. "Did Pamela tell you that while she was laid up she began learning more about old clocks? I found books for her from the library in Halifax."

Tania did not add that as soon as her injuries permitted Pamela had foresaken that interest in order to give more time to running Canning's.

The Nortons were an entertaining pair – unintentionally providing more amusement for Tania than either of them suspected. Unused to company, these days, their excitement made them resemble wizened children, while their years had endowed a disregard for discretion.

Never once thinking to lower their voices, they

commented gleefully on the clothes people were wearing, hairstyles, and the right or otherwise of those who had taken up the most prestigous chairs. As they relaxed, they grew more vociferous, remarking on who might be filling their plates to overflowing, yet totally disregarding their own repeated forays to the long buffet table.

Everyone but Tania appeared unconcerned, intent on enjoying the occasion and strengthening family friendships. Eventually Andre made a brief speech calling on all present to toast the future of his own son, and of Dorothy and Charles's tiny daughter.

". . . I hope that the children will grow up to be friends," he concluded. "I have always been struck by the warm-heartedness extended towards me by Pamela's mother and all her family. I can only hope that the future will strengthen our connections."

Tania gave him a look. He must be saying merely what he felt was expected from him. His refusal to even contemplate her engagement to Ian certainly did not indicate any eagerness to increase such involvement! All at once she felt quite exhausted. Behaving immaculately *was* such a strain; how could she forget that so many of those present seemed intent on condemning her to be unhappy?

Even Ian himself was giving her the impression today that he was becoming indifferent to her. He had hardly glanced her way since arriving at Stonemoor House. When he was not laughing and talking with his cousin Charles he was speaking at length with her own father. Could Ian not understand that, unless Andre relented, his forbidding her to marry had ruined their father-daughter relationship?

It was only some hours later that Tania realized that Ian might have been encouraging her father to reconsider his verdict. Now that some of their guests had departed, she succeeded in taking Ian aside to ask if he had had any success.

Ian simply grinned and shook his head. "It was nothing like that. I was asking him if they played football in Russia, or if they preferred rugby."

"What on earth is rugby?" Tania demanded scathingly.

"Don't you know? It's played with a different shaped ball – and played very differently an' all, with its own rules. Then there's both League and Rugby Union— "

"No," Tania interrupted, her hopes falling yet again. "I do not wish to hear if all you can think of is some stupid game."

"Nay, don't be daft," he reproached her. "You've got to have some kind of an interest, haven't you, hobbies?"

She shook her head. "I would have thought it was more important to concentrate on work, if only to save for the future . . ." She paused, swallowed. "For a home."

"There's time enough for that, isn't there, when they won't consider us getting wed for years?"

Tania might have been reassured that he was mentioning their marrying at some future date, but she was not. Ian's cheerful acceptance of the circumstances was goading her to pursue the argument. But this was still the day when she meant to show Mildred Baker (if not her own father) that she was imperturbable.

Sensing that she and Ian were heading towards a disagreement, she walked away from him and hastened across to sit where Pamela and Dorothy were talking across the heads of their now sleeping infants.

"Hello, love," Pamela greeted her warmly. "Thanks for all you've done to make today such a success. Dot's just been saying what a nice little hostess you are."

"Thank you," said Tania and nodded towards the sleeping babies. "It looks as though this is the best time to come and chat."

"It is an' all," Dorothy agreed. "Although they both were on their best behaviour in church, weren't they, bless 'em."

"Where is Jim?" Tania enquired, glancing around for the toddler.

"Charlie and Tom have taken him out into the garden. Plenty of space out there for him to let off steam. He's at an age now when he's into everything, and you've so many lovely things here that it's quite a job keeping an eye on him."

"It must be very interesting, though, seeing him develop."

"Aye, Tania, it is that! Not that there's as much time for him now this young madam is on the scene."

"But you are very fortunate, I think, to have two children. They will be happy to grow up together."

"Or will fratch like the devil, and drive you crackers!" Pamela exclaimed, but relented when she saw her stepdaughter's expression. "All right, just for today, we'll pretend it's all sweetness and light. I know you can't wait to start having bairns of your own."

* * *

95

Mihail had been so good throughout the day of the christening that Pamela had thought how very fortunate she was. Within a week, however, he became so restless that she began to feel exhausted.

During his first few weeks he had been such a quiet baby that she had concluded that his premature arrival was being compensated by the need for a lot of sleep. If that had been the case, that need must now have been sated. From sleeping most of the night and a large portion of each day he changed to wakening every two or three hours in the night and remaining awake during much of the day. And whenever his eyes were open he was learning to demand attention.

Andre was practising the violin more regularly as the concert season proceeded, and could idolize his son without relishing the screaming that frequently interrupted rehearsal of important pieces.

Not wishing to trouble her, he had said nothing to Pamela, but he already was deeply concerned about his own playing. Two of the northern orchestras who had been anxious to engage him for concerts the previous year had failed to offer him a booking for this 1949–50 season. Neither had given any reason, and his agent seemed as nonplussed as he himself by their lack of interest.

His one firm engagement so far was in Manchester, and he had now decided that he must look to the London concert halls. Since his marriage he had been reluctant to spend time away from home, a feeling which had increased since Mihail's arrival. The fact remained, though, that he could never bear to give up the violin, and nor would he readily accept that he was being denied bookings because his ability had deteriorated.

"I have instructed my agent to try and secure me an audition, at least, with one of the London orchestras," he told Pamela one evening while she was attempting to settle Mihail for the night.

"Why not?" she said cheerfully. "I'm only surprised that you've been content this long to perform in the cities around here."

"Oh – you know how it has been . . ."

"Not really. Tell me . . ."

Andre smiled into her eyes, which today appeared especially blue and brilliant. "I could not bear to be parted from you, for even a short time."

"You mustn't worry on my account. There never seems a spare moment these days, I'd be so busy with Mihail that you'd be home again before I'd time to turn round!" And, she thought to herself, I might engineer some time for keeping a closer eye on that business of mine.

She couldn't be happier about this son of theirs, but she was missing the challenge of her old job, to say nothing of additional adult company. The buffet the other Sunday had been fun, but it also had reminded her that she rarely saw anyone outside her immediate family. Making up the wages to hand over for Ted Burrows to pay out was about the extent of her involvement with Canning's now.

The difficulty wasn't only Andre's opposition to her returning to her career, but that the injuries she had sustained in that fall all those months ago still continued to trouble her. The fracture had healed tolerably well, but had left one leg weaker than the other. Standing for any length of time now exhausted her. She had hardly mentioned this at all to either Andre or her stepdaughter, chiefly because she always had intended to return to the work she loved. But renovating and redecorating was a physical occupation, she was afraid she might have to accept that putting in long hours would be difficult.

Throughout her pregnancy Pamela had used her condition to excuse her reluctance to remain on her feet, now that she could no longer employ that as the cause, she was beginning to feel quite alarmed.

This would be the time to find out what she could manage. With Andre away from home even for two or three days, she might test herself by trying a few hours of working alongside the men. She could find that the leg was not so debilitating as she feared, in which case she would then set about convincing her husband of her need to work.

Almost before Pamela was ready, Andre arranged to go off to London, and she hastily began assembling plans. Just before leaving, though, he shook her by making a suggestion which she hadn't anticipated.

"I want you and Mihail to come with me," he told her. "I have reserved a room in one of the London hotels which suffered little damage in the war and now is up to a good standard. The change of scene will be beneficial for you, and I shall love having you there."

"Oh, Andre, I wish you'd mentioned this before," said Pamela, trying to think quickly and provide a satisfactory reason for not going. "I can't just drop everything like that."

"I do not see why not."

"Because of Canning's, of course, darling. I may not play a very active part, these days, but I am still the boss."

"You have a good assistant manager, I feel sure he would take on further responsibility."

"Happen he would." And happen I don't want him to, she thought. "But I'm not entrusting calculating the men's wages to him, for a start. The minute one gets to know what all t'rest of them are earning, you're in for trouble."

"We should not be away for even one full week. Surely, you could do the wages either before leaving or on our return . . .?"

Pamela could not agree, was determined not to agree. Hadn't she been relying on this opportunity for tackling some real work?

Reluctantly, Andre was obliged to accept that she was adamant. He continued preparing for his trip, but without enthusiasm. He felt let down because Pamela had refused to come with him, he also felt more anxious than he would have admitted. He had relished seeing his son each day, revelling in the boy's growing attachment to them and in his very dependence which was quite touching.

Andre had never anticipated that he in turn might depend upon Mihail so greatly. He had been shaken to discover how much he needed the boy. At no time since leaving his native land had he ever sensed so deeply who he, Andre Malinowski, was. And where he belonged. Even to himself it seemed odd, but the fact remained that young Mihail had increased his own sense of identity.

*   *   *

On the day that Pamela drove her husband to catch the London train, Tania was rehearsing for a performance the following week. After waving Andre off and putting Mihail back into his carrycot in the car, Pamela continued up the hill from the station and along the Calder Valley where russet-toned leaves were scattering about her.

At the large house, on the hillside beyond Hebden Bridge, where her team was working, Ian was the first to spot her car, and waved from the window where he was graining the woodwork.

"Where's Ted, do you happen to know?" she asked from the doorway of the room after lugging the carrycot and the now crying infant indoors.

"Him and the others are upstairs, I think. Shall I give him a shout?"

"No, thanks, love. I'm here to give a hand, that's all. Thought I'd have a word first." She did not mean to antagonize her assistant manager by walking straight in and taking over.

"My word! You've won Andre round, have you?"

Pamela did not put her brother right. The fewer people in the know the better, especially if she eventually was obliged to admit defeat. She had no intention of having anyone mention this experiment to Andre unless it should prove successful.

Ted Burrows was, if anything, even more surprised than Ian that she had come here to work, but Pamela did not let his raised eyebrows daunt her.

"I'm hoping to get back into harness one day, Ted. But I need to know how this bairn of mine is going to react to spending time in a strange house." No mention of her own uncertain limbs, and none of

100

the sudden anxiety that had arisen merely through putting her dreams into practice.

Feeling perturbed in her work environment was so unlike Pamela that it decreased her faith in her own stamina even before she had got her hands dirty. Following the brief consultation with Ted Burrows, she had chosen to begin preparing the woodwork in one of the bedrooms.

The house was mid-nineteenth century, not so old as Stonemoor, but almost as large, and being adapted now for occupation by a further generation of the present owners. A pleasant couple in their sixties, the Chapmans had decided to accommodate their son, daughter-in-law and three children, to make better use of the space now that there was a hope of supplies of decorating materials improving.

The rooms undergoing renovation had seen little in the way of redecoration for many a year. Pamela had noticed when providing estimates that Mr and Mrs Chapman had been content to lock up any parts not required. The cupboards in this bedroom were large, running the length of one wall, and their doors had suffered blistering as years of sunlight streamed in through the windows that faced them.

Beginning slowly at first to rub down the paintwork, Pamela realized that she was faced with a very long job which did not feel at all so enjoyable as she had imagined.

Don't be such a fool, she silently told herself, you're making the work harder than you need already, just by thinking how long it will take. Where's all your spirit? This will be nothing like the task you took on at Stonemoor House – and that was tackled on your own.

No sooner had she stilled her own misgivings than Mihail broke in on her concentration with the now familiar wail that prefaced his demand for attention. Setting aside her tools, Pamela wiped the dust off her hands on the seat of the overall that she had donned as soon as she arrived. Talking reassuringly to the baby, she crossed the room to the carrycot. She had never resorted to giving him a dummy, and she would not do so now, but she would have welcomed some miracle means of silencing him.

She could appreciate that Mihail might feel intimidated by the strange smells and even stranger sounds in these new surroundings. But when his initial wailing turned into heart-rending sobs she began to be perturbed. She also was acutely embarrassed. Ted Burrows and the other men would know now that she hadn't quite got the hang of keeping this son of hers contented.

A tentative knock on the open door of the room and the appearance of a grey head and worried brown eyes behind silver-rimmed spectacles only increased her embarrassment.

"Oh – Mrs Malinowski!" Mrs Chapman exclaimed, coming through to investigate the carrycot. "I never expected to see you working here."

"Didn't you?" said Pamela, her voice sharpened by her own discomfiture. "I don't believe in being just a figure-head, you know. I've always considered myself one of the workers."

"But with such a young baby? Is it wise, do you

think, bringing him here? It can't be good, surely, disturbing his routine?"

"His routine, Mrs Chapman, has not yet been established. As you can see he's young enough yet to adapt. And adapt he will, given time," she added grimly.

"What was that, dear?" Mihail's unwillingness to adapt was so vociferous that it had drowned out his mother's assertion.

Pamela shook her head. "Nothing, nothing. Just that I'll soon quieten him."

Mrs Chapman had retreated to the door. "I shall close this behind me. My husband isn't at all well, you know. All this work here is disturbing him quite enough as it is."

Her leg was hurting. Pamela could not believe it, but after less than a quarter of an hour here, the pain was quite intense. Mihail's cries gradually were subsiding so that she was able to move away from him, but now this wretched leg was becoming another distraction.

She forced herself to continue working for a few hours, but the baby interrupted her quite frequently and the pain in her leg grew progressively worse. Tomorrow will be better, Pamela vowed as she packed up for the day. She would prove to herself then that working was still practicable.

The baby, if no one else, seemed to have benefited from the outing, for he slept soundly that night. But Pamela was disturbed by the pain from her leg which was uncomfortable in every conceivable position. She also was missing Andre far more than she had expected.

The following day at work was no better, Mihail seemed even more unhappy, crying so regularly that Mrs Chapman twice came fussing into the room with reminders that her husband was unwell and needed quiet. What was more, Pamela's leg ached unbearably. It's no good, she thought dejectedly, I can't pretend I'm up to this sort of a job now.

She would have to concentrate on the business side of running Canning's and leave the actual redecorating and renovation to the men. Ted Burrows will be pleased, she realized as she went to explain that she would not be coming in the next morning. She herself felt miserable.

Andre had arrived home before her, a full day earlier than she had expected him.

"Where were you?" he asked, meeting her at the door and taking the carrycot from her.

"I just went over to where the men are working," she said hastily, after kissing him. "It seemed like a good idea since you were away."

"You were missing me?" he suggested, and she noticed the strain evident in his dark-circled eyes.

"Of course. And I thought – well, now you're back we'll be able to spend more time together if I don't have to go and check on them."

Andre nodded, but still he appeared perturbed. Suddenly, he inhaled and smiled, but without any light returning to his grey eyes. "You need not worry, Pamela, I have not signed up to perform in London."

"Why not? But, darling, you mustn't neglect your career for me. Much as we like being together, we're both old enough to be sensible if we have to be apart."

"It was not that . . ." He stopped speaking, sighed, and then forced the smile back on to his lips again. "Why are we talking about work? We have been separated, now we are together. And how is my boy – has he been good?"

Pamela grinned. "Forceful's the word, I believe. He is beginning to understand that yelling guarantees that I'll rush to him!"

"So – now there are two of us to attend to him. You look tired, my love, I shall insist that you take some rest."

Having Andre at home again made Pamela realize that for the time being, she could enjoy his company along with their combined delight in each small amount of progress that their infant was making. Tania was out of the house quite a lot, engaged in practising with the band as well as her singing classes and performing in classical concerts. Although her relationship with her stepdaughter had improved so greatly, Pamela was at times glad to have Andre to herself.

There was, however, a cloud which seemed to envelope him on occasions and even though he professed to be all right each time that she enquired, Andre continued to appear worried.

Tania was thankful to be singing with the band again, if only because that ensured that she would be seeing Ian. On several occasions recently he had claimed to be working over and unable to meet her. She had felt quite torn – on one hand she was glad that he seemed to be intent on saving for their future, but niggling away at the back of her mind was the suspicion that he could be finding excuses for not seeing her. Once or twice recently she had sensed that he wanted to delay making any firm commitment to her, and all those old insecure feelings that she did not really belong with anyone had returned.

She had learned that his mother, while still saying that she liked her, had been telling Ian that he should remain free to take out other girls. Tania herself could not dispute that, as yet, they both should have that right, but that wasn't what she herself wanted.

Since singing was a more individual art than playing as a member of the band, Tania did not attend so many rehearsals as the instrumentalists who had to work at combining to produce the required sound. When she was present she often had the feeling that she did not quite fit in – the others had more shared experiences, jokes even that meant nothing to her. Ian was still very friendly, of course, as were several others, especially Gerald Thomas, their solo trumpeter. And she noticed, of course, that being the only female there attracted to her the young men who would make a fuss of anyone wearing a skirt.

It was one evening when they had finished their rehearsal that Ian became annoyed with Harry, one of the lads who had made himself conspicuous by giving Tania the eye every time she was singing. As soon as the band began packing away their instruments the young fellow made straight for her, and slipped an arm around her waist.

"Nice to see you here again, love!" Harry exclaimed, giving her a squeeze. "It doesn't half brighten up the place when you're around."

"Thank you," said Tania, and smiled nervously,

wondering how to proceed. She had no experience of dealing with unwelcome attention and although Harry had not really been overfamiliar, she sensed that was something which could quite easily happen.

Ian saw her smile, and the conflict already existing in his emotions immediately increased. He couldn't bear to watch Tania encouraging anybody else. He wanted her for himself, longed to get her right away from everyone, especially from lads like this who thought nothing of making a pass at every attractive girl. If he'd been allowed to place a ring on her finger, he could have warned others off. As things were, Harry wouldn't take a bit of notice, not when there was no way of showing that he and Tania belonged together.

Harry was still talking away to her now, that arm was still round her waist. Ian was beginning to believe that Tania was enjoying it.

Without knowing what he was going to do or say, he started striding towards them.

"Do you want a lift home as usual, Tania?" he asked her.

"She can come with me," Harry asserted very smartly. "We go in the same direction."

"It's all right, thank you, Harry," said Tania and smiled at Ian. "Ian always drives me home."

Tania chatted all the way out to the car, asking how work was going, and if Tom and his mother were well. But Ian could not quite dismiss the unease he had felt while she was with Harry.

"Do you fancy him?" he heard himself asking as Harry gave them a wave as he got into the car parked next to theirs.

Tania laughed. Discovering that Ian could be jealous was something new, and really quite ridiculous when he knew how desperately she yearned to spend every minute with him.

"He is good-looking, I suppose," she teased. "Tall, and with all that dark wavy hair. But— "

"But nothing," Ian interrupted, starting up the engine. "You're obviously flattered because he makes a fuss of you."

"Oh, Ian, don't," she said, contrite now, for she would not hurt him for the world. "You know that you are the one I want. If only we could, I would marry you tomorrow— "

"Well, we can't, can we?" he said as he drove off. "You know as well as I do that they'll not let us. And besides, we couldn't afford to, not really." He had been calculating how much setting up a home would cost, and had found the figures quite alarming. And the fact that Tania lived in such a large elegant house made everything far worse. He'd never be able to earn enough to furnish a place in anything like the style her father had provided.

"Have you taken my earnings into account?" she asked seriously. She did not mean Ian to be weighed down by too much responsibility. "I am hoping to give more performances this season than last, and already they are offering higher fees."

"I can't take your money." It wasn't right that a woman should have to earn to keep their heads above water. He had seen how the struggle to bring in a few pounds had worn his mother out.

"Please do not be foolish, speaking in this way,"

Tania persisted. "If we intend to marry, then we must work together for our future. The money I bring in will help to give us a nice home."

"*I'll* provide us with a nice home, you don't have to worry about that. It might take a bit of time but— "

"And that is the point which I am making," Tania insisted. "We may not have to wait so long if we use my money."

Ian frowned. He was not enjoying this discussion. It seemed to him that Tania was trying to influence him against all his instinctive caution. Thinking things over, he'd had to admit that in lots of ways his mother had been right, and so had her father. Tania was roughly the same age as himself, but girls did seem to get ideas about settling down while they were much younger. One of them had to be sensible about it, and accept that waiting would do them no real harm. He had reached the conclusion that by the time he was twenty-one he would have saved enough for a deposit on a decent little place, and maybe even sufficient besides to set them up with furniture.

All this talk of hers now, about wanting to put in some brass of her own, was only making him confused. Even if they were able to persuade his mother and Andre to consent, were they themselves ready for buckling to and making a go of it? There would be precious little left over for going out and having a good time. He'd have to think twice before having a drink with the lads, as the others were tonight, as they did after each band practice. Tania would have to stop buying so many clothes – which you only had to look at to know how expensive they were.

And what if they had a baby as soon as they were married?

"What is wrong?" Tania asked anxiously after Ian's prolonged silence.

"Eh, I don't know – *me*, I'm afraid. Can't seem to think straight."

All this business of wanting a girl, and not wanting to tie all that responsibility round his neck was getting him down. He felt it was beyond him. He'd changed, that was the trouble. Years ago, he'd always believed there was a way out of any difficulty. He'd had the guts then to have a go at anything. The trouble was, folk had clamped down on him so much that he had almost lost his initiative. He was the first to admit now that some of his schemes had been a bit near the mark. He could have been in real trouble if he'd continued to have an eye on making a few quid, no matter how. He might have turned out to be a right spiv by this time. Even so, having his ideas curbed while he settled into a steady job had drained something out of him.

They had reached Stonemoor House and Tania was about to get out of the car. He kissed her warmly on the lips. He could sense that was what she expected, and in any case she was hard to resist.

"See you Friday night," he said.

Tania trudged towards the front door, and did not even turn to wave when he drove off. *Friday*, not before then? That was days ahead. Was Ian no longer as keen even to go out with her? She felt sick with disappointment. She was prepared to fight for their future, but not for having to fight Ian himself.

Chapter Six

Pamela wandered from room to room, noticing how the afternoon sunlight patterned the walls in each. In one the tracery of a tree, bare-branched since an autumn gale had stripped its leaves, produced shadows that shifted as the breeze stirred. The next bore the outline of the tall window's narrow glazing bars, the third the silhouette of a bronze statuette of the Duke of Wellington which stood on an antique table.

Smiling, she crossed to study the bronze which Andre had bought her when Mihail was born. She was delighted to possess such a beautiful object, and one that echoed the period of Stonemoor House.

From the corner of the room their longcase clock chimed the hour, and she turned now to nod approvingly in appreciation of the sheer pleasure it evoked. But that clock, the wedding gift from the Norton sisters who had been so happy to return it to its old home, also aroused her guilt. She'd had so many good intentions about discovering that clock's history.

There had been books, several of them, read while she was recuperating following that accident to her leg. Only she had done the books, along with the

111

clock, less than justice, reading with half a mind while she willed away time until she was no longer housebound.

Reluctantly at first, Pamela now began to consider possibilities. She had been depressed since that abortive attempt to do some real work for Canning's, she also silently condemned her own depression.

She had a lovely, healthy son, a good husband, this exquisite home – what right had she to feel discontented? Even without her active participation in the work, Canning's was doing well. Increasingly, they were taking on permanent craftsmen where a year ago they had used casual workers. Ted Burrows was a sound assistant manager who only occasionally tried to usurp her decision making. And there was Ian. That brother of hers was proving himself time and again: skilled and reliable, with promise of gaining the ability to become her successor even before he officially came of age.

Pamela supposed it could be that the very fact that Canning's was operating quite well without her had become a major factor in this dissatisfaction. She needed fresh stimulation, a new interest to take her thoughts beyond home and family, fond though she was of both.

The clock chimed the quarter, jolting her into realizing that for fifteen minutes she had remained immobile, thinking. A rare luxury in this household.

For once, Mihail was quiet. Since the unsuccessful experiment of taking him to work with her, she could have sworn that her son was enjoying his own home. And, whilst she was pleased that he suddenly appeared happy simply to be in the house that he would inherit, she herself was missing his demands for attention. Now that Mrs Singer had finished for the day, she and the baby were alone here. The other two had gone out for a meal together. Tania was singing with the band and Andre had delighted her by agreeing to attend. All too often, his own attachment to classical music, plus his opinion that his daughter ought to concentrate on her more serious concerts, tended to keep him away.

Pamela quite frequently attended when the band performed, she was more comfortable with music that, to her, seemed more accessible. Despite her increasingly good relationship with her stepdaughter, though, she was well aware that Andre's presence mattered more to the girl. These days, she was conscious also that neither he nor Tania seemed particularly happy.

Ever since Andre had returned from London without securing any further bookings to perform, Pamela had sensed that something was alarming him. Something far worse than the failure by various orchestras to acknowledge his talent.

No matter how often she encouraged him to confide, he did not do so, but reminded her instead of the old Andre: the one who before their marriage had always chosen to contain his troubles.

Tania was hardly more forthcoming. From the day that Andre (and for that matter Pamela's own mother) had refused to allow her to marry Ian, the girl had made her unhappiness plain enough.

Pamela sighed, and then smiled a little ruefully. Perhaps this evening Tania would accept her father's interest in her performance as a move towards a truce, and also as his genuine concern for her well-being. And maybe she herself should be using this time for planning some means of introducing more interest into her own life. If one quiet day with Mihail left her feeling at a loose end, she must find a means of caring for him and at the same time employing her brain.

Most of those books about antiques had been obtained from the library, but one had been bought by Andre just a week before their son's early arrival. Pamela had left it in the nursery to be read whenever Mihail was slow to take his feed or to settle. After a quick glance towards the carrycot where he now was investigating his own fingers, she ran upstairs to get the book.

She already knew that the clock which the Norton sisters had given them was somewhat older than Stonemoor itself, and that it was the work of one of the Halifax clockmakers. She remembered now that Thomas Ogden was his name and this style of clock was admired for the fine arch above its dial where phases of the moon were shown.

Finding his name, Pamela learned that he was a Quaker, and that a further speciality of his work was an arch outlined in silver engraved with the names of countries. On such clocks, she gathered, the sun rotated within the arch and was complete with a pointer to reveal the hour when noon was reached in each country indicated.

She would love to see one of those. But the book told her more about their own clock, she became absorbed in comparing it with an illustration and discovering more about its refinements.

114

The brass dial itself was interesting, and quite elaborate with a chapter ring of silver where the hours were marked in roman numerals. A narrower outer ring of brass bore the minute markings, five, ten, fifteen, round to sixty, and these were in Arabic numerals. The inner part of the dial was engraved with leaves against a dull surface which, Pamela read, was termed matted.

Beyond the outer ring of the dial, decorative corner pieces featured cherub faces and were, she learned, called spandrels. Reading on, she found that the designs of these often were useful in identifying the period of a clock.

Mihail reminded her of his presence with a cry that seemed to protest that he finally had objected to being ignored. Pamela laughed and set aside the open book to hurry across to attend to him.

Feeding the baby, bathing him and settling him for the night, she felt happier than for some time. Having another interest was making her appreciate all the more the satisfaction of having an infant.

After she had made a meal for herself and eaten it whilst listening to the wireless, Pamela went upstairs to check that Mihail was sleeping soundly before returning to her book. The news on the wireless had disturbed her so much that she needed a distraction.

Details emerging over several days were confirming Joseph Stalin's approval of the new German Democratic Republic. A special BBC report had made her more aware than before of the spread of Communism. Since 1945 Bulgaria, Czechoslavakia, Romania and Poland had become Communist, now East Germany stood alongside them. She knew from the small detail Andre had told her, that their citizens would experience little freedom of any kind. And Russia had not demobilized. She had heard it said that all the Red Army needed to reach the North Sea was boots.

Her book had fallen open at the next chapter which concerned silver and Pamela was glad to take her mind off international threats by reading. Thumbing through the pages she located information on silver of the period when Stonemoor House was built, and was particularly impressed by a picture of a silver-gilt tea urn in the Egyptian style. Its date of 1806 confirmed its origin as being around the time when this house was having rooms decorated with sphinx heads, scarabs, lotus plants and palms – all to mark the campaign in Egypt. She would enjoy explaining all this to Mihail when he grew old enough to understand. She thought yet again how glad she was that she had talked Andre into having her restore so much in the correct period.

Illustrations of other less ornate pieces soon were beginning to convince Pamela that she could become almost as interested in silver objects as she was in clocks. Without really knowing where it was leading, she felt exhilarated by her day's reading and, by the time that Andre and his daughter arrived home that night, quite optimistic.

Andre had enjoyed taking Tania out before the concert for what these Yorkshire people called high tea. Following their awkwardness in the car (when he had been acutely aware of his daughter's continued disappointment about his verdict on her marrying) he had been afraid that they could have a difficult few hours in prospect. But they had talked on as soon as they were shown to a table and made their choice from the still rather limited menu available.

He had asked about that evening's performance but Tania had laughingly shaken her head before declaring that she did not mean to spoil his surprise. But she herself had produced another topic.

"Did you know that for my next classical concert they have suggested that I sing several operatic arias?"

Andre had not known, but was thankful now that she was confiding in him again. "Which ones?" he asked, and listened intently while she told him.

Tania then enquired what he was to play in forthcoming concerts.

"There are not many of those, alas," he admitted, but he did not want her to be anxious for him. He went into considerable detail about the pieces lined up for the only concert that was arranged.

Andre was relieved when Tania did not use the opportunity to pester him for permission to marry Ian. He hated to deny her anything, but could not encourage committing herself to anyone at such an early age.

On the way to the hall, where the band were to perform, they talked of the old days, of family members left behind the Iron Curtain, and of how Andre felt that he must wait now before again attempting to reach any of their relatives.

His sister had refused to come to England some time ago, even despite his journey back to his homeland.

All the preparations that had been laid on for getting her away had been wasted.

"I am afraid that I must not try to get anyone else out. There is so much mistrust now between the Eastern block countries and people in the West that I should not be at all sure of returning to Yorkshire."

"Then you must not go, promise me you will not," said Tania urgently.

Andre smiled at his daughter. "I have said, have I not? I would not attempt anything of the kind for some long time."

They were among the first few people to arrive at the hall. When Tania had dashed off to join the musicians backstage, Andre decided to look around. This hall was one which Canning's had renovated. In fact, the one where his wife had fallen down the staircase.

Heading towards that staircase now, Andre willed himself to ignore the rush of emotion surging to his throat. That fall, although serious, could have had far more dreadful repercussions, but he must ignore that aspect for tonight. He did wish to see the wall painting on which Pamela had been engaged at the time, the one since completed by her brother.

He liked Tom Baker who, now sixteen, was progressing well in the art department of a local magazine. Although the younger, he often seemed to Andre to be more practical in outlook than his brother Ian.

Unfortunately, Ian often made him feel uneasy. From the start, he had been too ready to respond to Tania's beauty. But it wasn't only a father's instinct to have the best for his daughter that generated these reservations, he saw in Ian too much impatience about making headway. He always appeared reluctant to wait for anything. It was not only his wishing to rush into this marriage. There was his desire for promotion which seemed, as yet, hardly justified.

But Canning's is not my concern, thought Andre, and immediately felt glad. He could foresee all kinds of difficulties ahead when Ian really began to pursue advancement in earnest.

Tom, on the other hand, possessed similar determination but *his* was expressed in quiet persistence of the kind that worked quietly and steadily to perfect a skill.

And skill it was indeed! decided Andre when a turn of the stair brought him face to face with that mural. Pamela had told him it was inspired by a Degas painting, but he needed no such explanation. The shades used and the style, together with sheer grace, had combined to evoke that artist in an exquisite fashion.

Stepping nearer, he examined the brush strokes, marvelling that Pamela and her young brother had achieved such an effect. He had been impressed by everything she had done whilst renovating his own home but, although many varied skills had been employed there, none had seemed to be this artistic.

I must tell her tonight, he resolved, smiling. Perhaps then she will realize that I do regard her work with great esteem, however much I insist that she should now resign herself to taking a less active part in the company.

Some little while later when the curtain went up Andre gazed from his seat to the painted backdrop before which the band was playing. Briefly, he had forgotten that this mural was his wife's handiwork, and hers alone. We should have found somebody to sit with Mihail tonight, he thought, I wish she was here beside me. I need to tell her now how proud I am of all that she has done.

When first they met, Pamela had told him how she had inherited Canning's on her husband's death at the end of the war, and how before they both went into the forces he had taught her all he knew about decorating. But that had been simple work, making houses look cleaner and brighter, nothing on this scale, nor of this quality.

The entire hall was light and well painted, a credit to all his wife's team. And he should not forget that Ian was included among them, nor that he himself knew well enough that Pamela expected, and got, from every one of them the very best of craftsmanship.

The band had finished their first piece, a now popular tune from the film *The Red Shoes*. It was followed by one of the Glenn Miller melodies to which these young men in their pale suits still seemed greatly attached.

And now his Tania had appeared, walking forward confidently, yet without any air of self-importance. He saw that Ian's gaze was drawn towards her, along with that of several bandsmen, especially the tall young fellow who played the solo trumpet.

I'm getting old, Andre thought, my daughter's becoming a woman, for only a few years now will I be able to influence her against making hasty

120

decisions. Or against acting before contemplating consequences.

As the first few notes had played, she opened her mouth to sing and, as ever, Tania demanded complete attention.

Andre did not like the song, he never had when hearing it innumerable times over the wireless. 'On a Slow Boat to China' always seemed to him to emphasize feelings that were too facile, to conjure up dreams of a relationship relying too heavily on attraction, and neglecting the element of responsibility.

They *were* young, nevertheless, as were a large percentage of the audience, and Andre could not fail to be delighted by the applause his daughter had generated. For once, he was happy to hear her entertaining with these lighter tunes. Provided that she continued to pursue her classical career.

Tania's second song came immediately before the interval, she had two further pieces in the second half. The last one of all was more to his taste – 'Riders in the Sky' possessed some additional, and to him quite haunting, quality. And Tania sang it to perfection.

Andre went backstage to wait for her, and bumped into Ian almost at once. They chatted amiably enough while the young fellow was packing up his sheet music and placing the saxophone in its case. And then Tania was running in their direction, thrusting a hand through an arm of each of them, smiling from one to the other.

"You were splendid, my sweet!" Andre exclaimed. "You have a good range, as I have told you before."

"Thank you, thank you," she said, her grey eyes

121

glowing. "And what have you two been talking about? Has Ian said anything?"

Andre shook his head. "Said? About what?"

"Getting engaged. We were talking earlier."

Her father could feel his mouth setting grimly, he stifled a groan; but Ian had flushed and appeared even more perturbed.

"I didn't say I agreed it should be yet," he said. He had had time to think since that day when Tania so nearly had swept him along by her impetuosity.

Tania frowned angrily, turned away and began running.

"Eh, I am sorry!" Ian exclaimed, his brown eyes clouding.

Andre squeezed his arm. "Do not be. I am pleased that you are being sensible. There is all the time in world for you both."

"Aye, that's what I'd decided, after I'd thought for a bit, like."

"Then do not worry, Ian. Tania is very fond of you, she will come to see the wisdom in your thinking."

Andre caught her up on the front steps of the hall. Looking as though she had already shrugged off her fury, she was talking animatedly with the tall young man who played the trumpet.

"I do not believe you two have met," she said, and smiled, although Andre saw now that there was no light in her eyes. "Father, this is Gerald Thomas – he lives not far from us, in Hebden Bridge where his father owns a factory."

They remained only long enough to be polite. Andre's evening had been ruined now, and Tania seemed drained.

In the car nothing was said about her attempt to accelerate engagement plans. Andre had decided that avoiding the matter was the wisest course. The whole subject must be allowed to cool. Now that Ian himself seemed determined to defer any decision there was every chance that Tania would be influenced into waiting.

They had turned off the road at Mytholmroyd and were well on their way up Cragg Road towards Stonemoor House when they noticed a distant flashing light, and heard an ambulance siren. For some reason, however irrational, Andre felt alarm tearing right through him. God, don't let that be Pamela or our baby, he silently pleaded. Beside him, he sensed Tania stiffening in an alarm that matched his own.

Neither of them said a word as the ambulance rushed around a bend towards them and went hurtling past. His foot hard down, Andre sped the rest of the way to their home.

Pamela came to the sitting room door as soon as they entered the hall. Her smile and immediate question about how the performance had gone reassured them at once. She kissed them both while Andre enthused about his daughter's singing.

Tania, he noticed, looked pale but seemed to have put her annoyance behind her.

"And did the band play all right?" Pamela asked when they finished telling her about the songs which the girl had sung.

"They all were very good," said Andre. "Some of those young men are too talented to merely be semiprofessional."

He mentioned the ambulance while they were drinking hot chocolate beside the fire.

"It was old Mrs Fawcett from the tiny shop," Pamela told them. "It must be serious, they were even ringing the bell on the way up here. It sounded so near I had to look out and see what was going on."

"Is she very old?" asked Tania. "I do not know her."

"Nor do I, really," her stepmother said. "I've only ever been in there once or twice, when we'd run out of something and I couldn't be bothered to go any further."

"It is such a dark little place, scarcely tempting one to venture inside," Andre added.

"*Was* the concert OK?" Pamela asked him when Tania had gone up to her room. "Tania seems a bit quiet."

"The performance went very well. It was afterwards that the silly girl invited her own distress. By trying to persuade Ian that they should become engaged."

Pamela sighed. "Not again! I suppose we shall have to make allowances, she's only young."

"Yes, well – from what he said tonight, Ian is less eager than she is to make a match of it already. Let us hope that now she will let the matter rest, at least for another year or two."

Tania, her head held high, sat beside Pamela as they drove towards the station. Andre had offered to drive her right into Leeds where she had a singing engagement. In fact, Pamela had made a similar offer. She knew that they both thought that she had declined because of all the upset about her relationship with

Ian. She had heard them discussing her reaction to his refusal to consider becoming engaged. Learning that they supposed she was being temperamental was no surprise – she had known for a long time what they both believed her to be. At times, she even acknowledged that their opinion might be justified. On this occasion, however, although Ian had hurt her she was too busy planning ahead for giving in to disappointment.

Tonight, for instance, she had her own reasons for discouraging both her father and his wife from remaining for the concert. Everyone might believe that she had become entirely obsessed with the idea of being engaged to Ian, but before long they would be proved wrong. Just as she would waste no more time over regrets, she now would cease making a fool of herself over a young man who could speak so coldly of deferring their plans.

Ian *was* fun, he also was kind and so attractive that she often literally felt dizzy with longing whenever they were together. But he was the one who had curbed their outings recently. She wanted him, but what she needed more was to believe that Ian could not live without her. He could not be as indifferent to her as he appeared! Surely, he would recognize quite quickly that he had made a mistake. They loved each other, she did not doubt that, but *her* mistake could have been that she was too readily available. She was about to change all that. Only for a short while, of course, just . . . long enough.

In the train, after her stepmother had dropped her off, Tania smiled to herself. It all had fallen into place so readily. As well as her feeling that this had been meant to happen, there seemed an odd kind of justice in the fact that if Ian had not been so offhand with her she would not even have been chatting with Gerald.

His compliment about her voice had come at a moment when she could barely croak because of the huge lump filling her throat. But Gerald had said lots of very nice things, and had gone on to ask about the other side of her singing, the classical part which she had believed never interested the members of the band.

He had insisted that she must get him a ticket for this evening, and insisted also that he must drive her safely home afterwards.

"We can have a meal somewhere, if you like, on the way back," he had promised. Tania had remembered then the isolated occasion, before she had grown so fond of Ian, when Gerald Thomas had taken her out one night. She had sensed then that he certainly knew how to look after a girl, how to make her feel special. This seemed to be just what she needed if she was to avoid becoming paranoid about Ian's uncaring attitude.

The concert went well, Tania had practised the arias in private as well as at rehearsals, she had even studied the entire works from which they were taken. Not yet accustomed to opera, she meant to do her best to demonstrate that she possessed some degree of dramatic interpretation.

The warmth of the applause told her that she had achieved almost as great a success as she had hoped (what artist in any field ever felt wholly satisfied that they could not have done better?) And the smiles from the surrounding orchestra revealed that she might believe that she had impressed her fellow professionals. But tonight even more important to her was Gerald's wholehearted approval when he came round to her dressing room to collect her.

"You were breathtaking!" he exclaimed, his blue eyes shining as he caught both her hands in his and gazed down at her. "I've always known you'd a good voice, but this evening was magnificent. Promise me you'll always let me know where you're performing."

Tania left the concert hall on his arm and in a state of euphoria never matched in the past. His car was in a nearby street, and he opened the passenger door with a flourish that would have enchanted a princess.

"There's a club I know where we may eat, if that suits you?" Gerald suggested. "And if you need to telephone your people from there, you could tell them you may be late home, but not to worry."

Tania wasn't sure about ringing them. She had explained that a musician would be driving her home, but had not contradicted their assumption that he was a member of the orchestra playing that evening. If she said too much now, she might reveal more than she intended.

"It's all right, I don't need to say anything else," she heard herself reassuring him. "They know that you're seeing me safely back to Stonemoor."

The club was small, but the elegance of the decor and of its clients witnessed to its tastefulness. Tania was impressed, and really quite surprised. Gerald spoke beautifully and his clothes always looked expensive, but she had not associated him with attending somewhere this sophisticated.

He advised as she selected something from the glossy menu, and then while they chatted and waited for their meal to arrive, they watched the dancers moving slowly around the tiny floor.

"Why don't we have a go?" Gerald suggested when another number began.

His hand was warm on her elbow as they walked between tables, and then warm on her back where it was bared in a deep 'V' intersecting her shoulder blades.

Gerald danced well, she discovered at once, and seemed a considerate partner who made allowance for her inexperience with English dancing.

"Did you dance in Russia?" he asked, smiling into her eyes.

"A long time ago, and nothing like this, traditional dances, I suppose you would call them."

He was holding her close, making her feel protected, a delicious sensation that became welcome when she realized that the performance had tired her.

They saw a waiter heading towards their table and met him there to approve their dishes. Gerald drew out her chair before the waiter might do so, and held it for her. Tania could not help being entranced by his manners.

A pale wine accompanied their food, it went to her head at once and she decided she must limit her intake of it. Somehow, though, talking as they were, she sipped the wine continuously, and talked with even greater animation.

Gerald was smiling a great deal, his blue eyes glittering in the light of the candle set between them. He seemed more handsome than she had evernoticed in the past, and his eloquence impressed her.

He had spoken already on innumerable subjects, many light and inconsequental, but with the insertion of the occasional particularly astute remark. She had expected music to be their principal topic, but they had ranged from the theatre to cinema and books, from the Olympics held the previous year in London to international events of more serious consequence. And best of all he was skilful in drawing conversation from her, inviting her opinion, convincing her it mattered.

They danced again when they had finished eating. Her limbs, weakened by the wine, felt seriously afflicted but Gerald was unperturbed and steadied her against him.

He had been watching the time, a conscientious escort determined not to ruin everything by keeping her out too late. He knew how old she was and that her father was inclined to be overprotective.

The interior of the car was comfortable and warm, and Tania was tired. As soon as she sank back into her seat she was happy to accept that Gerald had been right to drag her away from the night-club.

"I'll take you there again," he promised, and squeezed her fingers before starting up the car.

Tania felt reassured. Knowing that Gerald was always going to be happy to see her removed the pressure from her longing to marry Ian.

On the way home he took a slight detour and parked where a steep escarpment provided a vista of darkened hills, and lights from distant houses and cars gleamed like fireflies against black velvet.

After the engine stopped the interior grew cool, but Gerald drew her to him now, enveloped her in his arms. They kissed at once, and she wondered why she should be surprised.

What really surprised Tania was her own response. Until tonight she had supposed quite seriously that Ian was the only young man who made her feel this intense attraction. Suddenly, she was compelled to recognize that Gerald generated a similar degree of desire – a desire that was driving away reservations until she was the one drawing close against him, kissing him fervently.

"I wish you were mine," he murmured into her ear, his breath caressing her neck while he ran his fingers deep into her hair.

She had worn it in a new style for the concert, coiling it at the back of her head, but with tendrils tumbling in curls to either side of her face. She could feel the pins loosening at his touch, and relished the sense of freedom induced when the full length of her hair swung down about her shoulders.

Gerald buried his face against her neck. "You smell gorgeous," he said huskily before turning so that he could claim her lips once more.

Tania noticed then the scent of his shaving soap which seemed to accelerate all her senses as she felt his hand on one shoulder, warm and loving, assuring her that she mattered to him, and then his fingers reached her breast. She quelled a moan as her need surged.

The gear lever was pressing into her leg while

Gerald leaned across, his mouth devouring hers and his fingers caressing ceaselessly. She felt her own body stir, restless with urgency, and noticed then that he was stirring too, willing her compliance.

"We mustn't, Ia— " she began, and remembered. This wasn't Ian. And even if it were, she should not permit this to progress any further. "We must not even kiss any more," she amended hastily.

Gerald eased away from her and smiled, "I know. I do know, sweetheart. You're adorable, but you're too fine a young lady for this to be an appropriate setting. Just promise me there'll be other occasions together . . ."

Tania promised, of course. He *had* treated her like a lady tonight, had made her feel mature and, more importantly, that she was needed. And Gerald was protective, preparing now to drive her home. He might have been feeling an alarm as powerful as her own, on account of these strangely insistent longings.

The whole experience had been a curious blend of excitement and assurance. This euphoria which she was feeling would not simply evaporate. She could not deny him one final kiss when he stopped the car in the road that led to Stonemoor.

"I will see you again," Gerald asserted, opening the door for her. And somehow Tania knew that everything was changing. This young man would teach her all about going after the things she wanted. He would never permit others to take charge of his future plans.

Chapter Seven

"You shouldn't be worrying like this, Andre. She told me how well this Gerald looked after her."

Andre shrugged. "You do not understand, do you? I was so sure that she had said someone from the orchestra was to bring her home."

"Are you perturbed simply because this fellow was only from the band? Is that all that's troubling you?" Pamela had wondered from the start if Andre thought that nothing but classical playing counted. Had he really objected to Ian because neither his job nor his music were good enough for *his* daughter?

"Not at all. You have missed the point – I cannot help feeling that Tania set out to mislead me." Andre paused, thinking, then smiled ruefully. "Am I creating a terrible fuss?"

Pamela smiled back at him. In his dark suit, and a black tie contrasting sharply with that white shirt, he looked far too prepossessing to be so distracted by his daughter's actions.

"I'm afraid you are rather, love. Tania is eighteen, after all – and if you don't wish her to become engaged, you might have to concede that the alternative should be exercising the freedom to see other young men."

He raised a hand. "Oh – please. Do not sound so

very rational, or, by contrast, I shall appear even more paranoid."

Pamela crossed swiftly to hug him. "You're a lovely father, and I believe I do understand how natural your anxiety is. I just don't want you to antagonize Tania by restraining her too much."

"I shall try not to. With your help, I might even begin to succeed."

The discussion ended when the longcase clock chimed, reminding them that they should be ready to go out. They were attending old Mrs Fawcett's funeral that afternoon. Even though they had scarcely known her, they had been shocked to hear that the lady had been dead by the time the ambulance arrived at the infirmary. When, following the announcement in the *Halifax Courier*, the Misses Norton had called at Stonemoor House to ask if they knew more details, Pamela and Andre in turn had learned more about Mrs Fawcett.

Once a regular worshipper with the Nortons at the local church, the old widow had no brothers or sisters remaining and, it seemed, few friends of her own generation.

"We shall pay our final respects, of course," Hilda Norton had affirmed while her sister Sophie nodded and wiped away a tear from behind gold-rimmed spectacles.

"And so shall we," Andre had announced. He did not like to think that the only people present could be the handful of parishioners whose work allowed them to attend a weekday service.

Pamela was pleased by her husband's insistence on going to the funeral. Although her own attendance at church had become infrequent whilst Canning's was devouring so much of her time, she had begun to miss her visits to St Paul's, but hadn't yet gone to their church in the valley here. About his own beliefs, Andre had said very little and she had been happy to accept him as he was. So much about his life in Russia seemed painful that she hesitated to enquire into the feelings that had developed from the situation in his homeland.

The neat church with its square tower was set near Cragg Brook, down the lane which led eventually out to Withens Clough reservoir. The building chilled them as they entered, but more chilling still was the sight of a mere half-dozen mourners assembled in the front pews.

The Norton sisters were not among them and Pamela and Andre headed rather hesitantly towards the first unoccupied pew on their left.

Music was playing furtively on an organ which, even to Pamela's untrained ear, was in need of renovation. The vicar emerged from the vestry, glanced about him and then at his watch, and began walking extremely slowly towards the west door.

They heard a vehicle draw up outside, and Pamela prepared to rise for the coffin as it was carried into the church. But instead of the even tread of pallbearers, she heard scurrying feet, and urgent feminine twittering.

"Oh, dear, how late we are!" Sophie Norton exclaimed as she and Hilda scuttled along between the pews towards them.

The sisters knelt to pray, and instantly jerked

upright again as the solemn progress of the old lady's coffin commenced.

In any other setting, the sisters' arrival would have amused; here, it seemed only to add further pathos to a departure from this life which could hardly have had fewer witnesses.

"We must visit this church again," said Andre as they left the graveside after seeing the old lady interred.

"Oh, you must, you must!" Sophie encouraged. "Our father was a churchwarden here, you know. And most faithfully he served the parson of his day."

"Until he was crossed," Hilda reminded her. "You can't have forgotten all that dissention before the old vicar was replaced."

Pamela and Andre exchanged a smile. The sisters seemed to brighten the dank November day which had felt particularly miserable while they stood at the graveside. Bare trees had dripped moisture produced by the fog still drifting around the grey stone church.

Pamela invited the Nortons to Stonemoor House for tea, but as the four of them were getting into the Wolseley a bronzed young man detained the sisters.

"Excuse me – I don't believe you remember who I am, but I haven't forgotten you. Miss Sophie and Miss Hilda, am I right?" While the pair were still looking perplexed the man continued. "Mrs Fawcett was my great-aunt, I'm afraid I am the only family she has remaining. And I've lived in Australia for years."

"Vincent? Vincent . . .? Dear me, I can't recall

your surname now!" Sophie exclaimed. "But I do know you, yes. You visited your great-aunt on at least one occasion."

"And you were very kind, both very kind, letting me roam around your garden. You live at the big house, don't you?"

"Not any longer," said Hilda and went on to explain, and then to introduce Pamela and Andre.

When they learned that Vincent had flown back to England alone, and was about to inspect Mrs Fawcett's old home, Pamela invited him to join them first for tea.

After they had reached Stonemoor, Vincent admitted he had been hoping that he might have persuaded the Nortons to hold a key for his great-aunt's property until it was sold. "However, since you are no longer living in the neighbourhood, that wouldn't be practicable."

"But we might help you there," Pamela suggested. "You'd better tell us what it would entail."

"I hardly know that myself. My sole intention is to rid myself of the house and its contents – the shop included, naturally. I've already arranged to put this in the hands of her solictor. But my hope was that someone local could just keep an eye on the place."

Over tea it was decided that Pamela and the Nortons should join Vincent afterwards as he began to assess Mrs Fawcett's old home. When Sophie and Hilda could be prised away from their admiration of young Mihail, they left Andre in charge of his son.

The tiny shop which occupied the front of the building was only of interest as an example of 1930s' premises – and stock which, in some instances, looked almost as old! The room to the rear, however, and the living quarters on the floor above made Pamela gasp in amazement.

Mrs Fawcett evidently had been quite a connoisseur of antiques. From furniture that clearly was genuine nineteenth-century to silverware, from clocks to paintings and porcelain, all her possessions witnessed to knowledge allied to good taste. Best of all, to Pamela, was a longcase clock very similar to their own.

"Ah," Hilda sighed, gazing around. "I remember now what an eye she had for a good piece. You must engage someone knowledgeable to value this lot, Vincent."

"But who'll want this, it's so old-fashioned!" he protested, and seemed surprised when the other three were appalled.

"Miss Norton is right, I'm sure," Pamela put in. "I've recently been reading up on all kinds of antiques, and they really can represent a lot of money."

Vincent shrugged nevertheless and his grey-green eyes became anxious. "But I can't spare the time to go into all that, I've my own business back home. There is no way I can hang around here until this lot has been assessed, then sold piece by piece."

His reluctance to give much time to obtaining good value for disposing of the place and its contents, meant that no decision had been reached when Vincent was leaving. He was to travel back to London the following afternoon before beginning his flight home to Australia on the next day. He gave his home telephone number and that of his

London hotel to both Pamela and the Nortons, and thanked them all for their help as he departed.

Her mind full of the exquisite antiques that she had seen, Pamela spent a restless night. She would give anything to have access to such interesting things, to examine them and discover their dates. The grey dawn of late autumn was paling the outline of their bedroom window when she admitted to herself that what she wanted most of all was to be allowed to sell those fascinating pieces.

Andre was encouraging when she put the possibility to him during breakfast. "It is allied to the work you have done here and elsewhere," he remarked. "And I can certainly understand why you find them so intriguing."

"There is all the information I've picked up from reading about antiques. Do you think Vincent would be willing to sell me the whole place?" She was beginning to have an idea concerning its future. "Not complete with contents. But perhaps with the proviso that I would dispose of them, and then maybe simply deduct my commission from the proceeds."

They discussed the idea of taking it on, and when Andre did not object to the prospect Pamela telephoned Vincent at his hotel.

He had spoken with the solicitor handling Mrs Fawcett's affairs, and also with several of the major auction houses. The latter had not been particularly enthusiastic, Vincent felt, and had left him eager to rid himself of everything in that house as swiftly as feasible.

Pamela's suggestion came as such a great surprise

that he actually laughed down the line as soon as she reached the end of her explanation.

"You can't really wish to go to such lengths, Mrs Malinowski?"

"But I love old things, the history of them and everything. Of course, you would have to obtain a proper evaluation of the entire contents of that house. Only in that way would you be sure that I was getting fair prices on your behalf."

"That could be arranged, certainly. But about the property itself, are you sure you wish to take it on?"

"I have money sitting in the building society. I was always too busy running that business of mine to spare much time to enjoy spending. Now this seems as if it might be an ideal way of relishing a new investment. The building would be off your hands almost immediately, and we both stand to make a profit . . ."

Vincent was only too happy to agree. All he'd really wanted was to dispose of his great-aunt's home and belongings quickly, in order that his own interests would not suffer neglect. He and Pamela talked for quite some time, thrashing out details, and agreeing a time-scale for sorting out the legal side.

Andre seemed amused rather than disturbed by the speed with which she'd set everything moving. Pamela was glad this was one of her ideas that he did not oppose. Quite suddenly the prospect of trying to make a go of running an antiques business had become exciting.

* * *

139

Tania was entranced when shown around Mrs Fawcett's old home, and immediately enthused about Pamela opening up the shop there.

"It is so near to Stonemoor that you will not become tired by travelling every day, and you will be able to have Mihail here with you until he is old enough to go to school."

Pamela laughed. "Always providing that I can keep the business going that long! There's no means of knowing that I can make it succeed."

"You will, I am sure. And Father and I will be thankful that you no longer do such physical work."

"And happen *I* shall be as well," Pamela confessed. "When I did try tackling that again, it felt quite daunting."

"You have studied previously, to make a success of Canning's. This time you will become an expert in furniture of every period, and in all the things that give a home an especial character. When I have my own little house I shall expect your advice."

Pamela smiled and thanked her, but inwardly was disturbed by Tania's compliment. Was the girl seriously considering setting up home in the near future? Had nothing that they had said dampened her determination to marry Ian?

Pamela would have been even more perturbed had she known how actively her stepdaughter was investigating the possibility of purchasing the house she coveted.

The meal out with Gerald Thomas had led to a Saturday afternoon together when, on learning of her interest in that house on the moors, he had driven her out to see it. On that occasion they had been unable to contact the estate agents in time to obtain a key, but Gerald had admired the exterior and its setting. He also had insisted that he must help her ensure that she should inspect the place.

"Setting your heart on somewhere is important," he had told Tania, the smile in his blue eyes endorsing his words until she felt thrilled to have won his approval. "It is good to have sufficient spirit to try and make your dreams come true."

On the day that he picked her up to return to the little house Tania was feeling elated. If only it were Ian who was taking her there, she would have been ecstatic. As things were, she was grateful for Gerald's practical help, and for his understanding of her enthusiasm. He was kind, and generous with his time, and best of all he treated her as the adult that she felt she had become.

In the car that morning Gerald talked almost as excitedly as Tania herself. If she hadn't felt she knew him well enough to entertain no such doubts, she might have wondered what he thought to gain from this excursion. Discounting his having any ulterior motive, Tania enjoyed his company. And she reminded herself quite frequently that not everyone was alike; she must not condemn Ian for having misgivings about surrendering his freedom at a mere eighteen.

Girls did mature more quickly than young men, yet it was the man who expected to shoulder responsibility. She could understand that the prospect of taking on so much might feel daunting. It was easy for Gerald to endorse her ideas when he was not obliged to tie

141

himself down. In any case, Gerald was five years older than Ian, and apparently from a family who had not been hit by a shortage of funds.

The estate agents was a busy place on that Saturday morning, several couples were looking at details of the properties displayed, one or two of them with children of assorted ages who were increasing the agitation of the two men in charge.

When Gerald finally attracted the attention of the elder of the two and explained their purpose, the man turned aside to locate a folder.

"This details the accommodation the house contains, together with the asking price. Can't say when I'd be free to take you round, though. Have you come far?"

"Actually, we have," Gerald told him. "No chance of letting us have a key, I suppose?"

The man looked dubious for a moment, but glanced down at the details of the house and smiled. "Why not? It says here that the place is empty – I remember now that the only furniture left behind was practically worthless."

"Did he mean that he didn't know whether to trust us there?" asked Tania when they were back in the car. She was prepared to be quite indignant if that were so.

Gerald smiled. "There's no need to be offended by his caution, Tania. Every estate agent has to have a strong sense of responsibility. They can't let just anyone have access to a person's property."

"I had not thought of it like that." And now she felt ridiculously naïve. Gerald must believe she was gauche! If she was to convince him or anyone else that she was capable of taking on a home of her own, she needed to learn to think more carefully before speaking.

All ideas of containing her thoughts were forsaken as soon as he parked the car outside that tiny house, and helped her out of the passenger seat. Tania bounded up the path to the front door and waited impatiently while Gerald locked his car and strode towards her.

She ought to have taken charge of that key herself, she thought, even these few seconds delay were trying. When the key seemed stiff in the lock, and Gerald had to employ considerable force, she shifted from foot to foot, but then reminded herself not to appear immature by fidgeting.

Entering the living room at last compensated for any time wasted. Tania was enchanted by that first glance all about her. Some long time ago, the walls had been papered in a flowery design in which roses predominated. Although now faded, the pattern seemed perfect for a home situated like this, deep in the tranquil countryside.

The windows were small, but on such a wintry day as today that seemed an advantage rather than a fault. Tania had enough experience of cold climates to recognize that any place out here would require a lot of heating.

Gerald had taken a quick look at the kitchen. She heard him groan as he turned away. When she crossed to examine it, however, she could see no reason for complaint.

"What is wrong with this? There is even a gas oven."

"If it works! The thing is ancient. And there are no built-in cupboards."

"I shall buy a fine wooden dresser," Tania declared. "I can picture rows of beautiful plates set out upon it. I shall ask my stepmother to help me find exactly what I want." Her grandmother in Russia had had something of the kind in the farm kitchen.

The staircase was narrow and twisted awkwardly near the top where it also was quite dark. Tania was glad when Gerald turned to offer a hand. The bedroom was large and occupied the whole of the first floor. Gerald frowned as he gazed around.

"But where's the bathroom?"

Tania shrugged. "I don't know, but there will be one." She was scarcely listening. She had crossed immediately to the window where the view entranced her. Below them the rear garden looked quite tidy considering how long the house seemed to have stood empty. Somebody had cut the lawn at the end of summer, and had trimmed back various clumps of flowers which the autumn frosts had attacked. Against the far sandstone wall some climbing shrub was magnificent with scarlet berries. Tania began to wish that she knew someone who might teach her about English gardens.

Beyond the wall the hillside rose steeply, scrubby grass for the first few yards and then heather that became interspersed with black rocks where the slope grew more rugged, extending towards the moors.

Tania yearned to live here. She could be quite alone with the man she loved, away from everyone else and allowed to concentrate on him.

An arm came around her waist and she was drawn

144

towards the warmth of his tweed jacket which felt welcome in the chill of the draughty room. Instinctively, she leaned sideways, resting her head against him while she continued to absorb the view.

"You want this place, don't you?"

Tania was startled. That wasn't Ian's voice! She struggled to appear composed. But she had nearly lost herself while contemplating this lovely house and its surroundings. Even now, she felt transfixed, quite unable to summon the will to move.

"Thank you for sharing your dreams with me." Gerald sounded far less assertive than usual, she could almost believe that he also was experiencing the euphoria that being here induced in her.

She sensed him moving slightly to glance over his shoulder.

"I'm sure you'd have a magnificent view of the moors while lying in bed," he remarked.

Tania hauled her attention away from the window and turned to discover that the room wasn't quite empty. A well-worn divan stood against the wall to their right.

"Where do you think the sun rises?" she asked, hurrying across to test the view from the bed. "I would love to watch it creep above the top of the hill."

Stretched out on the divan now, she leaned her head against the cold wall. "Even from here, you can see more hillside than sky – *and* the tops of the garden trees. Come and— "

But Gerald didn't need prompting, he was here, easing himself down beside her on the creaking bed that smelled quite musty. "God, but it's cold, Tania! Here – lean against me instead of the wall."

145

He was still warm when he placed an arm around her, so warm that he seemed to lend reality to her being in this empty house where its strangeness was evaporating already while she visualized how beautiful it might become.

"You're right, there's a splendid outlook from here," Gerald declared, shifting to her the responsibility for recognizing its potential. He turned his head, brushed the side of her cheek with his lips. "If you want to live here enough, you can make it happen."

Having got this far, Tania suddenly began to feel quite daunted. She did not even know how people in England set about buying a house. If only it were Ian who had come here with her she would have admitted how little she understood and he would have explained. They could have discussed every aspect of what action they should take next.

"Why didn't he come here with you?" asked Gerald softly.

"Ian?" She shrugged. When she continued her accent sounded stronger to herself, as it did so often when she became perturbed. "It is not his fault. At least – they have tried to put him off. My father and his mother. I think that Ian himself is beginning to be convinced that he is too young."

"But no one has put you off the determination to find yourself a home like this."

"No. I would even buy it for myself – alone – if I could do so. But I know so little about such things . . ."

"I could help you, I should be glad to."

"Really?" Her eyes lighting up, she faced him.

Gerald smiled as he nodded. "You need someone to help you make those dreams come true." Having Tania here could be interesting, he thought.

She felt his lips on hers then, tenderly at first so that the kiss seemed to be just one more facet of the curious serenity that she had found in her tiny house. His mouth became more firm, possessive, yet still she felt no alarm. Gerald was so warm, the sweater beneath his jacket so smooth textured that she was reminded of being enveloped against her grandmother's shawl.

And when his kisses deepened and grew exciting, he soothed her with murmured words. "I'll take good care of you, Tania."

Gerald had drawn her closer to him, curving her to the warmth which seemed to be the only life in the coldness of the room. His kisses went on and on, thrilling her now as she recognized that this man was aware that she was attractive, and had no reservations about anything.

His mouth left hers, he smiled and moved away. Tania smiled also, relieved that she need not fear he might expect too much from her.

"Have you seen enough of this house?" he enquired, and headed towards the top of the staircase.

Tania didn't reply immediately. Lowering her feet to the floor, she had glimpsed a corner of something white underneath the edge of the divan. Recovering it, she gasped.

She was gazing at an old photograph of a garden. That it was the garden here, she could not doubt. And in the centre of the lawn, within a coach-built pram, lay a curly-haired baby.

"One day," she whispered to herself, clasping the picture to her, as she listened to Gerald's footsteps descending to ground level. One day I shall live here, she thought, and *I* shall have a child who means all the world to me. It would not matter then that everything at Stonemoor House had become so different following Mihail's birth.

Andre was looking after his son while Pamela made yet another visit to Mrs Fawcett's old place. He smiled to himself, thankful that his wife's latest idea would keep her so close to their home, and that it would more readily accommodate her caring for young Mihail.

He loved tending the boy, even just watching him as he had for the past hour. This son of his had acquired the ability to hold up his head and constantly delighted with his air of being interested in everything. Andre himself, however, could not be lulled into believing that Mihail's development was enough to keep them happy. This winter concert season had begun disastrously for him, and he would be obliged to exert more effort to find work. He would shortly be compelled to tell Pamela of his fears, to explain to her what it was that had caused these orchestras to cease offering him engagements.

She seemed oblivious to the potential devastation for his career which was inherent in the increasing mistrust felt by the Western Powers for his native country. Pamela had been occupied with the baby, he knew, and so had missed a great many of the murmurings against Russia. And he himself, he freely admitted, had done his best to ensure that she remained undisturbed by the unease developing between their countries.

Since 1948 at least, over in America there had been suspicions of spying and of the existence there of a Russian fifth column. In September this year news of a Russian Atomic bomb had increased rumours that espionage and the skill of British physicists had been engaged. It was no wonder that mistrust of his fellow countrymen was spreading throughout England – and so perniciously that few people appeared to listen to explanations that not everyone from the USSR was of Communist persuasion.

He could feel the unease now whenever he went to audition. No matter how well he played his beloved Stradivari – and he read in their faces that his music delighted – they always found some excuse for not offering him a contract.

He was dispirited by the monotonous succession of refusals, worn down by it all, and hurt by the irony. For so long after first coming to Yorkshire, he had considered it unwise to draw attention to himself by performing. Yearning to play the violin again, he had suppressed that feeling until, only a little more than a year ago, he had first appeared in public over here. There had been no hint amid the rapturous receptions of his work that so short a time would elapse before he was out of favour. And through no failure of his ability.

Andre heard a car in the drive and Tania calling 'Goodbye' to someone. Glancing out, he saw the car was not Ian's, and was not surprised. Ian would have come into the house with her. Or – once, he would have. Since disapproval of an early marriage between the pair was voiced, no one could be certain what Ian might do. And, for that matter, Tania's behaviour had become even less easy to predict.

She was cheerful, however, on this Saturday afternoon, delighting Andre when she paused to give him a hug and then again when she rushed over to her half-brother.

"Are babies not adorable?" she exclaimed, glancing over her shoulder towards her father as she extended a finger for Mihail to grasp. "I can imagine nothing more wonderful than seeing your own small person growing and progressing, as this little one does!"

Thankful that she evidently had shed all resentment, Andre went to put a hand on her shoulder as she remained there, making approving noises. This seemed to enchant Mihail who preened himself, gazing from one to the other of them, his blue eyes sparkling.

Pamela came in while the three were united in this way, smiled to herself and hastened towards them.

"And how's my lovely family? It's good to see you all happy together. And I have news that will make you feel even better."

"What is that, my dear?" asked Andre after kissing her. He was pleased for her, but would have been more contented if *he* was the one bringing news of success.

"About the shop. Everything is going so well now. Evaluation of all Mrs Fawcett's exciting things has started. And I've heard from Vincent again. It shouldn't be too long before I can open up for business. I was wondering, Tania, if you would

150

like to spend some time there with me, just until I'm rather more organized,"

Tania gazed back at her, the expression in her eyes curiously unfathomable. "I am not sure, Pamela. That would depend upon when you needed me."

"Any time you're free. It's only that you're so good with Mihail, and until he becomes used to being at the shop and I have it properly organized, I could do with some help."

Her stepdaughter smiled. "I will if I can, but I think I might be about to be quite busy on something of my own."

"Another concert on the horizon?" asked her father, wishing with every scrap of his being that he was accepted as readily as Tania on the concert platform.

Tania only grinned at them and shook her head, making her long blonde hair swirl around her shoulders. "You must wait and see, I think. It is too early to tell you very much."

Chapter Eight

Tania told Ian about the house almost as soon as she saw him. She hadn't entirely contrived the outing with Gerald in order to evoke a response from her old friend, but Ian had responded. On the Wednesday of the following week he had telephoned her to invite her to go to the theatre with him.

"In Halifax, at the Grand," Ian had said. "It's only repertory, but they're a very good company – the Lawrence Williamson players."

Tania had been delighted to accept. Ever since seeing her house near the Lancashire border she had known that living there alone wasn't really what she wanted. It was to be a family home, one where she would be part of the loving triangle that included the baby which would make her feel complete.

Their theatre visit was on the Friday evening, and because Ian was working late Tania offered to meet him in Halifax. Going into town by bus was something of a novelty for her, and she was so excited about seeing him that she ran all the way along Southgate to Corn Market where he was waiting outside Boots the Chemists.

They kissed, though only on the cheek, but as they began to walk on Ian took her hand. His fingers felt strong and familiar, and Tania's spirits started to soar. Deep inside her attraction awakened an insistent beat.

"You went out with Gerald Thomas, didn't you?" he said before they reached Northgate. He could not contain this need for reassurance.

"Only because he offered to take me to a place that I wished to see. Being with Gerald means nothing to me."

"It seemed to mean a lot to him, are you sure you didn't give him the wrong idea?" At last night's band practice Gerald had made a point of telling him about spending so much time with Tania.

"Wrong idea? What do you mean?"

"You know, that you – well, fancy him, like."

"You were like this that other time, when I spoke for a few minutes to Harry. But people like them are only friends who happen to be male. You have no need to be so suspicious, Ian. There is only you."

"Oh, aye? I'm beginning to wonder. It seems to me there's allus somebody you're making eyes at."

"Ian, please. Let us not quarrel," she said, her accent thickening. All the elation of meeting him again had waned.

He gave an awkward shrug and sighed. "OK, forget it." But he could not forget, not when Gerald had related details of visiting that house which interested Tania.

The play was good, or so she supposed, all around them the rest of the audience were listening attentively and then applauding. Tania herself was unable to concentrate. Where had she gone wrong? She had wanted Ian to be aware of how seriously she intended to have her own home, but not to have him disturbed by believing that she might settle there with just anyone in order to have the place.

During the interval that followed the first Act she began to explain. "I only wanted to see the house for myself so that I should know whether or not I really wished to live there. If you had persuaded your mother to let us at least become engaged, I would have asked you to go there with me. But it seems as though you have given up." And *she* could not even contemplate surrendering to their parents, would not be able to wait. The longing to have Ian love her was storming now in every heartbeat.

"It's not only my mother who objects, it's your father as well. You needn't make it out to be entirely our fault."

"But I could talk him round, I know I could, if he was the only person holding out against our marrying."

Ian grunted. "Actually, I dispute that. But it's irrelevant really, because there is a lot of sense in their advocating that we wait. We'd have more behind us then for setting up house."

Tania gave him a sideways look, challenged him to deny her fears. "You do not want to marry me, do you? You have changed your mind."

"No, I haven't. I haven't at all. All I'm saying is that we'll be better waiting a bit."

"But that house is for sale *now* – and it is so beautiful."

The curtain was rising for the second Act, so Tania was obliged to suspend her pleading, even though she continued watching the play with even less enthusiasm

154

than earlier. When the lights went up for the next interval she turned to Ian.

"This is a waste of time," she said agitatedly. "I would much rather talk. We need to decide what we are going to do."

Ian sighed heavily, rose, and took her arm as they left their seats. "We could talk in the bar," he suggested. He had planned this visit to the theatre in the hope that it would be an enjoyable evening which would restore their good relationship.

Tania shook her head. "No, we should have longer in which to decide something so important. Shall we go for a meal?"

Ian, who had spent most of his spare cash on theatre tickets, began to feel embarrassed as well as depressed. "No, I'm not in the mood. We'll pick up the car, I'll drive you home."

"Why not come with me to see that house tomorrow?" Tania suggested as soon as he had opened the passenger door for her.

He was frowning when he slid in behind the steering wheel. "I've said – because there's no point. We're not able to get married yet. You ought to be capable of seeing that as well as I can. We are too young, there are no two ways about it."

Tania felt the hurt of rejection overwhelming her. This was dreadful. Ian meant something far worse than that they should not marry in the immediate future: he was trying to exclude her from his life now. He'd no longer be her special person. She was being shut out of all the fun and the excitement that had developed in their friendship, shut out even more firmly than she was from the happiness that belonged to her father and Mihail and Pamela. Trying to prevent Ian seeing her tears, she stared out of the side window as she spoke.

"You do not wish to grow up, that is the real trouble. I never thought that you were too soft to want to leave your mother."

"You're talking proper daft! I shall be happy to leave, love, but only when I'm sure that I can provide for my wife."

"That is just an excuse. You know that I earn also, I told you that this season I have more professional bookings than last. I probably shall earn enough to pay a deposit on the house— "

"You'd better get on with it then," Ian interrupted. "You evidently don't need me at all," he added, still smarting from the fact that she had gone to view the place without him. Tania had no room to talk about folk not being grown-up – she was worse than a bairn, wanting everything straight away.

Sensing that he couldn't trust himself not to say too much and ruin everything between them for ever, Ian clammed up. Only when he finally dropped Tania off at Stonemoor House did he express the hope that she would calm down and want to see him again.

"Calm down, calm down?" Tania snapped, scarcely capable of a coherent sentence while distress combined with the intense yearning surging within her. "You think that you are calm, but all you are is dormant!"

Pamela and Andre were in the nursery. Tania heard them cooing over Mihail as she began running up the stairs to her own room. Passing the open door, she glimpsed them both as they turned to look, but she continued on, longing only to weep out all her anguish, alone.

Her half-brother was crying too, if she had been less distressed she would have realized that this was the reason he was receiving so much attention, but she was past thinking.

Five minutes later her father knocked on her bedroom door and, when she did not respond, came into the room.

"What is it, my sweet?" he enquired sympathetically, prepared to rush to the bed where she had thrown herself.

Tania did not answer.

"I thought you were meeting Ian tonight?" he persisted. But he had never been very good at coping with his daughter's tears. "If you do not tell me what is wrong, I shall not be able to help, shall I?"

"You do not care, anyway," Tania muttered into the pillow. He had taken such an age to come to her. And she had not needed that delay to emphasize how preoccupied Andre always was with his son.

"You and Ian have quarrelled, I suppose?"

"And would not have, if you were not so unreasonable. You should be satisfied now, you not only have stopped us marrying, you have ruined our friendship."

Tania heard Pamela's footsteps and the creak of the bedroom door as it opened wider. Pamela murmured something to Andre.

"A little tiff, I fear," he began to explain.

"It is not little, whatever 'tiff' means," Tania

retorted, sensing that the word conveyed something far less important than this major conflict. Her entire body felt racked by the upset, and still tormented by this longing as well – a longing she barely understood, and which would not go away.

No one would ever console her. When Mihail again began crying Tania felt almost relieved that Pamela hurried along to the nursery.

"This is not the end of the world, my dear," Andre began. "You and Ian will become friends again."

She shook her head violently from side to side. "No, no."

Tania heard Pamela's footsteps once more, and then her voice. "Just take hold of him for a minute, Andre. He's been sick, poor mite. I'll have to change all his covers."

"Sick? Is it serious, do you think? Should we call the doctor?" Andre sounded extremely worried.

"He'll probably be all right now, just his feed that's disagreed with him. He seemed tired when he was taking it. But we'll move his cot into our room for the night, keep an eye on him."

"So long as you are sure. I will carry him downstairs until you have the cot ready, sit with him beside the fire where it is warm."

You do that, thought Tania, look after the boy, he is the one who matters. Why should you care that my heart has been broken? That I am here in this country that frequently feels strange, and that my true friend has deserted me.

Half an hour later she had relented, was beginning to feel anxious about Mihail. Was he all right? Or was this sickness the start of an illness, something

158

life threatening even? She did not really resent the attention that he needed. He was tiny still. And he was a lovely little thing. Please let him be better in the morning, she prayed.

Mihail appeared to be in perfect health at breakfast time, beaming at the three of them, looking enchanting with his golden curls gleaming in the wintry sunlight flowing in through the tall window. Tania crossed swiftly to give him a kiss, then smiled at both her father and Pamela whose relief was showing in happy faces.

"As you see, he is completely fit again!" Andre exclaimed.

"That is good," said Tania. But being pleased about her half-brother did not affect her own deepest emotions.

She had decided, though, that she was going to do something about this awful misery. She'd known she could have to fight. Now she would show them all, and especially Ian, that she was not about to let their suppression of her ideas render her as ineffectual as Ian himself.

Tania set out by bus for the estate agents and whilst deploring the slowness of the journey was conscious of using the time to marshal her thoughts. She would see her little house again, what was more she would find out exactly how much was being asked for it, and what a mortgage would entail.

She was earning good money, after all, hadn't she brought with her concert programmes that proved how frequently she was engaged to sing, and with prestigious orchestras?

159

The estate agents was even busier than on the previous Saturday, but after quite a wait Tania attracted the attention of the man who had assisted them previously. He seemed delighted that she wished to inspect the house again, and impressed when she spoke of taking her interest a stage further. It was then that he glanced about him, and shattered her with his next question.

"But your young man – isn't he with you today?"

"No, he – he could not come. But it will be all right, I am quite sure that I can find my way there."

"Ah – I'm afraid that is not at issue, my dear. The fact is – well, to be frank, you do not look quite so mature. How old are you?"

"Almost twenty," Tania lied.

"Then I am sorry. We would not contemplate issuing the key to anyone under age. Company policy, you understand. You do understand?"

Suddenly last night's tears seemed to threaten again. She could not, *would not* make a fool of herself here. Tania drew in a long breath, and swallowed twice. "Perhaps you would arrange for someone to accompany me to the house?"

The man shook his head. "Unfortunately, everyone else is out, showing people around other houses. Obviously, I cannot leave— "

Tania interrupted by turning on her heel and heading smartly towards the door. But this was not admitting to defeat. She had Gerald's telephone number in her diary somewhere.

He sounded impatient at first when he answered, but his tone warmed instantly on hearing her voice.

160

"What are you doing?" Tania asked, unable to delay until they had exchanged niceties.

Gerald laughed. "Working on an old car, if you must know. I'm restoring it when I can find the time. Why?"

Tania told him how difficult the man at the estate agents had been. "But he let you have the key without any fuss, did he not?"

Her accent made her sound particularly appealing. "I'll meet you there if you like," Gerald offered. "But I'll have to wash and change, give me an hour, no, an hour and a quarter. Go and have a coffee or something."

She strode out along the pavement to the nearest store and then up in a lift to the restaurant. It was an elegant place, even despite the restrictions on food which still had not been relaxed after the ending of the war.

Feeling very adult, Tania ordered coffee and cakes, and glanced around her until the waitress brought them to her table. Most of the other clients were ladies, all of them so well dressed that they evoked her silent assertion that she would always appear equally sophisticated.

The fact that the home on which she had set her heart did not exactly match up to such impressive standards did not strike her. The means of judging these people here was not related in any way to her consideration of that dream house. But she did know already that she could dress to look elegant. Her contemplation of her future home was on a different level. It was becoming so essential to her life that she would not believe that it had any shortcomings.

Warmed by the coffee and comfortable surroundings, Tania wandered through the rest of the store, admiring coats and dresses, trying on hats which added ten years to her age, and slipping her narrow feet in and out of innumerable pairs of shoes. She would purchase nothing, of course: today she could glean ideas for the future without needing to carry anything away with her. The assurance she sought would be of her eventual ownership of that house; about everything else she was engaging the strictest economy.

Only when I have that place, Tania promised herself as the plateglass doors swung to behind her, will I begin to think of other necessities. She passed the next ten minutes in a music shop, looking through records as well as sheet music before noticing the time and rushing along the street to meet up with Gerald.

He was late, but she forgave him gladly, so relieved by the access he provided to that key, that she thrust a hand through his arm as she gazed up at him.

"Am I thankful to see you, Gerald! You would not believe how foolish I felt when they refused to let me go alone to inspect the house."

Gerald was smiling down at her, giving no sign that her interruption of his day perturbed him. "If only you had said that you wished me to go with you again, I'd have been happy to arrange it."

But I could not have known how difficult Ian would be, she realized, and consigned that thought to the back of her mind. "It does not matter now. You are here." Soon they would be in her lovely little house.

*   *   *

"Do you seriously want to live here?"

It was half an hour later. They were in that upstairs room again, having inspected the whole of the rest of the house for a second time. Tania wondered why Gerald sounded so incredulous, but did not comment on that. While she needed his help she must not question the value of his opinion. But she surely wanted this house, and nodded fervently.

"Oh, yes. Indeed, I do. It is the thing I wish most in all the world."

"But it's in rotten condition, Tania. Look at it. There's no proper bathroom, only that terrible lavatory out at the back."

"There is a bath, in the kitchen."

"But who would want to use it?"

"It is not so bad. And besides, there is room to build on at the side here."

"That would cost a packet. Have you thought, really thought, about the cost of this place? Where would you find the money in the first instance, let alone for renovations?"

"I think I could raise the deposit. And – and my stepmother is in that line of business."

"A builder, you mean?" His incredulity was increasing.

"Well – doing interior renovations. She restored my father's house." Tania refused to even think about the fact that Pamela would oppose all this just as aggressively as her own father would.

Gerald shrugged. "Up to you, of course."

But Tania suddenly felt overwhelmed by it all, and yet again tears began pricking at her eyes. Of course, the house needed improvements, but it was still such a sweet place. She couldn't be so disloyal to her dream that she would ever agree that it would require too much renovating. And it was in such an idyllic location . . .

"Would you really wish to live on the edge of the moors like this?" Gerald asked her as they went downstairs again. "Think how cold it will be in a hard winter."

"I am used to severe winters," Tania reminded him. But her voice quivered. She was thinking of her grandmother's tiny farmhouse, which seemed farther away today than at any time since her arrival in England. What am I trying to do, she wondered, why am I so determined to make a home out here? But there seemed no way now of going back. She would look such an idiotic *child* if she admitted to anyone that the whole prospect now seemed entirely daunting.

"Why didn't Ian come with you today?" Gerald enquired. "I'd have thought he'd have wanted to look at the place, at least."

Tania shook her head, and now her eyes filled with the tears she had struggled to restrain. She gulped. "Ian? Oh, that is finished, I told him yesterday . . ." A sob choked her.

Gerald drew her to him, held her while her body shook with the emotion that had only been suspended because she was so desperate to be practical. To make things turn out the way she wanted.

"All right," he said, "all right. Forget him, and think about this house, you evidently need something to cheer you up."

His words seemed to have little effect. Perturbed,

164

Gerald leaned against the side of the chimney breast and held Tania close against him, her head pressing into his shoulder.

Several moments later he kissed her wet cheeks. She clung to him, her arms reaching up about his shoulders, and then their lips met in a kiss that startled her out of despair.

Unaware that Gerald had waited only to learn that Ian was out of the contest, Tania surrendered to the relief of having arms enfold her. She had been so afraid that no one cared about her now.

Even when his kisses grew insistent and he continued to crush her against him, she only felt comforted by the warmth of this man who seemed to understand her.

By the time that she had recovered from weeping and insisted that they continue their tour of the house, Tania's attitude was changing – and not only towards the practicalities of purchasing a home. She had always considered Gerald a reliable friend, she was discovering now that he was more interesting than she originally had thought. And so mature that she no longer could dismiss him merely as someone who could be useful if other people refused to take her seriously.

Gerald seemed to know a lot about houses and, even while he was pointing out all the shortcomings of this one, had convinced her that his advice was worth remembering. Tania wanted to show how adult her own ideas were. Straightening her shoulders she spoke briskly.

"Maybe there is a lot needing attention here, but they should reduce the price. When we go back to the

165

estate agents I would like you to ask how large a deposit is required, and then perhaps you could tell to me how I must obtain a mortgage."

Gerald sighed. "Ah – there we have a problem. I'm afraid that until you are twenty-one you are unlikely to be granted a mortgage."

"But that is stupid. I earn good fees now whenever I sing."

"I don't really think that will make a substantial difference."

"You will find out for me though?"

Gerald's promise was reassuring. Refusing to be downhearted, Tania gave her mind to enjoying the rest of the day. Even when the estate agents' response proved to be very much as Gerald had anticipated, she felt herself relaxing. No matter how strangers behaved towards her, she could not be miserable while this attractive man was beside her, treating her like a mature woman.

"What are you doing over Christmas?" Gerald enquired as they drove up through Cragg Vale towards Stonemoor House.

Christmas? Tania shuddered as gloom threatened to envelope her again. She was perfectly able to feel content while Gerald was beside her. But that would only last for the next five minutes. Dashing off, as she had today, had allowed no time for realizing how catastrophically her break with Ian affected everything. For ages now plans had being going ahead for Mihail's first Christmas. Mildred Baker and both Ian and Tom were to stay with them. Her father and Pamela had been purchasing expensive gifts for the baby. Tania recognized with a jolt that made her feel sick that she would not be able to endure those days of family celebration.

Incapable of speech, she shook her head and eventually turned her brimming eyes towards Gerald as he parked the car.

"Then come to us," he said, reached for her hand and squeezed it. "I'll square it with my parents then telephone you with the details."

"Thank you. Oh, thank you!" Anything would be better than remaining at Stonemoor now that she and Ian no longer belonged together.

"Where is Pamela?" Tania asked as soon as she walked into the house and saw and heard her father practising the violin.

Andre stopped playing to come and kiss her. "She has gone out, to see an old friend over in Halifax."

"Dorothy, you mean?" Pamela had been saying recently that she never found the time to call on Dorothy and Charles.

"No, not Dorothy."

Tania shrugged. "Has she taken Mihail to show to them?"

"No, he is in the nursery. Pamela took him along to Dr Philipson this morning, but he seems quite well again. Just sleepy as a result of that restless night." Andre himself was satisfied that this provided the opportunity for practising uninterrupted. His music appeared to interest that son of his, with the result that no work was done. And he needed to improve his technique – although he was already utterly convinced that the absence of engagements was caused by something more perturbing than flaws in his performance.

167

Today, he was doubly glad to concentrate on his violin. Pamela had been deeply disturbed, as had he himself on her behalf.

She had been cheerfully unpacking a crate of glassware recently purchased for her shop at an auction in a neighbouring village. All at once, she had uttered such a strange cry that Andre had run to her believing she had cut herself.

She was smoothing out a piece of newspaper, and moaning under her breath. "Oh, no – oh, dear. Poor Roger."

After taking several seconds to regain composure, Pamela had explained. "It's here, in the deaths, the name caught my eye and – and it's Leslie Rivers. You remember – the chap that Roger went to live with? It doesn't say what he died of, or owt like that, but he couldn't have been more than thirty-five or thirty-six."

Unable to obtain an answer on the telephone, Pamela had become convinced that Roger was at the flat alone, and inconsolable. "It'll be so dreadful for him, with not daring to risk talking about – about their relationship. He'll be having to face it all on his own."

She had set out almost immediately, and in such an agitated state that Andre was concerned about her safety at the wheel of the Wolesley. He had offered to accompany her, but their housekeeper did not come to Stonemoor House at weekends, and going anywhere would have involved getting Mihail ready to go too.

In the car, as she headed towards Halifax and then out beyond in direction of the flat beside Ogden

168

reservoir, Pamela was feeling physically sick. She had known for years that she owed Roger a great deal. He had been so supportive throughout those appalling months following the death of her first husband. A close friend of Jim, Roger had been there for her whenever she needed help, sorting Jim's affairs and then encouraging her to continue with the decorating business. And Roger had taught her to drive. To this day, she remained certain that she had so lacked confidence at the time that no one else would have succeeded in teaching her.

Despite all that he had done, she had subsequently avoided Roger until guilt combined with awareness of her own neglect, and even the shortest encounter between them made her acutely embarrassed.

But she had not known that Leslie Rivers was unwell. Sighing, Pamela admitted that she had not known for the simple reason that she had wished to learn nothing further about either of them. Even while Roger was still visiting her own mother's home, coaching Ian in playing the saxophone, she herself had refused to mention his name.

Briefly, Pamela acknowledged that this evasion had partly been generated through her dread of blurting out some hint of what was taking place at that flat out in the country. From the day Leslie had revealed the nature of the relationship she had been terrified that she could be responsible for such a slip resulting in their arrest. With Roger a sergeant in the police force, his punishment could have been even more severe than for someone in a civilian occupation.

The flat now had its own entrance, a stone flight of steps on the side of the building. Determined to get the initial awkwardness over and done with, Pamela ran up them and knocked on the door. Standing there, listening as she waited, she began to believe that Roger was out on duty. She could have wept, her reluctance to confront him was altering into an urgent longing to put things right between them.

She knocked a second time, and was about to turn away when the door was opened.

Roger looked nearer seventy than forty, his brown eyes red-rimmed in a face grown haggard. He tried to smile, cleared his throat.

"Pamela. You'd better come in . . ."

The flat still appeared bright, the pale green walls that she had painted, as clean as on the day when she completed them. Only the atmosphere was dark, heavy with Roger's loss which almost felt tangible.

"I'm most terribly sorry," she said. "I've only just seen it in the paper. I had to come."

"Thank you. You know what I am going through."

Pamela nodded. "I know." The death of a partner, no matter their sex, was like being torn apart. She wanted to ask what had happened, could not find the right words, and began to feel increasingly inept.

Roger told her anyway, but not before indicating a chair and waiting until she was seated. He prowled while he spoke, an action all the more unnerving in a room that seemed cluttered with furniture.

"We thought it was flu at first, Les complained about getting an attack at the start of the winter. I made him stop in bed, managed to look after him myself, being on shifts helped in a way. I was always here at some part of the day.

"He didn't eat much, in any case, even from the

start. And he wouldn't have the doctor in, not for a long while, any road. Well, you don't, do you, just for the flu? When the doctor arrived, though, he came back into this room with a face like somebody who's not used to seeing illness. 'It's pneumonia, I'm afraid,' he told me. And then that Leslie was refusing to be moved. If they could get him into hospital, it might be all right, if they were able to put him in an iron lung.

"They treated him with some of them new drugs used for the first time during the war, but it was too late. I blamed myself – for not insisting that the doctor was called, for letting Les believe he might recover at home. He wouldn't listen to that. Over and over again, he said how he was an adult, had made up his own mind about what he would do. I still know it's my fault."

Pamela rose, rushed across the room and gathered Roger to her. "I'm sure you did your best for him."

"I tried, I really did try, when it was too late. It was the condition his lungs were in, you see. Before the pneumonia. He'd had infantile paralysis, you know, polio. That was why he limped. It was years since either of us really noticed that. But I ought to have remembered, I ought to have *thought* . . ."

Her arms still around him, Pamela continued to steady Roger against her.

"I shouldn't have let him be so dismissive about the doctor. If only I'd insisted . . ." he began again moments later.

"Has he – have you had the funeral yet?"

"It's to be on Monday. At Illingworth Moor

chapel. That's why I'm off work today. Getting ready. Not that there'll be so many folk there. His mother, naturally. Mine – well, my mum and dad haven't wanted to know, not about either of us, since they found out. I'm hoping there'll be a few chaps from the band, but most of them we grew up with have left."

"I'll be there, if – if you'll let me."

"You?" Roger had stepped back from her, now he gave her a look.

Pamela flinched. "I know. I've been rotten to you. All this time, rotten. And after all you'd done. It was just— "

"Shock. You don't have to explain, everybody who's learned the truth has been shocked. Not that many have known." Roger sighed, nodded to himself. "I'll be glad to have you there. Aye, I will."

He made a pot of tea and they sat in comfortable chairs, but he remained comfortless, unable to speak of anything but the weeks preceding his lover's death.

Being made to picture it all seemed to Pamela a just means of eradicating her guilt for those months when she had neglected this dear old friend.

"Looking back now," Roger told her, "I can see caring for Les as the privilege it was. At the time, though, it was bloody depressing. There was so little I could do. I've never felt more useless."

She could understand that when he described the days and nights of being unable to do more than ease things for Leslie, washing his body as it grew increasingly emaciated, attending to other, more personal needs, feeding him until the time came when Les could neither eat nor drink.

And all the while Roger had been obliged to continue to work, going out daily to a police sergeant's world where every sense was required to remain acute, and no account was taken of exhaustion. There was no compassionate leave when love featured someone of your own sex: only the threat of imprisonment if anyone chanced to discover its existence.

"I'll be there on Monday," Pamela reminded him when she finally prepared to leave.

The wind stung her face when she emerged on to the stone steps. Fearfully cold, it was tearing across the reservoir from the moors where the Brontë sisters had roamed. Pamela shuddered, stared for a few moments across the expanse of water, then turned up her collar and hurried towards her car.

All the way home to Stonemoor she had to force herself to concentrate just to stay on the road. Roger was so isolated out there. She would never rid herself of the image of that bright little flat, and the dark and the despair that had developed within its walls.

Chapter Nine

It could have been because of Roger's presence, but whatever the reason, Leslie's funeral brought back to Pamela her first husband's death far more forcibly than the recent interment of her neighbour.

She had quietly joined Roger in the front pew as soon as she had seen that old Mrs Rivers was the only person at his side. Reaching them, Pamela realized that the two were in no way together, but rather had determined individually that no one should oust them from that position. Her own sadness immediately increased. Several rows behind sat three members of the brass band in which both Roger and Les had played. The minister and undertakers were the only others present.

Beside her throughout the chapel service Roger appeared composed, his lips moved in each required response, but scarcely a murmur emerged. If he had confided that words were all but impossible, he would merely have confirmed what she sensed, but Roger would confide nothing. The only words that seemed to gleam through the tragedy of Leslie's shortened life and make a bit of sense were quoted by the minister from Henry David Thoreau:

'Time is but the stream I go a-fishing in. I drink at it; but while I drink I see the sandy bottom and detect how shallow it is. Its thin current slides away, but eternity remains.'

At the graveside, Mrs Rivers swayed. For one dreadful moment Pamela was afraid the angular lady might fall on to her son's coffin. But Roger was there with a steadying hand. Pamela noticed that his hand was dashed away within seconds.

"Are you a pal of *his*?" Mrs Rivers asked her afterwards, jerking her head towards Roger.

Pamela quelled a sigh and fixed her steady gaze on the lined features and heart-wrenchingly defeated eyes. "Yes. Roger's always been very good to me. He was my late husband's friend."

"Oh, aye?" The woman's sniff owed nothing to her intense sadness. "If it had only been up to me, I'd have had a cremation, you know." She turned to glower at Roger, glanced down into the grave for one last time, then turned again to walk towards one of the black cars.

"She refuses to come back to the flat," said Roger dully.

Pamela, who originally had intended going straight home to Stonemoor to feed Mihail, tried to smile. "Come on, love – we'd best be getting there and putting the kettle on. Are the fellows from the band coming with us?"

Roger shook his head. "They – have things to see to."

They talked about the brass band, though, sitting either side of the table in the living room. Roger was only thinking about Leslie, she knew, but his mouth formed the words which ranged beyond this unspeakable sadness.

175

Pamela contributed to the verbal duet, raking up memories of days before the war when her Jim, and Roger as well, had lived for those concerts. The subject exhausted at last, she hauled up memories closer to hand, of her early days renovating and decorating, and how she had depended upon him in order to survive the loss of her husband.

"Don't ever forget now that I shall be there for you," Pamela insisted. "Andre will understand. As a matter of fact, he's understood all along about you and Leslie."

Somehow, though, when she finally was compelled to leave, Pamela sensed that Roger would turn to no one as he struggled to survive this grief.

As soon as she arrived back at Stonemoor House Andre came out into the hall to greet her. "How did it go?"

"About as I expected. There were pitifully few people there, and Leslie's mother's resentment of Roger made everything worse. She blames him, I could tell. As if she's blinded herself to it taking two to create that sort of a relationship."

"Let me take your coat," said Andre, longing to hold this wife of his, to kiss her until every other thought but of themselves might be driven from her. But Mihail had wailed for most of the past hour, had refused to take the bottle that Pamela had prepared before going out.

"I am afraid we have an unhappy son," he admitted ruefully. "In fact, I feel certain it is only because he senses that you are here now that he has ceased yelling."

"Didn't he take his feed?"

176

Andre shook his head. "I fear that he finds me a miserable substitute for his mother!"

"And where's Tania? Couldn't she persuade him either?"

"Tania went out, shortly after you left. And no, she did not say where she was going."

He was perturbed about his daughter, she seemed so young to refuse to reveal her destination or whom she was meeting. But, for once, Andre was even more anxious about his own news. The telephone call this afternoon from his agent had confirmed all that he had been dreading. The situation now was so serious that he could no longer continue to spare Pamela by keeping his fears to himself.

He followed when she went to the kitchen, watched while she checked that Mihail's bottle was still of the right temperature, then followed again as she went towards their son's fresh cries of indignation.

Sitting nearby while Pamela began feeding Mihail, Andre found that the sight of his wife and their now contented baby eased his pangs of alarm, but not sufficiently to deflect him from the conversation which he had decided they must have.

"I am sorry to raise this matter when you so evidently have had such a distressing day already," he began. "But I must not conceal the truth."

What truth is this? Pamela wondered, shaken enough by the truths hammered home a few hours previously. Truth, *facts* about life were swiftly becoming all but unendurable.

"My agent has been in touch, but I really needed no one to declare what has steadily become obvious over the past few months. There seems no solution

177

to my inability to secure engagements on the concert platform."

"But you play so well, magnificently— "

"And that is now of no consequence, it seems. Because of who I am, of where I am from. Too many over here, more still in America – and I need not remind you of the influence they have – are developing mistrust of everything Russian."

Horrified, Pamela could hardly believe what she was hearing. "You mean – they're not giving you work because of what's going on behind the Iron Curtain? Andre love, are you sure? That can't be right."

"Not right in the ethical sense perhaps, but true of the situation. You have been busy, I know, too busy for reading newspapers. It is everywhere now, a massive mistrust of anyone of Russian extraction."

"Not everyone surely? That doesn't make sense."

"And when did sense entirely govern people's reactions, a nation's? It is all around us now, I know. Suspicion, doubt, the fear that spy-rings grow up overnight like mushrooms."

"That can't be happening, not here in the heart of Yorkshire."

"Not yet, maybe, not in our valley. Unfortunately, our neighbourhood is not graced by concert halls. In order to play, I must travel. And now my agent confirms my own growing fears – that I am no longer to be welcomed."

Pamela moved as though to set the baby aside and go to hug Andre, but Mihail's hungry mouth emitted a fierce yell of protest.

"Later," she told her husband, saw his smile, but wished that it were echoed in his grey eyes.

Tania came in even before Pamela had finished feeding the baby, preventing her from comforting Andre, and then increasing their upset with the words that followed her cheerful greeting.

"I thought I would tell you now, Father – Pamela. I shall be away, staying with friends at Christmas."

"But . . ." Andre began, his expression which had lightened with Tania's arrival blackening swiftly.

"Where are you going?" Pamela enquired softly, sensing that Andre was in no mood to avoid the unpleasantness of a major confrontation.

"Tania is not going anywhere," said Andre coldly, but Pamela again interceded.

"Please let her at least tell us what she intends."

Andre shrugged, but her stepdaughter's smile rewarded her. "It is nothing that either of you need feel perturbed about. Gerald's parents have invited me to stay for Christmas, that is all. They are very nice people, with a lovely home, it all is very refined."

Pamela stifled sudden amusement. Tania had been justified in anticipating that her proposed visit would be vetted, it appeared that her assessment had been quite accurate, and she was taking appropriate steps to allay their fears. She was not to know that Andre was already so depressed that the prospect of the Christmas holiday without his daughter seemed appalling.

"We did encourage her to look around her more, to balance her friendship with Ian against seeing other folk of her own age," Pamela reminded him.

"As you say," Andre observed, but his grey eyes appeared as relentless as a winter's sea.

179

They talked afterwards, when the long evening ended and Tania went up to her room, but Pamela felt that she was unable to help him. Nothing anyone could say would lift the gloom induced by his daughter's decision, just as nothing seemed likely to alter the attitude of those orchestras now refusing to engage him.

"Where's Tania then?" Mildred had come rushing into the house, leaving Ian and Tom to bring in their luggage and, of course, a mass of presents.

Andre smiled into the blue eyes so much like Pamela's. "I am afraid that you are to be disappointed. Tania has gone to stay with friends."

"Oh – I see." She digested the news, gave a tiny shrug and hugged her son-in-law. "Aye – well, she's growing up, isn't she?"

Pamela came into the hall with Mihail in her arms. She kissed her mother, asked how she was, and had the baby taken from her before an answer was given.

"I'm all right, love, thanks," Mildred then replied. "And all the better for seeing this little chap. He's grown, you know, since last time. You'll not notice, I suppose, being with him every day."

"I notice he's getting heavier," her daughter remarked.

Ian hurried in through the front door with Tom on his heels. Pamela noticed Ian looking around, clearly expecting to see Tania. She saw his sherry-brown eyes veil for a second and then he smiled towards Andre. Setting down the things he'd brought in from the car, he crossed swiftly to shake his brother-in-law by the hand.

180

Tom was already making a fuss of the baby, causing Pamela to smile indulgently. This young brother of hers was always perfectly natural, and would not dream of disguising feelings that to many a sixteen-year-old lad might seem soft.

Pamela couldn't have been more thankful that Andre evidently had relinquished regrets about Tania's absence and was prepared to make the most of Mihail's first Christmas. Ever since beginning to love Stonemoor House she had longed to celebrate the season here, now that she had a child she was not going to permit anything to spoil the next few days. She could make allowances for Tania's wish to avoid any awkwardness, and forgive her for not staying at home.

Only today it had occurred to her that her step-daughter could have chosen to go away because of feeling usurped by the baby. There had been instances that showed how sensitive she had become to occasions when Mihail was demanding a lot of attention.

She's only a lass herself, Pamela reflected, and she has suffered the loss of her mother followed by that separation from Andre. Happen I haven't done enough to make really sure that she feels included in everything that involves the family, she thought.

Andre immediately threw himself into entertaining their guests. While Pamela and her mother were busy in the kitchen or with the infant he took Ian and Tom upstairs into the room adjoining the nursery.

"I want your advice," he told them. "And, if you do not object, a little practical help."

He went to a cupboard and showed them what he had bought for Mihail.

"Isn't he a bit young yet?" Ian asked with a grin.

Andre was taking out yards and yards of miniature railway track, followed by steam-engines and an assortment of rolling stock.

"Pamela learned of these whilst attending auctions to stock up her shop. I could not resist them. They are all pre-war, you see, and it will be quite some time, I think, before trains of such quality are manufactured again."

The lads set to, sorting out track and helping Andre to lay it in a huge circle around the floor. They then began to examine the trains that he had bought.

"This is going to take days!" Tom exclaimed, smiling, when their host insisted that every item must be inspected, and any requiring repair put to one side pending attention.

The task did indeed continue at intervals all over Christmas, and filled many an hour when time might otherwise have dragged for Pamela's brothers. For Andre himself, his wife and mother-in-law, there seemed too few hours in each and every day.

Mihail was becoming an enchanting child, more interesting than ever now that he was trying to sit up, intent on watching everything around him. Resisting his smile was well-nigh impossible, and only when he was asleep did his mother and grandmother freely concentrate on anything else.

With so much cooking to be done, Pamela had taken to placing the carrycot in the kitchen, and was thankful that she and Mrs Singer had prepared a great deal of food in advance. Keeping an eye on

Mihail always seemed to mean pausing to play with him, and encourage him to respond.

"I'm surprised about Tania, you know," Mildred remarked on Christmas morning. "I'd have bet any money that she'd never have wanted to miss her brother's first Christmas."

"Happen the novelty of having him around has waned a bit by now," suggested Pamela.

Her mother shrugged. "I can't believe that, she seems to love bairns so much. No, I thought she'd be fed up before now wherever she is, and wondering what's going on at home."

"You have made me so welcome here! I feel as though I have known you both for a very long time."

Tania was smiling as she walked towards her host and hostess across yards of exquisite carpet. They were assembling for drinks before dinner on Christmas Eve, and she already felt at ease with his parents, even when Gerald was late down.

The lateness was her fault, so he had said, but that was their personal secret. And Thelma and Barry Thomas were not the kind of people likely to require an explanation from him.

Tania knew no one else so relaxed about everything, no parents who expected young people to decide things for themselves, and without constant questioning. Of course, Gerald was several years older than herself, less liable to suffer interference. Even so, she sensed that he had always been treated as someone responsible. Which he is, she thought to herself, while listening as his father began describing some of the drinks that were unfamiliar to her.

183

"I shall enjoy learning all that you can tell me," she enthused. "I have not yet acquired much experience of what is available over here. My father has not entertained a great deal."

"Not even since his remarriage?" Thelma enquired.

"Only for special occasions, like my half-brother's Christening."

Following her host's description of the drinks she might sample, Tania accepted gin with a generous portion of lime. Although a little uncertain about the fragrance rising from her glass, she liked the limey taste which seemed to quench her thirst. She had been given red wine at lunchtime, and had noticed how dry her throat remained afterwards.

When Gerald finally appeared, he hastened straight to her side and placed an arm around her waist. Tania continued to smile to herself long after she turned from responding to the grin he gave her. Gerald had a way of making her feel special, and that their friendship mattered a great deal to him.

He chose gin as well, confirming her own selection, but he took his with tonic water, something she had never tried. As soon as she said this to him, he offered his glass for her to sip.

Their eyes met over its rim, and his were laughing when she gave a tiny shudder.

"I prefer it with lime, I think!" Tania exclaimed.

His father was at her side immediately, one hand extended for her own glass. "Then I must top that up. You're to have everything you like best while you're here with us."

Gerald's fingers tightened significantly on her waist, their touch reminiscent of the interlude an hour ago when he had awakened all her senses so tantalizingly.

Thelma was talking now of friends who would be joining them for drinks before lunch on the following day, but Tania was unable to give her hostess her complete attention. Gerald was standing very close, his possessive arm conjuring reminders of lingering in the heated conservatory where the scented blooms had seemed no more heady and exotic than his kisses and caresses.

"I must send you off to prepare for this evening," he had said, finally, his voice husky and those deep blue eyes hazed with longing.

She had read in his need to despatch her the greater need that had been contained, and had liked him better than ever in the past for deciding that their passion should be curbed. Learning she was so evidently desirable to someone as mature as Gerald had been a surprise, but one which made her feel infinitely better about Ian's neglect.

Dinner was a beautiful meal, served in the relaxed atmosphere that owed much to Thelma Thomas's having a resident housekeeper. Freed of the need to dart between kitchen and dining room, Gerald's mother was proving to be an interesting raconteur. Her membership of the Local History Section of the Literary and Scientific Society gave her a wide range of subjects, and what sounded to be a fascinating circle of acquaintances.

Enthralled by details of the old days around Hebden Bridge, Tania listened, and ate with enthusiasm, and drank the wine that the men seated to either side of her replenished so frequently.

Gerald took her arm as they went through to the sitting room when the meal was over. Realizing how unsteady her legs were feeling, Tania suppressed a tiny giggle and was thankful for his support.

Barry Thomas was the pianist from whom Gerald had inherited his musical talent, and they sat around while he played a succession of popular tunes which he followed with Christmas Carols.

Glad that her own voice would never let her down in company, Tania joined in fervently, helped by the book that Gerald provided as soon as he discovered that some of the English words were unfamiliar to her.

Happy though she was, Tania had begun feeling so drowsy that the prospect of bed seemed overwhelming attractive when her host eventually rose to his feet.

"Thelma and I are going to church at midnight, we always do," he announced. "We'd be delighted if you would come with us."

So pleased with them that she wished to please in return, Tania was about to agree, but Gerald answered for them both.

"We'll go to morning service instead, if you don't mind," he asserted, while his tone indicated that their 'minding' would not affect the decision.

"I could see you were too tired for going out," he confided when his parents had left them in order to get ready for church.

Tania smiled at him. "You are very considerate, I think," she told him, and yet again relished his concern for her.

After Thelma and Barry had said good-night on their way out, the housekeeper came to ask if they would be requiring anything further. Gerald checked with Tania before confirming that they had everything that they wanted.

"I feel as though I shall not do justice to all that food tomorrow," Tania confessed. "Tonight's meal was so delicious that I could not resist a thing."

"What you need is some exercise," Gerald insisted, taking her hand and drawing her to her feet.

"I am not sure I could . . ." Tania began, but he was crossing with her towards the record player.

"Only gentle exercise," he told her.

The record was one of Glenn Miller's, so familiar that Tania instantly began swaying to the rhythm. Gerald drew her against him, enveloping her in his arms so that she forgot how unsteady her legs had felt. He danced her slowly around the room while she closed her eyes and gave herself to the music. The tune was followed by another, then a third, a fourth, and with each one she grew more entranced with the beat, and with her partner.

Their kisses seemed a part of the music, simply an additional means of expressing its insistence. While he stirred against her Tania noticed only that their dancing appeared more exquisitely attuned.

"It's getting late," Gerald murmured into her hair. "If we're to be up in time for church in the morning, we'd better turn in now."

Holding her closely to his side, he took her up the elegant staircase and along to her room. The melodies to which they had danced were echoing through Tania's head, affecting her entire body, bestowing the drifting sensation that made her thankful for Gerald's arm about her. When she sank on to the bed and shut her eyes again, the whole room appeared to whirl about her.

But Gerald was there to steady her against that unnerving lurching, pressing her to him so that now she felt secure. Sighing as relief mingled with her happiness, she curved closer against him.

His lips teased the lobe of her ear, travelled across her throat and then fastened on to her mouth in a kiss that began as reassuring then deepened and intensified. Tania could only respond, matching his need when the force of her own passion surprised her.

He had made her so happy today, had taken away all the hurt of feeling shunned. This yearning to give seemed only one facet of the special relationship developing between them.

Gerald's hands through the silk of her gown felt warm, as gentle as the delicate conservatory blooms that witnessed those earlier kisses. Kisses which were no more than promises. Tania remained motionless while he began easing up her skirt, his skilled touch over her fine stockings so soft that it might have been imagined.

It had been such a perfect day, such a blissful evening, this awareness of herself felt like coming alive. Her heartbeat had quickened, developing new pulses to race through her entire body. She wanted to sing out her success. She had proved all the others wrong, she was not still a child, she had coped without them all.

"You make me so happy, Gerald," she murmured huskily. And clung to him.

He smiled into her eyes, his own dark and intense, mysterious. And when he made her his Tania knew only that he was creating release for all her months of tension.

He undressed her tenderly at some time during the night, lay with her in the bed, and much later loved her into full consciousness as the wintry dawn sent a chink of light between the heavy curtains.

Seated beside Gerald in the unfamiliar church that morning, Tania marvelled that everyone seemed oblivious to the way that she had changed. To her own eyes, her reflection in the stylish glass in the Thomas's guest bedroom had looked infinitely more adult, intensely happy. Gerald was different too, smiling frequently with that knowing look which revealed how mature he was. How he had matured her.

Throughout Christmas Day their altered relationship was to increase Tania's enjoyment. Gerald would not have needed her, had he considered her immature. If she were not desirable, he would have invited some other young lady home at such a special time of year.

Glancing sideways, Tania noted his fine profile, the handsome features, the pleasing shape of his head. And then he grew aware of her interest and smiled.

Gerald's smile was the best thing of all, the sharing of a confidence, the very private world that they had made their own.

His parents' friends were at the house when they returned from church. Tania noticed at once how delighted Gerald seemed to be when he introduced her to them. She also saw a momentary glance exchanged with his father, a glance which on Gerald's part seemed to convey triumph.

189

He has not always been happy, thought Tania suddenly, he has needed to overcome some obstacle. Believing that she herself, somehow, had helped, her already high spirits soared.

Their meal was eaten quite late in the afternoon, following the departure of their guests and Thelma's disappearance in the direction of the kitchen.

"We give our housekeeper the opportunity to spend the day with her own folk," Barry explained.

Tania smiled and nodded, and assumed that Gerald's considerate ways were inherited.

Although a great deal of the food had been prepared in advance, Thelma seemed grateful to be offered assistance. Tania herself was glad that the occasions when she had helped at home made her appear useful. She liked Gerald so much. She wanted to impress his family. That Gerald himself was impressed was very evident in his steady gaze throughout the meal, and in his attentiveness afterwards when the four of them were relaxing with their drinks.

Happy though she was, Tania felt that the rest of Christmas Day suddenly began to pass quite slowly. From time to time, across the room, Gerald's eyes sought her own and in their intensity echoed the longing that had surged through her for hours. She was beginning to understand why lovemaking became so obsessive.

If he had not come to her room that night she would have lain awake, aching to have him near. But Gerald returned to her, of course. How could he have kept away?

On the day that he drove her home to Stonemoor

House Tania was a little regretful, but they had made too many plans for her to feel entirely miserable.

Knowing Gerald Thomas was proving heady. He was so different from Ian whose reluctance had hurt her so much. Gerald would never make her believe that she did not really matter to him. *His* enthusiasm was infectious, an encouraging force, so exhilarating that it constantly generated all this passion.

"You must come and stay again," he had asserted, even before he had begun to drive away from the Thomas's front door. "And in the meantime we must get together whenever possible. I've been thinking that we ought to book into a hotel next time you go away to sing somewhere."

Tania was still wondering what her father would think of that idea when Gerald grinned.

"You only need tell your dad that you'll be too tired after the performance for facing the journey home."

Tania admired the way he always had an answer to hand. And the prospect of staying in an hotel excited her. In the old days, in Russia, with family and friends scattered across those parts of the country which they might visit, hotels had been unnecessary. Since arriving in Yorkshire she had not ventured far from her new home.

"We could even go to London if you wished," Gerald suggested as he drove up Cragg Road. "All you have to do is arrange to sing there, I'll make certain I shall accompany you."

Even her concern that he might not get away from work was dismissed with a smile. "Leave that to me, Tania. I can wangle a few trips now and again to

191

represent Dad's firm, don't forget. That's if I need a reason – I'm sure the parents wholeheartedly approve of you already."

The approval of Thelma and Barry Thomas meant a great deal to Tania. She had needed reassurance, especially after the way that Ian's mother had shaken her by disapproving of the prospect of their marrying. She had felt bewildered, let down by Mildred Baker just when she had begun to believe that she had her wholehearted support.

Tania was glad, nevertheless, to see that Mildred was still at Stonemoor House. Ian had returned to Halifax, no one said what reason he had given. Tania resolved that his absence would no longer be permitted to dilute her own happiness. Looking back to what might have been was pointless, especially now that Gerald painted such an exciting prospect for future outings together.

Unlikely though that seemed, Mihail appeared to have grown during those few days that she had been away from Stonemoor, certainly he was extremely animated – prising himself up against cushions as he constantly made attempts to sit up. He is becoming really interesting now, Tania decided, and yearned again for her own baby. It struck her then that having a child might not be so impossible as she had thought only a week ago.

Gerald was so very mature, and must be itching to have a home of his own. Agreeable though his parents were, he should have somewhere in which to be his own master.

Dreaming of the infinite possibilities ahead of her, Tania chatted with her father and stepmother, with

Mildred and with Tom, and sensed that they all were noticing her new self-assurance. Only wait, she thought, and you will see before very long how well I can take on everything that life might bring me.

Chapter Ten

Andre offered to help Pamela on the day that she opened up her antiques business after the New Year. Initially surprised, she had realized within minutes that he was making the offer to counteract the gloom induced by the absence of any further engagements to play the violin. All over Christmas he had valiantly presented a cheerful face, but it seemed his good spirits had departed with their guests.

"I can certainly use a strong pair of hands," Pamela assured him now as she unlocked the door of the newly-converted shop. "And I'll be thankful to have you keeping an eye on young Mihail, here, as soon as he wakes up again."

Their son was sleeping in his carrycot, having roused himself reluctantly and only for long enough to be fed. They had had a disturbed night which Pamela at first had attributed to her own sudden unease concerning this new work she was tackling. She had soon discovered that she wasn't the only one who wakened repeatedly. Mihail was teething now and had painful gums which had troubled him several times. On the last occasion, she had just settled him at four o'clock when she heard Tania moving around.

Her stepdaughter was still in bed when they set out to walk this short distance to the shop. Andre had been annoyed by his daughter's non-appearance at breakfast, but Pamela had decided to play down the occurrence. Andre had enough to perturb him.

"I expect it's all those late nights catching up on her," she had said. They had heard an account of the partying that had gone on over Christmas, and Gerald had taken Tania out on two evenings since then.

"I have told her she must put in some practising today," Andre had stated solemnly. "Her voice production classes do not begin for another week yet, and I have not heard her singing at all recently."

"Well, she'll soon make up for lost time, I'm sure. Happen she's as entitled to a holiday as the rest of us."

Andre had snorted. "I think perhaps that some holidays are too long."

Pamela had concealed a smile. Today, her husband resembled a great Russian bear, one with a headache perhaps. Or an aching heart, she reflected, thinking again of the violin that had not been played in public for too many weeks.

The interior of her little shop looked quite pleasing now. She had engaged her own team of decorators, naturally, after all old Mrs Fawcett's shelving and counters had been removed.

The walls were distempered in a delicate eggshell blue which she had selected to provide a foil for the furniture now ranged around them. The good lady had left some splendid pieces in mahogany and walnut of periods varying from Regency to late Victorian. Some were so beautiful that Pamela coveted them, picturing how they might look in certain rooms of Stonemoor House; but she had promised to obtain for Mrs Fawcett's nephew the best possible price. In fairness to him, she must at least delay until learning whether they might command the sort of figures suggested in the evaluation.

She was happy meanwhile to inspect the few purchases that she had made at auction, items which now would be arranged to fill in the gaps between Mrs Fawcett's former possessions. There was, for instance, the glassware carefully washed at home before being conveyed here.

Although clocks still remained of prime interest to her, Pamela was becoming fascinated by glass, and especially of such fine quality as the French *millefiore* paperweights from the Baccarat factory. There were English specimens also – a collection of wine glasses which, in time, she was determined she would date. For the present, examining their differing shapes and types of stem provided further interest.

"What do wish me to do?" Andre enquired, having placed Mihail's carrycot away from the draughts that drifted through the old building. "Did you say that you must rearrange your display of clocks?"

"That's right, love. If I'm to make a real feature of them, I've got to have them near the front of the shop. Except for that longcase with the sun in the arch. It's taken that long to get that to work properly on this uneven floor that I don't want it shifting."

Andre glanced from the clock to his own watch and back again, and smiled. "It is accurate now, certainly. You have been very patient, my dear."

Pamela grinned over her shoulder from where she

was setting out a quartet of cut glass scent bottles. "Well, that clock's worth a bit of patience. If I never see another as good, it's one to remember always."

Once, he would have bought that clock immediately for their home. Now, however, with this huge cloud hanging over his professional future, Andre had grown cautious. He experienced a sudden and quite intense hatred for the people whose mistrust was creating this terrible situation.

Even with the smaller things that she hoped would attract customers who might hesitate to offer for any of the larger items, Pamela had not expected to entice many people into her shop in the middle of winter. She was all the more pleased, therefore, when a Humber Hawk drew up outside and an imposing man, in an overcoat that clearly was expensive, entered.

"I couldn't just drive past!" he exclaimed in response to her greeting. "You have such a splendid display of good solid stuff, and I'm furnishing a house I've bought just over the Lancashire border."

Invited to look around, the man spent nearly an hour inspecting the dining table and chairs and both bedroom suites that Pamela had agreed to dispose of, and also several of the clocks. Glad that she was able to pass on the details from that recent valuation, she chatted freely, and began to relish the prospect of making a career of selling.

In the end, the man only offered for one suite of bedroom furniture, but he promised to return with his wife to consider the dining set, and at least two of the clocks.

The only other potential client was a spinster lady whom Pamela had seen from time to time passing along the road to her cottage on the edge of the moors. Today, she suspected the lady was merely curious to see what was going on at the shop, although she did study the scent bottles and enquired if Pamela dealt in silver.

"Any particular kind of silver? I only have a few bits and pieces at present," she explained. "But I shall be stocking up all the time, and would be happy to look out for anything special when I attend auctions."

The woman shrugged. "I don't know really. It's more a matter of wanting summat to catch my eye. I used to get about a lot myself, seeing what was going at house sales, and suchlike. Nowadays I don't venture so far."

Pamela smiled sympathetically. "Well, you're always welcome to look in and examine whatever I've acquired. And I'll bear silverware in mind next time I'm buying in."

Making her first sale had encouraged her to think of filling the place with a wider range of desirable objects.

Heartened by that first day's work, Pamela was chatting animatedly to Andre as they walked up the hill to Stonemoor House. They both were surprised to see an unfamiliar car in the drive, and further surprised when the house seemed very silent as they entered.

"Are you there, Tania?" Pamela called from the hall while Andre placed Mihail's carrycot in the first room he came to, then hurried through the others seeking his daughter.

Pamela had removed her coat and was walking

198

towards the kitchen when Tania leaned over the bannister and called down to them.

"I'm up here. I have been showing Gerald right through the house. He was longing to see how beautifully you have decorated all of it."

Gerald, when he was brought downstairs to be introduced, was not at all as Pamela remembered from his playing in Ian's band. Without the pale suit, and wearing instead a dark worsted, he looked years older.

He was charming, nevertheless, and really quite impressive. He also seemed so genuinely interested in all that she had done to the house that she soon began explaining how the place had first appeared to her and about all the work entailed in its transformation.

Invited to join them for a meal, Gerald accepted but immediately insisted on telephoning his mother to explain that he would not be eating at home.

He seems a considerate young fellow, Pamela reflected, and wondered why she still felt quite uneasy about arriving home to find him there.

Concern about Gerald's friendship with her step-daughter was thrust to the back of Pamela's mind before that first week in January had passed. The man who was purchasing the suite of bedroom furniture returned with his wife and the request that Pamela should try to locate a round eighteenth-century table with matching shield-back chairs. His wife had seen an illustration of a Hepplewhite chair which she had decided would be ideal.

Andre agreed to take charge of the shop whenever Pamela attended likely sales on their behalf. "After all, I am doing nothing else that is of any use," he added bitterly.

Setting out for an auction to be held in a large house out beyond Halifax at Northowram, Pamela willed herself to concentrate on the task ahead of her. But concentrating on anything seemed harder than ever today. Andre had ceased even to practise the violin, and only last night had admitted that he feared he would never again be asked to play anywhere in England.

If she hadn't known him so well, she might have suggested that adopting another name could help him become more acceptable. But despite leaving the land of his birth, Andre had remained intensely proud of the good things of his Russian heritage. I don't want him to change, she reflected, but deep inside her she ached with concern for his frustrated talent.

Although the auction that day offered no furniture of the kind she was seeking, Pamela invested in several items of silver, including an elegant early Victorian wine ewer from Edward Barnard and Sons. Best of all, however, was a skeleton clock complete with its glass dome.

She was feeling quite cheerful when she halted her van outside the shop at around four-thirty.

The first shock was that the door was closed and locked, but the greater shock was to follow when she arrived at the house. Tania was away in Manchester, rehearsing for a concert, but Mrs Singer (who normally went home much earlier than this) was taking care of Mihail.

With the baby sitting contentedly on her lap, the housekeeper was seated in the doorway between

200

the kitchen and entrance hall. This made it obvious enough that Mrs Singer was looking out for her, the alarm in her eyes revealed that the news she had was very worrying.

"What's happened?" asked Pamela. "Wherever is Andre?"

The frustration that Mrs Singer perpetually endured because of being unable to speak seemed particularly distressing. Turning aside after handing Mihail to his mother, the woman tore a sheet of paper off the pad she always kept by her in order to communicate. Glancing rapidly to the page, Pamela recognized Andre's handwriting:

'I am sorry for being obliged to close your shop. I know that Mrs Singer will care for Mihail until you return home. You must not worry, please. It is only to answer some questions that they have taken me.'

"Taken? But where to?" Pamela demanded.

Mrs Singers' eyes filled with tears as she lip-read the urgent words. She had been scribbling a note while Pamela was reading her husband's message. Sighing, she handed it across.

'They didn't say where they were taking him. They brought him here in the car that had picked him up at your shop. I am that sorry . . .'

There were no words for Pamela's own sorrow and alarm. She could only think that the people

201

taking Andre away were officials of some kind, and were investigating him because of his origin. And this was such a shock! Until this moment she had never seriously thought that anyone could ever believe Andre should be investigated. She felt as if she'd never cope, how could she even begin to weigh up what she ought to do? Without knowing who these people were, or what grounds they might have for suspecting Andre of being involved in something untoward, she hadn't a clue how to help. Or where to turn.

Mrs Singer had to be allowed to go home, of course. Alone with Mihail, clutching him to her, Pamela began walking from room to room, unable to sit still, unable to struggle against the impulse to surrender to panic. God help me, she prayed, longing for guidance from someone who knew what was happening. But she had neglected God.

Desperate to talk to somebody, she telephoned her friend Dorothy's number, only to hear it ring and ring unanswered in the empty house.

After ten minutes a bit of common sense asserted itself, reminding her that inactivity was no solution. She needed advice, however undeserving she felt of higher assistance. Never in all the months since meeting Andre could she have anticipated something like this. But somebody, somewhere, would know how best she could help.

Is it the police who have taken him? she wondered, and instantly thought of Roger. He had been marvellous to her when Jim was killed, and to their whole family on the occasions when Ian was a lot younger and tended to flout the law. Roger might not have heard any hint of what was going on now, but he would be able to find out if his colleagues were involved. And even if they were not, he could be able to tell her if some kind of government officials might be responsible.

She hadn't seen Roger since Leslie's funeral and, although sorry that he hadn't turned to her, she had not been surprised. There had been so many reasons for Roger to conceal that relationship, how could anyone marvel if he had grown too self-contained for being able to share his grief?

He was not at home when Pamela telephoned. Mihail was beginning to whimper, she glanced at the clock, wishing she knew what time Andre had given him his bottle. And if Mrs Singer had fed the baby since he was left with her. She felt dreadful; she ought to have enquired into that before their housekeeper set off for home. Somehow, awareness of her being so preoccupied with Andre's crisis excused nothing.

Roger was at the station when she rang, and due to go off duty at six that evening. He listened gravely while she explained, admitted that he knew nothing of any investigation into Andre's background, but promised to ask around before driving over to Stonemoor House.

Glad of tasks to occupy her hands if not her agitated brain, Pamela prepared food for Mihail who was by now both wet and hungry.

Almost as though her own distress were contagious, the baby fussed and struggled in her arms when she began to feed him. He was still refusing to co-operate when Roger arrived.

"Thank God you've come, I've never been more

relieved to see anybody!" she exclaimed, opening the door to him while holding the restless baby to her. "Have you managed to find out anything at all?"

"Not a great deal, I'm afraid." Roger followed her through to the sitting room and waited until she was seated with Mihail on her lap before taking the chair she had offered. "It's certainly not a local police matter. I've made a few enquiries – very discreetly – and we think it's most likely somebody who's come up from London. Whilst we've heard nothing concrete up here, we're pretty sure investigations are going on into lots of – well, foreigners. That they have been since all that wretched anti-Communist hysteria in America."

"But Andre *isn't* a Communist."

"Happen not, love, but who's going to be assured of that, without looking into it? There's been that much bad feeling against the Russians, hasn't there, even after their blockade of Berlin ended?"

"But Andre's got nowt to do with politics of any kind."

"I know that, and folk like me might believe it, but there's others who are going to need more convincing. We can only hope that this investigation, or whatever, will bring the truth into the open once and for all. With a bit of luck, it could all be over tonight, and they won't be bothering him again."

Pamela sighed, shaking her head so anxiously that Mihail gazed up at her. His little squarish face looked just as perturbed as she was feeling. All at once, one of his hands shot out and he touched her cheek.

He might have been reassuring her. It was proper daft to think that a bairn like him could understand

204

and want to comfort her, but the feel of his fingers lingered on her skin for minutes after he had withdrawn them. It might have been his reminder of the devotion Andre felt towards her, and that there now was this additional person, however small, to perpetuate their loving concern.

"I can't really take this in, you know, Roger. Tell me again – have you any idea who'll have taken Andre for questioning?"

"Could be MI5, they'll have been involved as part of the Western intelligence services looking into folk. In the States, there's the FBI, and there's that Senator McCarthy stirring things up." Roger grew silent, thinking. "Has there been any sign afore this that somebody might have their suspicions about your husband?"

Grimly, Pamela nodded. "Aye, I suppose so. I've tried not to attach much significance to it, but he had a good idea what was wrong. Since the start of the concert season last autumn, Andre's been getting hardly any work. And he was doing so well before." Pamela paused, smiling reminiscently. "The previous season, when he took up playing the violin again, he was delighted by the reception over here. He appeared as soloist with all the best orchestras up north."

"But not this season . . .?"

She shook her head. "When hardly any of them offered for him to play, he went down to London, but it was no better there. It was if they'd all ganged up and decided not to engage him."

"As perhaps they had. Anyone using artists from abroad will be more aware than most of the crises occurring as a result of different loyalties."

205

"But Andre *is* loyal to Britain," she reminded him. "Why otherwise would he make his way here as soon as the war in Europe ended?"

The moment the words left her lips Pamela realized that there were those who could believe they had grounds for thinking her husband's nationality provided ample motive for spying.

"Oh, God, Roger – no one could believe that he's a spy, could they?"

"Let's hope he's able to prove them wrong."

Before Roger left her he telephoned some police headquarters' number somewhere. After a brief conversation he hung up the receiver and gave her the news that he now knew where Andre had been taken.

"He will be all right," he assured her. "They're obliged to look into everybody who could be working against the state, that is their job, but as soon as they're satisfied they'll let him go."

"But how long will that be, Roger? I can't bear much more of this."

"You can, love, and you will. But I don't think it'll be that much longer." Not for tonight, he added silently. But will this be the end of this wretched enquiry? Or only the beginning?

Roger knew from the inside that every branch of an investigative force was trained to persist, and never to let go until satisfied as to a person's innocence. If need be, that went forward to a trial. And he knew, didn't he, of the trials that were pending of folk suspected of allegiance to powers behind that Iron Curtain?

Tania came in while Roger was sitting alone after Pamela had taken Mihail up to the nursery.

"Who are you?" she asked with all the open curiosity of youth. "And where's my father, and Pamela?"

Thankful that he had changed out of uniform at the station, Roger tried to make his smile reassuring. "I'm just a friend. Your – Pamela needed a bit of help. She's putting your brother to bed. Your father's had to go out, love. Pamela will tell you all about it when she comes down."

Tania could not wait. This stranger was perturbed, she could tell, and her father's unexplained absence alarming. She bolted through the hall and, two at time, up the stairs.

Pamela was leaning over Mihail's cot, and tears were pouring down her cheeks.

"Where is my father? What has happened to him?"

Pamela started, turned and rushed to draw the girl into a fierce hug. "Nothing awful's happened to him, at least – he's not hurt or anything like that."

"It is the police, no? They have taken him away . . ." Her voice ended on a shrill wail.

Mihail, who had begun to doze, awakened instantly and screamed.

"Stop it, Mihail!" Tania shouted, glanced towards her stepmother and shrugged. "I am sorry, it is not his fault, I know. But if he screams and screams no one will be able to think. You must tell me, please – where is Father? What can we do? Is it the police?"

"Well, sort of – but it isn't a matter of anything criminal, you must understand that."

"I do know that. He – would not. But I am not a

207

child, I read the newspapers, I discuss things. Gerald has spoken with me, you know. He warns me that Russian people might be unpopular here, especially as McCarthyism spreads from America."

After settling Mihail they returned downstairs. Half-way along the landing, Tania had reached out to grasp her hand. Amid all the enormous anxiety, Pamela felt thankful. She and this stepdaughter of hers had healed a lot of aches.

They sat around listlessly while Roger talked, the only one sufficiently calm to speak coherently. Pamela blessed his knowledge of the law and its procedures which made their situation seem slightly less abnormal.

"I feel sure they'll not have any reason to hold him for more than a few hours," he said finally when Pamela, feeling guilty about keeping him from his bed, insisted that they would be all right now if Roger left them.

Her words were overoptimistic, merely what she felt she ought to say instead of taking up more of his time. The only good thing after he had gone was the way that all reservations between herself and Tania evaporated.

Side by side on a sofa, they each took comfort from the contact of another person and, although speaking hardly at all, somehow seemed to communicate the depth of their love for the man who was absent from their home.

A short while before midnight Tania turned to her stepmother. "They cannot send him back to Russia, can they?" she asked, the eyes so like her father's brilliant with tears.

"Of course they can't," Pamela asserted, and prayed that her supposition were not to be proved false. "He's married to me – that gives him a right to live in England."

They heard a car in the drive a few minutes afterwards and both jumped to the their feet and ran out to the hall. Tania was first to the door and flung it wide then hurtled down the front steps to rush into her father's arms.

Pamela met them in the doorway, hugging them both to her, kissing first Andre and then his daughter. All three were weeping as the tension flooded out of them.

"They proved nothing against me," Andre told them at last. "But – equally – they have not proved me innocent of any kind of spying. We can only be thankful that they have found no reason for detaining me. And hope to God that they never reopen that particular investigation."

Having said that, Andre became unable to speak further of the questioning he had endured. Pamela quelled her instinct to ask what on earth had given anyone the idea that he might have access to information useful to people behind the Iron Curtain. Tania, for once, also seemed to sense that this was the time to suspend her natural curiosity.

No one was sufficiently relaxed for going to bed yet, Pamela made hot drinks and Tania stoked the embers of the fire until the comfortable familiarity of the house helped their alarm to subside.

The incident made Andre even more determined to take up his career again. "I must get back to that concert platform, if only to show everyone that I have nothing to hide."

Together with his agent, he renewed the assault on all the major orchestras, resolved that before the season was out he would be playing that Stradivari once more.

Pamela was finding her new business interesting, although trade was slow, a fact hardly surprising given the time of year. These months of late winter brought snow along with the keen West Riding winds, and few strangers ventured over the hills to their valley. One or two local people and some from Hebden Bridge and Mytholmroyd called in at times, inspected her stock freely enough but purchased very little.

When she was in touch with Mrs Fawcett's nephew, Pamela was relieved that he was happy that she had sold some of the old lady's possessions, and seemed in no hurry to have her dispose of the rest.

The summer will be better, Pamela told herself, with more people using this road as they take outings. For the present, she could be content that Andre was safe at Stonemoor, and with Mihail around there was no end to the daily discoveries. He already seemed to be an intelligent child, taking an interest in his surroundings and, although too young to crawl, he often rolled on to his side, as though eager to become more mobile. They had bought him a playpen which now was set to one side of her shop and lined with thick blanketing to protect him against the coldness of the floor.

Surrounded by a selection of his toys, he amused himself quite happily whilst she was busy, and responded with a smile on the many occasions when she paused to play with him.

Andre had never confided what form that interrogation had taken, nor had he explained what, other than his nationality, had caused the enquiry into his background. Aware that he remained disturbed and on edge, Pamela decided not to ask him. She knew her husband of old, had experienced his determination to handle his own problems unaided. More than that, she believed she recognized in his silence that the matter caused him more pain than he admitted.

He had difficulties enough without further questioning, she discovered, when weeks passed and he failed to secure even one engagement to play in public. Their finances were suffering as a result, but worst hit by far was Andre's morale.

Thinking over the problem one day, she decided to enlist Tania's aid in trying to find some means of cheering him. Father and daughter had always been so devoted, surely the girl might be the one to recharge his zest for living. Tania herself certainly appeared to have a full life now, she sang quite frequently in classical concerts across Lancashire in addition to Yorkshire, as well as appearing with the jazz band. And Gerald certainly was widening her social life.

Whilst finding nothing to complain of in the young man, Pamela could not relinquish regrets that he appeared to have commandeered her stepdaughter's time so thoroughly. Even though feeling that Ian was too young for settling down, Pamela was fond of her young brother and hated the way that, these days, he avoided visiting Stonemoor House.

Their mother also had noticed how Ian had less

211

enthusiasm for the band that he had adored, just as he took no interest in other girls. Mildred had confided to Pamela only last week how guilty she felt for putting a stop to the young pair's ideas about marriage, and as a consequence ruining their relationship.

"Eh, Mum, you only did what you thought was for the best," Pamela reassured her. "And you weren't the only one to say they were too young. Andre was just as opposed to the notion as you were. More so, if I'm any judge."

"Happen you're right. Too late now, any road. I gather Tania and that Gerald are becoming inseparable."

"They're still young, though. Or she is, he's that few years older, of course," said Pamela, and hoped that Gerald was not wishing to rush the girl into marriage. Andre seemed low enough without having his daughter leave home just yet.

I really must develop that idea of involving Tania in giving Andre another interest, Pamela decided, still determined to use the family to support him through all the uncertainty. They could perhaps invite friends and family round to listen to good music. Dorothy and Charles could bring the kids, and let them sleep in the nursery. Looking out from the shop window, she gazed all around her to the steep sided hills with snow on the tops, and thought how lovely it was out here. Even in winter, folk might appreciate coming out into the country. Walking back to the house late in the afternoon, Pamela was running through her ideas, concluding that she would get Tania on her own and ask her how best to approach the scheme.

Should they involve Andre in the planning, or would that mean risking his early refusal to co-operate?

The steps leading up to the front door were in sight when Pamela sensed that she was being observed. Straightening her shoulders, she willed herself to ignore the sensation. She had never been a fanciful woman, this was not the time to give in to such feelings. She was tired, and the past few weeks had been anxious, but apart from those two facts, she had no reason to fear anything.

There *was* somebody watching her. She heard grass rustling over to her left beyond the drystone wall and one of the stones grated when it shifted under someone's touch.

The angry snarl startled her and she instinctively moved her son to her other arm, away from harm.

"That's it, missus, go on – get home to that Commi bastard!"

Determined not to run, Pamela strode steadily towards the steps. And then she saw, through the gathering dusk, the great slashes of red paint across their well-preserved door.

COMMUNISTS.

Chapter Eleven

Andre hurried to the kitchen doorway to greet his wife as soon as he heard her come into the house. He smiled, and held open his arms for Mihail then kissed them both, but his grey eyes remained haunted.

Pamela could tell that his day's efforts to secure an engagement had been fruitless, and wondered how on earth to begin to tell him what she had found on their own front door.

"Mrs Singer went off early – she had a headache," Andre said, taking Pamela's coat with one hand while still holding their son on his other arm. "I have prepared vegetables for our meal, there is a casserole in the oven."

"That's nice," said Pamela and took a long breath which sounded to herself like a bottomless sigh. "There's something you've got know, Andre. I'm afraid somebody's been busy with a paintbrush."

"Where? How? What is this? I do not understand."

"You'd better come and look. It's the front door."

He went striding along the hall and was there before her, opening the door already when she meant to prepare him.

"Oh, God! This is all my fault. Pamela, forgive me – for having you involved in something so despicable. If I catch whoever is responsible I shall . . ."

But you won't catch them, you *mustn't*, his wife thought immediately, and decided not to mention the person or persons lurking behind the wall. Here like this, at least Andre was safe.

"You must tell me what will best remove that horrible paint. From experience, you must know how to treat it." Andre touched the lettering, glanced at his fingers. "It has dried, I am afraid. That will make it more difficult to remove, no?"

"I don't really know, love. But it's nearly dark out there, any road, nobody can start tackling it tonight."

"In the morning then. At first light I shall begin."

"I'll see what kind of paint stripper I've got here after we've had our meal. Is Tania in?"

Andre shook his head. "She had a singing class this afternoon, Gerald was to meet her afterwards." And when she returns home she will see what they have done to me, he thought, wondering how he had deserved this situation where he brought nothing but distress to the people he loved most in the world.

Pamela fed Mihail and together they bathed him and put him to bed. This little lad is our only bit of brightness, she reflected as he gazed back at them, beaming his contentment.

"I have an idea," Andre announced when they had eaten and were sitting in armchairs with their coffee. "I had concluded before this happened that something must be done to convince people that I

215

am neither a Communist nor a spy. I am even more certain now that I must take action."

"But what can you do, love?"

"Tell my story, all of it – from the time when I was a small boy right to the present day. I shall leave nothing out, not the risks that I took in leaving Russia, nor the terrible loss of my first wife." He paused. "I am sorry if that will be difficult for you . . ."

Her blue eyes glistening, Pamela shook her head. "No, you must not think of me. We've got to make everyone understand. Until we do, there'll be no peace for any of us."

Pamela was aching to help, she was thankful when Andre insisted that he needed her to assist with his English. And they began that night, sitting either side of the dining table while he started a chronological list of all the circumstances and events which had preceded his escape to England.

"You must make a point of your getting Tania out as well, and the attempt to persuade your sister to leave Russia," she said. "We're going to need everything that will add up to your opposition to Communist ideals."

They were still working when Tania came in at eleven-thirty. Preoccupied as they were, they had almost overlooked the shock that she would receive from the slogan painted on their door.

"Whoever has done that?" she demanded, her grey eyes wide with anger and dismay as she stormed through the house to find them.

"We don't know, love," said Pamela gently. "Your father was somewhere at the back of the house,

216

we knew nothing about it until I came in from the shop."

"How can you be so calm?" her stepdaughter snapped, her accent intensifying. "Do you not care?"

"Oh, I care, all right! You'll never know how much I care. But I mean to channel my feelings about this into something practical."

"It is dreadfully unkind," Tania went on. "Even if it were true, no one should be branded for their beliefs, not here. This is a free country, this is England."

"It will not continue, my sweet," her father assured her, rising and placing an arm about her shoulders. He went on to explain what he and her stepmother were doing. "One day everybody will know the truth about me."

True to his promise, Andre was up early the following morning and had begun trying to remove the red paint from their door before Pamela was ready to leave for the shop. She paused beside him, and couldn't help smiling when she observed the vigour with which he was tackling the job.

"Oh, I do so love you!" she exclaimed.

Tania was staying at home that day, and Pamela was thankful that Andre would not be alone at the house. Mrs Singer's husband had telephoned that her headache was no better and their doctor diagnosed the onset of the flu.

On her way down the road, Pamela was beginning to wonder if the infection was spreading. Tania had been glad to remain indoors and had eaten no breakfast because she said she had no appetite. They had seen so little of her since she had become so friendly with

Gerald Thomas that having her around now felt quite odd. But was that the only reason why there seemed something different about her?

Concern for everyone's health was driven out of Pamela's mind as soon as she approached the shop. Across its large window and diagonally over the door the same word was repeated. **COMMUNISTS**.

Letting herself into the shop, she glanced hastily all around, checking that its stock had suffered no damage. Relieved that everything was as she had left it the previous afternoon, she opened the door again and tested the crude red lettering. As she had feared, the paint had dried. And her only paint remover was being used by Andre up at the house.

Whatever else, she would not have him further disturbed by learning what had occurred here. She had left Mihail with his father today, so she would be able to concentrate on removing every trace of that wretched lettering, but she needed a supply of the necessary materials. And she was longing to confide in somebody.

Pamela telephoned Ian at the house where he and her Canning's team were working. He listened sympathetically while she related events of the past twenty-four hours.

"I'll get all the wretched stuff off for you," he offered immediately. "At the house, as well."

She explained that Andre was tackling the door at home. "I think he needs to, poor love, he feels it's all because of him."

"I suppose it is, an' all," said Ian realistically. "Any road, I'll bring everything we'll need to the shop and give you whatever help you want."

"Is the job there going OK?" she enquired, before insisting on speaking to Ted Burrows. She didn't wish her assistant manager to believe she was going over his head in asking Ian to come out to Cragg Vale.

Pamela was very glad to see her brother, and to have his company as much as his assistance when they began removing the bold red letters.

"Andre's not a Communist, is he?" Ian asked quietly as they worked side by side.

"Indeed not, that's the reason he came out of Russia, isn't it?"

"That's what I thought. Folk are going to want some convincing, though."

"I know. We've already made a start on that. But it's going to take time. Andre's determined to tell his whole story, then somehow we've got to get it printed. Don't ask me how, I don't really know where to begin."

"In the newspapers, you mean?"

"I suppose so. Eh, love, I've not had time to work that out yet. It was only last night that they'd daubed that stuff on the door at Stonemoor."

"Newspapers'd be quickest. Then there's magazines – some of them don't take all that long to come out, especially the locals. You'll have had a word with our Tom, of course?"

"Eh, I must be proper daft! I'd never even thought about him working on that magazine. Thanks, love, for reminding me. Just shows what a state I've got myself into, doesn't it?"

"I'll have a word with him tonight, tell him what's happened— "

"Hang on a sec . . . It might be best if I ring Tom

instead. I don't want Mum worrying about all this, and she's bound to get to know if you two are talking it over." She could picture all too clearly that small living room of their mother's, knew how little scope it gave for private conversations.

Heartened by the thought that her youngest brother might be able to help to publicize the truth about Andre's background, Pamela worked furiously on removing the paint daubed across her shop front and, with Ian's help, soon every last trace was eradicated.

They were sitting over cups of tea when he finally mentioned Tania. "She – she's still seeing Gerald Thomas, I suppose?"

"I'm afraid so, love. It's a pity that she's my stepdaughter, in a way, it must be making it harder for you to forget her."

"I'll never forget Tania, no matter where she is, or who she's with," Ian declared fervently. "But they're not engaged or owt yet, happen she'll change her mind when she gets to know him better."

"I'm sorry you're taking it so badly, Ian. But there is time, as you say— "

"Don't go reminding me we're still young enough! If it weren't for being too young, none of this would have happened. Mum wouldn't have put my back up by refusing to let me get wed, and nor would Andre have stopped us." Ian paused for a moment, sighing. "And I wouldn't have been put off, as I have to admit I was, by the prospect of been tied to so much responsibility so soon."

There *will* be other girls for you, thought Pamela, but knew not to say so to her brother. She was shaken by learning how deeply hurt he remained as a result of Tania's friendship with Gerald.

"Happen he'll decide in the end that she's not mature enough, anyway. What is he really like, Ian? How does he strike you?"

He shrugged. "All right. As one of the chaps in the band. Well off, and likes to flaunt it occasionally. Fond of his own way, as are lots of folk wi' plenty of brass. Trouble is, he's been brought up to get what he wants."

The picture was not a glowing one, and nor did it indicate that, once having taken to Tania, Gerald would ever let go. The only good thing, Pamela thought, was that he did appear to have something about him. If the relationship with Tania developed, the girl should have a secure future.

After returning home, later that day, Pamela spoke to Tom over the 'phone, explaining what Andre needed to do and asking how best they might set about the task.

"If he comes up with an interesting article, angled to the local aspect – how he came all this way to settle in the West Riding and so on, I can see our editor taking it. I'd be happy to put in a word, if that'd help. They seem to trust my judgement these days – now they've found I'm not only concerned about making pages look attractive."

Tom also said that he might be able to interest one of the local newspapers to which the magazine was affiliated. "It might be possible then to syndicate to the nationals, but we'll go into all that when you've got something down on paper."

This sounded like a good first step, and Andre was

as pleased as Pamela herself that Tom could be able to assist with his story. He had been busy that day, enlarging on his initial notes, and this potential opening for his life story spurred him on to continue.

"I can work on it tonight," Andre asserted. "I have decided that I shall keep watch at your shop to ensure that nothing occurs there."

"Darling, no," Pamela contradicted, wondering for a moment if someone had told him that the shop had been defaced. "You mustn't. The place is insured, and I'm not going to have you risking your neck to protect it. Besides, Tania and I need you here at Stonemoor House to look after us."

"The house is well secured, as you know," he argued. "No one could break in here, even if they should wish to do so."

"Even so, I shan't consider you spending the night at the shop."

Andre smiled, it was good to know that, however much he wished to do to protect Pamela, she would not countenance his being endangered.

Andre became thankful, during the weeks that followed, to have this task of writing down his own history. Although much of what he had to relate brought reminders of events that had seared through him, he faced them all in retrospect. And almost felt grateful that everything he had suffered should now contribute to providing for himself and his family a more secure future. He might, for the present, have been prevented from performing on the concert platform but there now was something constructive for him to tackle.

As time proved the incident at Stonemoor House an isolated occasion, Andre began to believe that he only needed to get this article into print in order to win back the esteem once given to his playing. As an interlude in his writing, he took up the violin again, polishing his interpretation of well-loved pieces in the hope that by the next season he would be as sought after as he once had been.

Pamela was delighted to hear him playing, and pleased to have another topic for them to discuss of an evening or over breakfast each day. She was concealing too much from Andre for her to be relied upon to produce topics of conversation.

At intervals of only a few days in each instance, her shop was being defaced with a regularity that grew depressing. She deliberately had refrained from repainting the door once the offending word had been removed, in the belief that restoring its finish would invite repetition of the graffiti. Unfortunately, the perpetrators required no prompting, and on several occasions now, she had arrived there to be faced with the need for obliterating that same slogan.

Trade which had been only sparse before had now become nonexistent, but she concentrated on caring for Mihail, talking to him as she encouraged his early attempts at communication. He was an enchanting child who relished exploring the confines of his playpen, and showed a lively interest in the clocks chiming out the hours all about him.

"That's right, my boy!" Pamela exclaimed one day. "You learn to love everything here, just as I am learning." She relished her enthusiasm for old things, and promised herself that as soon as Andre's life story was written she would return to reading up on all manner of antiques.

These days, she was bringing with her to the shop whatever text her husband had written whilst she was away from the house. At his request, she was altering word order here, and changing a phrase there, so that his still too formal English might be easier to read.

On the day that she reached the narration of his first wife's murder, she was obliged to pause for a while and contain her own emotions. Told in words rendered stark by Andre's use of the simplest terms, the shooting of Anichka was particularly moving.

"We'll make it up to him again, won't we love?" Pamela said to Mihail, while he played oblivious to the existence of distress. She recalled then the way in which, several times before their marriage, she had longed to find some means of compensating Andre for all that he'd suffered. "We'll be a happy family again, somehow," she resolved. And smiling through a gloss of tears recognized afresh that this son of theirs was the promise of a happier future.

By the time that Andre had got everything that he wished to reveal down onto paper, Pamela had located in an auction a typewriter that should serve for producing his manuscript.

"It's old-fashioned, I know, but it does work," she assured him. "I made them produce a sample page before I would bring it away."

She had passed on her typewriter to Ted Burrows, who finally had convinced her that he could handle the clerical work for Canning's.

Several of the local auctioneers knew her by now and she was beginning to enjoy encountering familiar faces when she went in search of bargains. Getting out and about in this way had become essential to her peace of mind. Alone with the baby at the shop, with no customers as one day succeeded another, she readily grew despondent. Even telling herself, as she did, that this was only temporary failed to help. Pamela knew in her heart that even if and when Andre did succeed in convincing everyone where his loyalties lay, she would need to start all over again in her attempt to build up the business.

It is just as well that Canning's continues to thrive, she thought, her director's fees from the firm were helping their finances. She had never really known, nor had wished to know, how substantial were Andre's assets, but whilst he was no longer being invited to perform it was obvious that their resources were draining away.

Pamela offered to type up Andre's story, but he insisted that this was a task which he himself would tackle. Unused as he was to typing, and further encumbered by writing in a language that was not his own, the work was proving laborious.

Until she was able to check the finished manuscript for him, Pamela now felt redundant, and grew discouraged thinking how long they could have to wait before the work finally appeared and people were able to read the truth about Andre Malinowski.

We are going to need to stick together as a family, Pamela reflected. We've got to ensure that he does not feel defeated by this horrible business, even before this hope of his being exonerated materializes. She recalled then her earlier idea that Tania might be enlisted to organize something to help keep up Andre's spirits.

When her stepdaughter appeared in the bathroom doorway that evening it seemed like the ideal time for a chat.

"Hello, love, I wanted a word with you," Pamela said, smiling because Tania had sought her out while she was tidying up after getting Mihail off to sleep.

Down below them in the sitting room Andre was pounding away on the typewriter, so this certainly was an ideal time for a private discussion of what they might do for him.

But Tania herself seemed in need of something, she was looking pale, so pale that Pamela turned away from the bath to study her expression. Had her stepdaughter been weeping?

Before she could ask what was wrong Tania closed the door behind them and began to speak. "I have got to talk to you, Pamela. This is very difficult for me, will you please listen?"

"Of course I will, love. Why don't you come and sit on the linen basket?"

But the girl chose the edge of the bath, and clung to its rim until her knuckles turned white with tension.

"There is no easy way to tell you my news, Pamela. But I am so scared that I have to talk to someone. I am going to be a mother."

Immediate alarm sent Pamela's heart thudding in her ears so that she hardly could think what on earth to say. But Tania's grey eyes were beseeching her to assist, she must not her down. She was forced to muster a bit of composure in order to respond.

"I'll do everything I can," she promised. "But this isn't going to be at all easy. You are certain, I suppose?"

Mutely, her stepdaughter nodded. "I have missed for two months, and I have been to see a doctor."

"And what does Gerald say? It is his baby . . .?"

"Oh, yes. But I have not told him yet."

"You don't want to marry him, is that the trouble?"

Tania shook her head. "No, it is not. In fact, I believe he will provide well for us. But I do not know how I should go about this, my mother once told me how no young man will wish to marry a girl after she has given herself."

"Well – we'll just have to hope that Gerald isn't that old-fashioned."

"I am hoping that perhaps when you have spoken with my father he will talk to Gerald about our marriage."

Pamela gave her look. Trust Tania to expect her to tackle Andre about this! She could imagine how appalled he would be. But far, far worse than that, how deeply distressed.

"You'd certainly better leave this with me," she told her. "I'll try and think of a way to tell him that won't turn everything into a major crisis." But a crisis it was, and she knew Andre would consider it of gigantic proportions.

Despite sensing what his reaction would be, Pamela was unprepared for the way that shock drained every scrap of colour from her husband's strong features. For one dreadful moment she was afraid that he might even collapse.

But then he was speaking, his voice so strained that he sounded unfamiliar. "Please tell me that there could be some mistake. There has to be. Tania cannot be expecting a child. She is only a young girl herself."

Old enough to make love and to conceive, thought Pamela ruefully, but sharing such thoughts would do him no good at all. Instead, she swallowed and began speaking.

"If we're careful, we can probably prevent this developing into a catastrophe. They can have a quiet wedding, could even live here for a while until they've got a home together— "

"Never!" interrupted Andre savagely. "She will not marry any man who has taken advantage of her in this way. And he certainly will never be welcome in my house!"

Although she had not expected him to be happy about the situation, Pamela was shaken by how adamant her husband remained.

"I shall try to talk him round," she told Tania the following morning, and admitted privately that she had little hope of succeeding.

No one had reckoned with Tania's sudden decision to take charge of matters herself. As soon as she learned how difficult persuading her father would be, she confided in Gerald.

He was taking her to the cinema that evening and picked her up, as usual, outside Stonemoor House. When he had turned the car, but before they had emerged on to the road that meandered through Cragg Vale, Tania was speaking.

"There is something that I must tell you," she began in a rush, her only thought to get this out before something prevented her. "I am going to have a baby."

Gerald stamped on the brake pedal and the car slewed towards a drystone wall, so sharply that he over-corrected and narrowly avoided swerving into the wall on the opposite side of them.

"Hold on a minute," he said. "I'm going to park this thing before you have me driving us off the road."

Gerald did not speak again until he found a place where he could draw over onto a grass verge. By this time Tania was so perturbed that she was afraid of speaking in case tears overwhelmed her.

"Well . . .?" he prompted. "You are sure, I suppose?"

"Oh, yes." His astonishment roused her spirit. "And you need not sound so shocked – you cannot pretend you had nothing to do with it."

Gerald had the grace to grin. "I dare say you're right. Still, I never thought . . . Well, I'd been so careful."

"Careful?" Tania did not understand.

Gerald shrugged. "Not – you know, inside you. Or I thought I hadn't."

She still had not grasped what he was meaning, but she did know he sounded embarrassed about the outcome, disadvantaged. If she wanted her infant to have a father, this was the time for ensuring that he or she should have one. Something that she alone must tackle.

229

"You are not going to leave me to face the consequences alone, I hope? Whatever you intended, we are going to become parents. I should not like to think that you would be irresponsible now . . ."

Gerald was the only person she could depend on. Her own father had shattered her. He had refused to even discuss what she must do.

Beside her, Gerald shook his head as he put an arm around her shoulders. "No, I'm not the irresponsible sort. I'll do right by you. You can tell your father we'll be married as soon as possible. That way— "

"But he will not let us marry," Tania interrupted. "He told Pamela that, and he will not even have you in the house any longer."

"Not going there isn't going to bother me. Still, we shall have to gain his consent somehow, or there'll be no wedding."

"Do not say that, do not even speak of such a thing."

They did not go to the cinema, of course. With such a massive problem on their minds there would have been no point in sitting through a couple of films. No matter what they might have seen, any difficulties the characters were facing would have been far outweighed by their own.

Bolt upright in the front of Gerald's car they talked over and around the coming child, and reached no firm conclusion. What was worse, Tania became infinitely more disturbed as she gradually sensed that Gerald was not really happy about becoming her husband, or anyone else's. Without admitting as much in so many words, his whole demeanour warned her that he would not be sorry if her father failed to relent and give his permission.

"I think perhaps that little house will still be for sale," Tania reminded him eventually, her desperation to have him provide a secure future suddenly locating one gleam of hope. "It would make a nice home for us."

"Nice!" Gerald exclaimed. "I'm afraid that's not my idea of a home. But that's not to say I wouldn't buy it for you, if we're not allowed to marry. It would be big enough for you and the baby."

Tania shook her head vehemently, that wasn't what she had in mind. "I could never live away from you," she asserted, and wondered feverishly what she would have to do to make Gerald set up house with her.

"Only as a last resort," he assured her. "And maybe just until you are of age and need no one's consent."

Tania felt dreadfully hurt. Gerald was speaking as though he wished to shut her away somewhere, to keep her from his family and friends. And her own father no longer wanted her. How would she know what to do for a new baby? How, solely responsible for the child, would she manage to continue with her career? Who would take over its care – if only for an evening – so that she might earn from her singing? Whatever happened, she could not let Gerald deprive her of his support. She needed him, more perhaps than she needed his ring.

However much Tania considered remaining single out of the question, she was beginning to discover that there was a very real possibility that she might have to give birth without the benefit of a husband to help rear the child.

Her father was waiting in the sitting room when Gerald dropped her off at Stonemoor House, after her most depressing few hours in all the months since coming to England.

Andre greeted her with a smile, and although his beautiful grey eyes still appeared saddened, Tania felt hope returning. "I have been thinking, my sweet," he began. "I have put this idea to Pamela, and I believe she will agree in time that it would be the wisest course."

Dispirited already by Gerald's failing to fall in with any of her plans, Tania felt too uneasy to enthuse before hearing more.

"Are you listening?" persisted Andre, his earlier distress close to resurfacing now that he was confronted by what seemed to be his daughter's mutinous silence.

Dismally, Tania nodded. She would be obliged to listen, would she not? She could rely on no one else.

"We shall stand by you, naturally," her father continued. "Much as I disapprove of what you have done, you are just as important to me as ever you were. There is your career to consider also, nothing must be allowed to impede the progress you are making."

Minutes ago, she herself had been contemplating the effect a baby might have upon her professional life, but hearing her own father declare singing of prime importance shook her. It was all so cold and calculated, when he should have been thinking of his grandchild, of the place it would have in their family.

"I shall not neglect my career," she said stiffly, sensing that if he had been agreeing to Gerald's marrying her he would have said so. "But I had hoped that you would be more interested in giving your grandchild a happy future."

"And so I am, so we both are – I have discussed this thoroughly with Pamela."

Then perhaps, after all, there will be some warmth in what you propose, Tania thought, clinging to her memory of Pamela's quiet acceptance of her news, and of her willingness to speak with Andre on her behalf. It could well be that this result of their discussion might turn out better than she anticipated.

She swallowed. "I will listen to anything you suggest," she told him, her voice low and, she hoped, acquiescent.

But the suspense grew prolonged while Andre refined his speech.

"The plan is this," he continued at last. "Since you are far too young for taking on so much responsibility yourself, we shall accept it on your behalf. You will continue to live here at Stonemoor House, naturally, only leaving it very briefly for your – your confinement. Afterwards, once you are recovered, you will continue your singing."

"But I ought to be married, to Gerald," Tania protested.

"I think not, my dear. This is by far the wiser course. Pamela and I will always care for the child as though it were our own."

"You do not mean . . .?"

233

Andre nodded. Persuading his wife had been far from easy, but she had seen that in this way they would avoid all local scandal. A not inconsiderable matter at this time when they were struggling to remove all shadows from the name Malinowski. They would provide this coming child with a stable environment, and a share in Mihail's inheritance.

"For the child's sake, Tania – you must think of that. He will be reared as though he were another sibling of yours, with all the advantages. You would see him constantly . . ."

Tania stared incredulously at her father. They were planning to keep her baby from her: even before she had felt the infant stir within her, they were plotting to take it away.

Her only consolation, throughout all this dreadful anxiety since the first day that she had known the truth, had been the thought that she would at last have one person who really belonged to her.

"Never!" she screamed at him, and felt glad when Andre flinched. "Never, never, never, will I agree. If I have to go half-way across the world to keep my baby, that is what I shall do." Sobbing, she turned and ran out of Stonemoor House and uphill towards the moors.

Chapter Twelve

Charged by disappointment and distress, Tania hastened away that night, so swiftly that she was out of sight before Andre sped after her. She needed to think, to think and to plan. Away from everyone. This child she carried was *hers*, the one thing she wanted more than all the world. Heading uphill, to where the bleak summit of Blackstone Edge stood barely discernible from the darkness of the sky, she willed herself to use this wild freedom to inspire her. The cold bit through her thin spring coat. Out here the winters were slow to relinquish their hold, the keen winds all too reminiscent of her native Russia.

Thinking of her homeland generated a yearning to return to the country where she belonged. Her aunt lived there still, and would surely welcome her along with the coming baby. Her father would be dreadfully hurt. But wasn't he responsible for this situation now? How could he have expected her to agree to handing over her baby?

Tania felt more torn than ever in her life before. She stood in the lee of massive sandstone rock, leaned into its rough surface while her ragged breath shook her chest and the wind tore through her hair. Life was buffeting her even more fiercely than the elements out here, and she could find no protection. I won't give in, she vowed. They are all letting me down, but I am not a child any longer. I will make my own decisions. Her father could not take the baby if she refused her consent. No law would permit that.

And there was one possible solution. Even if Gerald did not marry her, he had promised her a home. The house on which she had set her heart. She would have to go back to Stonemoor, but only until she could move out there.

Andre's story was published the following day, initially in the *Yorkshire Post*, and it was good to have something to distract them from Tania's problems. Although edited quite severely, it so closely resembled the account that he had given Pamela before they married, that she felt emotion surging up into her throat. Tears blinding her, she could hardly get through to the end of the piece.

Perhaps because of the cutting, the article seemed all the stronger for its simplicity. Pamela read it a second time, and then again, growing increasingly convinced that no one could fail to be affected. Its title was mundane but the text soon belied expectations that it might prove commonplace . . .

ESCAPE TO FREEDOM

We are Russian, my daughter Tania and I – *White* Russian. Coming to make a home for her here in the West Riding was the wisest decision in all my life. It became, nevertheless, an aspiration requiring more determination than I would have believed I should ever possess.

My unease in our own country had begun

while I was a boy in Minsk. In 1918 my father joined a White volunteer army which was led by Tzarist generals. They allied themselves to the Cossacks. My father died in the conflict with the Red Army. I witnessed then the turmoil that my mother faced, but I was merely ten years of age, my sister four or five. My mother recognized that the only way for us all to survive was by feigning allegiance with Trotsky and Lenin.

For years afterwards I found it hard to forgive her the lip-service that she paid for the rest of her days to the Communist regime. Only now do I believe I understand. I almost would do likewise if that were to protect Tania.

So it was that we lived out this lie and, because my mother was a talented singer, we lived quite well. Even the revolutionaries could never bring themselves to destroy all forms of art. My mother began again to perform as soon as Russia had settled to a kind of peace. The conflict was within me, from the day that as a ten-year-old lad I had felt such an affinity with the British. I read avidly every account I could find of how their force landed at Archangel in 1918 to aid the White Russians. It was too late by then to help the Romanovs who had been executed, but hope was established within that young boy – hope that survived and led eventually to his escape following the end of this our second world war.

I would not pretend that everything in my own country was bad: my family ensured for me a musical training. Fortunately, I inherited

Mother's ear if not her voice. I played the violin professionally in many of the great Russian concert halls. But my appearances over there made me too well known for defecting easily without detection. From the hour that I set out to reach England I existed in perpetual dread that I was being watched.

Those in power were extremely reluctant to permit anyone to leave the USSR. Fortunately, I had friends, sympathizers who assisted. But our original plan was aborted as soon as my wife was killed. When Anichka was shot I found it impossible to feel thankful that I had survived, that my sleeve was grazed by a bullet but that was all. Because I dropped to the ground beside Anichka they were convinced I was dead. The men drove off, and I tried to carry her, but she was dying and knew it. She begged me to leave her – to stay alive for Tania. Leaving her was the hardest thing I have done. I turned back but Anichka pleaded with me again before lapsing into coma.

We were in the Ukraine, heading towards the Black Sea. I ran and ran through the forest that night, then set out in the opposite direction to foil the guards. I travelled overland on foot, always by night, avoiding all border areas. The journey took weeks, but I no longer cared for haste – I had left Tania where she was safe, with old friends from my university days. All I needed was to reach the West eventually.

Since arriving in England my only contacts with my native land have been in order to bring Tania to freedom and a similar attempt on behalf of my sister. Any future contacts will only be made if there is the opportunity to rescue members of my family.

Here in the West Riding the chances I took seem in retrospect quite alarming, and I abbreviate this account of my crossing to these shores solely to protect other people. My loyalty and my life have taken root in this land where openness engenders trust. I have thought this country quite small. Compared with the vastness of my own, England is tiny. But from the moorland heights surrounding our home the landscape appears to reach towards infinite space. I feel certain that it also contains the infinite freedom that I never remember in my homeland.

Reaching the end of the piece yet again, Pamela felt more tears trickling down her face. She was remembering the rest of the account of Andre's journey, crossing the Baltic aboard a tiny boat before stowing away on a merchant ship heading for Britain. A hazardous route that had been repeated in part when he returned to meet up with Tania and escort her to safety.

When first learning all this she had felt awed by everything that Andre had done, immensely thankful that some guiding force had brought him to her. Today, she ached with regrets concerning the ways in which their life together might have been better.

She had tried to be a good stepmother to Tania, but the girl's predicament now seemed to demonstrate how inept her own efforts had been. She had been determined to compensate Andre for past heartache, yet somehow they were in the midst of this massive turmoil where nothing promised to come right for them. She had let him see that she could do no more than acquiesce to his idea about Tania's child. She could never agree wholeheartedly to take it on.

Somewhere, over the far side of the house she heard Mihail chortling as Andre played with him. At least I have given him a son, she thought, and thanked God for that one achievement – so often now the boy seemed to be their only prospect of a better future.

A car turned in the drive, its doors opened and closed. Tania, she thought, and felt guilty when she cringed. How could they endure yet another confrontation? And how would Andre react when she herself failed to support his ideas? She was going to reconsider, she could not let Tania be deprived of her baby. They were so vital a focus for life. And I, she thought, and tried to forgive herself for being selfish, I would never be able to look after those two in addition to the second child of my own for which I am longing.

Picking up the newspaper, Pamela hastened into the hall and through towards the front door. I will show Tania this, she decided, to prove to her how deeply Andre cares for her. That he deserves more respect than she gave last night when she finally came down from the moors.

Tania was not alone. Gerald was beside her, his handsome features darkened by anxiety, blue eyes wary, and the generous lips narrowed as he steeled himself for the encounter.

"Hello," Pamela said, and motioned them inside.

"We want to speak to your husband," Gerald announced, as firmly as a quavering voice permitted.

"Of course," she responded, leading them towards the sitting room where she bent to take up Mihail.

Andre rose from his knees where he had been teasing the boy. She read the shock in his eyes as he saw Gerald in the doorway. When Pamela moved towards the door he detained her with a glance.

"You must stay, please."

The two young people did not sit when invited. Pamela noticed the way in which Andre straightened his back and squared his broad shoulders as he confronted them. He was finding this so difficult.

"Tania has explained this scheme of yours to me," Gerald began.

"I hope she made plain my concern for the well-being of the child, and that he or she would be second only to my own son, here."

Gerald nodded, but his eyes were grave. "She explained that fully. And also that she couldn't even contemplate your bringing up our baby. Nor, for that matter, could I. That is the reason I am here today."

He paused for several moments, marshalling his thoughts. "We've all read your story today, my parents as well. We've nothing but admiration for what you have done. I, for one, am thankful that you got Tania away from that place. That's the reason we can't understand why you're denying us the freedom which would mean so much to us."

"Freedom to live our own lives," Tania put in. "To

241

make mistakes, if we have to. We have managed that already, as you now know."

"Tania is young," Gerald continued. "I can appreciate that you might not wish her to take on married life so soon. But I am somewhat older, and it is time for me to shoulder responsibilities. Even if you feel you should keep us apart, I shall insist on providing a home for Tania and for the child I have fathered."

Pamela had watched Andre's expression altering, becoming flexible, irresolute, succumbing under Gerald's earnest determination. Aware of holding her breath, she listened for her husband's response.

"I cannot withhold my consent any longer," he told them wearily. "Marry as soon as you will, her stepmother and I both will be present to wish you good fortune."

"Oh, thank you, thank you!" Tania cried and flung herself at her father.

Pamela crossed to Gerald's side. "Well done," she murmured. "Just see you look after her properly."

Andre had similar admonitions and more besides, but now that the decision was made he shed much of the strain that had been evident since the day that Tania had first imparted her news.

"You must not expect a large wedding," Andre warned them nevertheless. He did not mean to broadcast the situation, or invite speculation concerning hasty arrangements. "Your people, of course, Gerald, a few friends perhaps, and Pamela's immediate family."

Not Ian, though, Pamela recognized at once. Poor Ian had been distressed enough while failing to even suspect that there could be a wedding and a baby on the horizon.

Mildred Baker refused the invitation as soon as it was issued, reminding Pamela and Andre when they called, that Ian was her son, and she could not support anything that disturbed him so greatly.

"You don't see him every day like I do, you don't know how he's altered. It were bad enough when we stopped 'em getting wed— "

"But they were both so young," Andre interrupted.

"I know, love, I know," said Mildred sadly. "And I was against it every bit as much as you were. Happen we were wrong, I'll never be sure. All I do know, is that I don't like what this is doing to our Ian."

"He'll pick up again, Mum," Pamela reassured her. "Because of how young he still is. There'll be other girls."

When Ian came in during their visit, however, Pamela wondered if there was much hope of his getting over losing Tania. Seeing him briefly, when dropping in at the house where the men were working, she hadn't noticed how thin he had become, how haggard his face. Today, he even walked wearily, as though an old man had been trapped in this young person's body.

"I'm glad I've seen you like this," he told Pamela now. "Away from Ted Burrows and the other chaps working for Canning's. You'd better know that I'm packing it in. Just as soon as I get confirmation of my new position."

Pamela was so stunned that she was too pre-occupied absorbing the blow to think of a reply.

Mildred, though, was shaken into delivering a torrent of words.

"Nay, Ian love, you don't mean that. You can't want to chuck everything away like that. Our Pamela's taught you all she knew, she's going to see you're all right, way into the future. If you'd seen the bad times that I have, you'd know the value of a secure job. There's prospects with the firm, isn't there – you tell him, Pamela."

"Ian's been told a long time since that as soon as he's twenty-one, he'll be given a lot more responsibility. Now that I've got my little shop to run as well, I dare say I'll be ready to think about handing over Canning's entirely."

"Then it'll have to be to somebody else. I shan't be here. I shan't even be in England."

"Ian?" Shattered, Mildred flopped on to a hard-backed chair.

"I think you'd better tell us what you're planning," his sister said gravely.

"I've applied to go out to East Africa. They're wanting young energetic men to get this groundnut scheme going properly."

"Africa! But that's ever such a long way away," Mildred said, her tired blue eyes filling with tears.

"Aye. That's what I need."

"But I've allus tried to give you a good home."

"I'm not denying that, Mum. But it was you that stepped in when we wanted a home of our own. Now look where it's got me."

"We only wished you to wait," put in Andre quietly.

"Oh, aye. And if you knew your own daughter,

you'd have realized that waiting is summat she never wants to do. Even when I began to see there might be a bit of sense in hanging on for a while, Tania wouldn't have that. Just as she couldn't wait to start a bairn," he added bitterly, turned, and hurried towards the staircase.

"Well, I don't know!" Mildred exclaimed as soon as Ian was out of the room. "I never thought he had any notion of going abroad. And Africa – I know nowt about the place."

"Happen it'll all fall through," said Pamela.

"Even if it does, if he's that set on leaving home, he'll be off."

As his mother-in-law finished speaking Andre crossed the few paces of the homely living room to place a hand on her shoulder.

"Whatever Ian does, wherever he goes, you may count on us always, Mother."

"Aye, I know. Thanks, love. Only it's not that. Our Tom'll still be here. But it's not me I'll be worrying about."

"I'll have a talk with Ian later on," Pamela promised. "I could offer him more responsibility in the firm sooner than I intended. That might make him see things in a different light."

Before she arranged such a meeting, though, someone else decided to take a hand in the situation.

Mildred had been to the King Cross shops one afternoon a few days later, and was taking off her hat and coat when she heard a knock on the door. Opening it, she was astonished to see Tania standing there.

"Are you going to invite me in?"

Mildred smiled. "Aye, love, of course."

"I did not know if I would be welcome here," Tania began, taking the proffered chair. "My father told me that you do not wish to come to my wedding."

"And did he also tell you why?"

"Oh, yes. And I am sorry – please believe me, very sorry. But I cannot think that I am to blame for not marrying Ian. Everyone knew that I wanted him."

"Only now it's somebody else you want."

"That does not sound like you," Tania remarked, shocked and upset by Mildred's tone.

"Oh, really? Aye, well – happen you'll find everybody here has changed. Towards you."

Tania rose, pulled on the elegant gloves discarded only moments earlier. "I think perhaps I should be leaving— "

Mildred hurried to grasp her arm. "Nay, lass, don't. I know I can be a bit outspoken."

"But I did ask for it?" Tania suggested, smiling slightly over her own adoption of a phrase her stepmother might have used.

"So, you do know. Happen there is still summat we can say to each other then."

"I did not plan this baby, you must understand. Nor did I plan to marry Gerald. I wish you to know that I would have liked to have had you for my mother-in-law."

"It's a bit late for that now. Your wedding's all arranged, isn't it? You've made your decision."

"Or had it made for me." Tania paused, considering, but she could not tell anyone of the dreadful plan that her own father had conceived with the hope of keeping her single and at home. She loved this woman whose weary eyes stared out from a lined face, but she loved Andre Malinowski more. "Do not be mistaken, I want this baby. And Gerald will provide well for us."

Gerald Thomas did indeed seem sure to provide cheerfully and well for Tania and their child. On the Saturday in late April, when he stood in the church at Cragg Vale, tall and personable, and smiling, he appeared the epitome of dependability.

Escorting Tania towards Gerald and, shortly afterwards, taking his place beside Pamela in the front pew, Andre wished that he could feel even fractionally content about his daughter's future. He stilled a sigh before it could disturb his wife, glanced sideways at her and managed to smile. Their own wedding was less than two years ago, he ought still to be regenerating the joy experienced in those early weeks.

He blamed neither Gerald nor Tania for the shortcomings of this day. Mentally he had adjusted – had made himself adjust – to the circumstances of their wedding. But his own situation was too fraught for him to feel happy about any aspects of their family life.

The small amount of favourable reaction to the piece he had written might have advanced his efforts to clear his name, but matters far beyond his control had worsened the Western attitude to all things Russian. He suspected it might always be that each forward step was cancelled by outside events to set him back by several paces.

In this instance, Moscow had announced that a US aeroplane had been shot down over Latvia. The

247

report had been followed only yesterday by the USSR's refusal to apologize to the United States. He sympathized with both sides in the unfortunate incident, but his own cause was helped by neither.

He sensed movement at his side, Pamela thrust an open hymn book into his hand, and again he smiled, this time shamefacedly. This was his cherished daughter's wedding and he was giving it sparse attention. He had become a poor father to Tania in recent months, and that was inexcusable. From this moment he would place his daughter's concerns before his own, relegate his declining career to the back of his consciousness whenever Tania needed him.

On that day, however, she seemed to need no one but Gerald. Gracious beyond her years though she was to his family and her own, throughout the reception at Stonemoor House which followed the church service, Tania appeared icily self-contained. Her eyes lit only for her bridegroom, the rest of her smiles reminded Andre of her professional face, the acknowledgement of an appreciative audience.

Noticing this, Pamela thought her stepdaughter was proving something. Showing her father, and Gerald's parents as well perhaps, that she was sufficiently mature to carry off this somewhat awkward day. And to survive unaided any days ahead which became difficult.

Pamela, just as much as her husband, was being misled. Tania had come close to calling off the wedding. Terrified of spending the rest of her life with this man she hardly knew, she yearned to be becoming the partner of someone she understood, her old friend Ian. But she was a realist enough to recognize that there could be no question of marrying Ian now. That dream had been destroyed by her own carelessness, as had her belief in the goodness of her own father. If she lived to be a hundred she would not, *could not* ever forget his suggestion that he would take her baby and rear it as his own.

Gerald alone understood how greatly she loved that unborn child. His offer of support had been the only good thing to shine through those days filled with dread. Frightened though she still was, Gerald deserved a smiling bride, one whose demeanour gave no hint of the tears now draining away somewhere deep inside her. She had learned to smile long ago, along with projecting her voice, maintaining perfect pitch, and all other attributes of a singer. For once in her life, she thanked God for the skills that ensured for this new husband of hers the response that he needed.

This feeling that no one else counted for her might pass, Tania hoped that it would. A world without her adoration of her father seemed a sad place in prospect. She was distressed also – and this surprised her – by the sudden mistrust which had arisen in her own attitude towards her stepmother. They both had worked at that relationship and had created something rather fine; so fine, that it was to Pamela that she had turned in trouble.

But Pamela would have taken over this child; so far as she knew, had failed to argue against such a heartless notion.

Gerald's parents were leaving, saying farewell to her father and his wife, expecting that she and Gerald would be leaving with them. Jolted out of her reverie, Tania slid her hand into her husband's arm and beamed up at him.

"Ready then?" he asked.

"Of course." Her case was in the Thomas's car, the rest of her belongings long since installed in the rooms that she and Gerald would share in their house.

I cannot say goodbye, she thought, and straightened her shoulders before crossing smartly to kiss and hug her father, then afterwards his wife. Pamela had young Mihail by the hand, he was standing now, clutching at her leg with his other dimpled fingers. Tania went down on one knee, kissed his gleaming golden head, drew him to her. Soon she would have her own infant, her only comfort.

On the Monday following their wedding, Gerald and Tania set out for a brief honeymoon high on the Yorkshire moors out beyond York. She had wanted to go there, most of all to get away from his parents. Living in their house would be very different from the light-hearted stay there, something that must be endured until they acquired their own home.

Gerald had disagreed with her over where they should live, a fact which had shaken her although she soon had realized that she might have foretold such a disagreement. The house she had wanted for so long was old, and did need a massive amount of renovation, he had condemned the place already.

"If that's a joke, I don't find it particularly amusing," Gerald had said when she had suggested another visit to her house once they were agreed that they should marry. "I'm not prepared to even consider taking my wife to a hovel like that. We may have to wait some little while before investing in a suitable home, but we've been assured that we'll have a roof over our heads for as long as necessary."

The house where they were staying for this brief holiday reminded Tania of the one she would have purchased. It was larger, of course, with several bedrooms to rent out and a further two or three occupied by their hostess and four children. She was widowed during the war, Tania learned, and now let rooms when she could to provide a better standard of living.

Tania admired her calm manner of coping, and resolved to tackle whatever life might bring to *her* with similar equanimity.

Gerald drove them out into the countryside each day, they ate at village inns or in picturesque cafés, walked quite a lot, and talked hardly at all. He seemed preoccupied here, scarcely aware at times that she walked beside him. Wondering how deeply he regretted the responsibility heaped upon his shoulders, Tania felt lost, unable to understand how to approach him.

During the third day away from the West Riding their walk took them through a wood, they heard dogs barking a little way off, children's laughter. After a few moments one of the dogs broke away from the group, plunged through the trees quite close to where Tania was walking, then charged off into the distance. On its heels, a man appeared from the same direction, hurtling after the animal, heedless of everything but catching it up.

She saw no more of him than light trousers, a toning sweater and the squarish shape of the back of his head where brown hair sat neatly above the polo neck. He was so like her father that she would have called after him. But through the trees the man's children appeared, all different ages and sizes. And now she wanted to weep, to sob out her fear and isolation, her longing for Andre Malinowski.

"Can we go home?"

Startled, Gerald looked down at her. "Sure, whenever you like. Didn't she say she was laying on a ham salad this evening?"

The house where they were staying was not home to her, and nor was his parents' house. Tania suspected that whatever place Gerald bought for them would not become her home. And Stonemoor House was her home no longer. The only terms on which she might have remained there had been unacceptable.

"I wonder how she is. *Where* she is . . ." Andre was even less happy today.

Pamela smiled sympathetically. She had insisted that she needed his help at the shop on this Monday afternoon. It was all a charade, with no customers in weeks and no incentive now to increase her stock, there was precious little for one person to do.

Mihail, bless him, was saving the day yet again. Having taken a sudden, vociferous dislike to the playpen, he was insisting on being allowed to roam. A couple of rooms stuffed with antiques was hardly the best place to accommodate a youngster who daily increased his mobility.

Andre's patience with the boy was unending. Relishing the sight of them together, Pamela felt refreshed simply by watching their mutual enjoyment.

252

She had so longed for this child, but she had never suspected that her greatest happiness would be in handing him over to his father.

Perhaps the next one would be hers more completely, she hoped for a girl while hesitating to even make the suggestion that they should increase their family. Andre so often seemed perturbed and, whilst the open antagonism that they had faced had disappeared, there still was no sign of the professional engagements which would renew his enthusiasm for life.

Physically, relations between them had ceased. She could date that cessation precisely, a fact that inhibited her from trying to put things right. Tania had come to her with the announcement of her pregnancy, she had broken the news to Andre, and he had withheld himself. Her own suspicion that he somehow was inflicting self-punishment was unfounded, no more than intuition, but it remained, a reminder that he felt inadequate. Pamela herself frequently felt that she was the one who was being punished.

Andre seemed no less disturbed when it was time to return to the house that evening. Pamela caught herself hoping that Mrs Singer would not have left for home yet, and wondered at her own reluctance to be alone with her husband.

Mrs Singer was still there, although slipping on her coat ready for departing. As soon as Andre set his son down in the hall the housekeeper bent down and held her arms wide for the boy.

Rapidly, and with eagerness making his progress look even more ungainly, Mihail crawled towards her. Watching as Mrs Singer clasped the child to her, Pamela realized how Mihail's friendliness had improved the quality of their housekeeper's mute world.

Andre was also watching. Turning to him, Pamela received and returned a sudden smile.

The moment restored some of the intimacy between them so that when Mrs Singer handed over their son and left them, Pamela began to believe that there was hope of rediscovering that original, very special element of their relationship.

Preparing Mihail's food and afterwards getting him ready for the night, Pamela was acutely aware of Andre's grey gaze following her. About to return downstairs and finish cooking the meal that Mrs Singer had left ready for them, she was detained by his serious expression.

"I wish that I might be a better father for him than I have been for Tania," he said gravely. "I have failed so badly with her, yet I so wanted to provide a good upbringing."

"You haven't failed," she reassured him. "You've always done what you thought would be best. You could never have guessed that she might go off and get herself pregnant."

"I should have instilled in her that there were these things that she must not do."

Pamela could not entirely keep the smile from her voice. "Knowing young folk, nowadays, I dare say you'd have only encouraged her to do just the opposite, if only to prove she was grown-up!"

Sighing, Andre shook his head. "I really do not know. In fact, I feel that I know so very little now.

I fear that Ian was correct, and I did not even know my own daughter. Or would not acknowledge that she wished never to wait for something she desired."

"It's not your fault if you've always thought the best of her – like not seeing how headstrong she could be, I mean."

"And if I am no better with Mihail, what then? A boy needs even firmer guidance. And you, my love – you need a husband always certain of what the next step must be. Of the shape our lives must form."

Pamela grinned, and slipped her arms about him, holding him against her. "Steady on a bit, Andre – I've never said I wanted all my decisions making for me. I've got to have a bit of latitude, if only to exercise a few ambitions."

And those, she reflected, are beginning to be overwhelmingly the desire to extend our family. Considering Andre's present mood, though, how on earth would she ever even broach that subject?

Chapter Thirteen

Tania and her husband moved into their own home five weeks after their wedding. The place was a Victorian terraced house in Hebden Bridge and it was rented. The third thing about it which Gerald hated was the hastily assembled collection of other people's furniture.

His parents had loaned several good pieces, as had Andre, and Pamela had insisted that they borrow a few useful items from the stock of her antique shop. He might be grateful that they need experience no real hardship, but this situation could not have been further from his ideal for setting up house.

Tania was happier now, and for that he was thankful. Her very evident misery in their home had all but driven Thelma and Barry Thomas to despair. In order to preserve good relations with his parents, as much as to placate his wife, Gerald had been obliged to find somewhere for them to live.

Although in better condition than the house Tania would have chosen, this place was inconvenient, a tall narrow building on four floors with its tiny kitchen on a different level from the room they reserved for eating. Twice already, Tania had dropped dishes on the dark staircase, and had asked him what he had expected when he made the mildest of comments about wasted food.

At times, he was compelled to recognize that some of her complaints were justified. She certainly was growing quite big now, a fact which must make negotiating so many steps difficult. Indeed, the very size of her was becoming a daily goad, reminding him that unless he wished their baby to be born in this place he must lay down the deposit on somewhere more suitable within the next few weeks.

Gerald was working harder than ever in the family firm. His father, quite rightly perhaps, had insisted that the salary increase he'd requested at the time of his marriage should be merited through greater effort.

Gerald did not mind that, or would not have done, if Tania were more capable in the house. As things stood, he frequently came home to find her laboriously tidying one or other of the rooms and their evening meal no more than a few vague ideas in her head. He was tired by the end of a working day and accustomed to his mother's well-run home, although he didn't need to remind himself of the compensations of having such an attractive young person as his wife.

Tania was, in fact, doing her very best to appear grateful that Gerald had got her away from his family to a place of her own. Young she might be, but she was no fool, and could understand that he would have preferred to remain somewhere more comfortable. She could not blame him for the fact that she spent so many hours alone here, and nor could he be held responsible for the days without rain and the ceaseless traffic a few feet from their door. She dared not complain that she found these rooms, whose small windows lurked behind layers of dust, infinitely depressing.

Several times she had been home to Stonemoor House while Gerald was away at the factory, and had called in on her way to chat with Pamela whose antique shop suddenly seemed to be becoming quite busy.

Her stepmother had shown her the magazine article which was virtually identical to the one in the newspaper, but with a photograph of Andre on the steps of Stonemoor.

Since that article was published, people had ceased to avoid Pamela's shop so rigorously. Best of all, Andre had been engaged to appear as solo violinist at a concert in Leeds.

Delighted though she was for her father's sake, Tania couldn't help feeling envious. It was ages since she had performed anywhere. Whilst preoccupied with wedding arrangements, she had not worried about the absence of engagements. Now she yearned for the satisfaction of singing before an audience. She also could have found a very good use for the money.

Travelling by bus while she was pregnant made her feel sick, if only she had her own car she might go anywhere she wished to alleviate the dullness of her domestic life. And by the time the baby was here, if she were able to drive she would relish taking him everywhere.

Tania had been to Stonemoor on the day when Gerald arrived home earlier than usual. For once, any problems in their factory had been resolved before the workforce clocked off, and his father had no reason to detain him for discussions.

He called to Tania as he came through the door, and was surprised when it was from their third floor bedroom that she called back to him.

"You are OK, aren't you?" he asked as she appeared way above him on a landing.

"Oh, yes. I was taking a bath, that is all. There were some workmen on the bus who smelled quite dreadfully of oil or something. I shall be dressed in a moment."

She was wearing a silky petticoat and as she turned to return to their room its gleaming folds revealed a length of bare leg which made her appear strangely vulnerable. With distance and this angle, Gerald could discern no sign of the child she was carrying and he was reminded of the passion generated in the early days of their relationship.

His initial irritation that dinner yet again would be delayed faded beneath the onslaught of a more exhilarating hunger.

Tania was holding a blue dress to her, testing its colour against her reflected skin in the mirror, when he came into the room.

"Forget that," he said, striding across to slide his arms around her breasts.

Tania bit her lip. Still unused to her own heavier body, she felt more sensitive to his touch. She also had been perturbed for quite some weeks when Gerald relentlessly made love to her. Would the baby be harmed? She could not imagine how such ferocious intrusion on its territory might have no effect upon that precious scrap of humanity. More than once she had intended to ask Pamela if lovemaking could put the baby at risk, but somehow she had been unable to find the right words. With her own mother so many things would have been so much easier.

Today, this husband of hers seemed so determinedly sensual as he drew her backwards against him that she felt doubly scared. If he persuaded her on to that bed there was no knowing what the extent of his passion might be.

"Not just now, Gerald, eh? I was about to get your meal ready."

"That can wait, this can't. You should know by now what effect your desirable body has—"

"But I am tired," she interrupted.

"You're not the only one who's tired," he retorted. "Don't forget I've spent my whole day working to provide you with something better than this wretched place. And there's no more sure release."

He was holding her quite fiercely now, invasive hands willing her to meet his passion. Struggling to free herself, Tania turned in his arms and was thrust still more firmly against him. He kissed her sharply then picked her up and carried her to the bed.

Gerald pushed the silken petticoat up to her waist and pulled off her matching underwear. Imprisoning her with one hand, he tore at his own buttons. Despite all her misgivings, Tania felt her need of him growing. When he stirred she echoed the movement and then he was making love to her as though he had waited for weeks for this experience, instead of a couple of days.

"You see, you enjoyed it, I knew you would,"

260

Gerald said triumphantly as he flopped sideways on to his own half of the bed.

"It is only that I cannot help thinking about the baby," said Tania, silently acknowledging that she did not wish to annoy him.

Gerald snorted. "And do you think that I can? But for that child, we wouldn't even be married. Or not yet," he added, though only following a noticeable pause.

Tania felt tears welling up behind her eyes. She had wondered if Gerald would have married her otherwise, but this confirmation so soon after his making love to her was a slap to her self-esteem.

He fell asleep immediately. She rose wearily to go to the bathroom. In the mirror her own face startled her. She might have been feeling tearful, but the gloss over her eyes looked more like the haze induced by desire, and those flushed cheeks did seem to imbue a certain glow to her whole appearance.

Perhaps Gerald was not so entirely wrong after all, she reflected, going downstairs to begin making their meal. It could be that he understood more than she did of what was acceptable whilst she was expecting. He might even have asked his father's advice. As she would have enquired of her own mother, if that had been possible.

During the next few weeks Tania yearned more than ever for Anichka Malinowski, pausing frequently to offer short little phrases into the air: snatches of their news, details of how the baby now was moving inside her, and earnest pleas for help in comprehending these changes which she was experiencing. And it did seem to help, to provide a little of the reassurance that she might have received from some source beyond her own world.

Gerald noticed, of course, that his young wife often appeared distracted, and he grew alarmed. Disappointed though he was by her lack of capability around the house, he was fond of Tania, and he'd no wish to even contemplate that unhappiness was inducing this strangeness. He wanted to restore their old familiar life.

"Do you know what?" he began one evening while they ate. "We haven't appeared with the band for ages. Not since we were married. I think, don't you, that it's time we did something about that. You need an interest outside the home."

Tania immediately thought of Ian and how she could not contemplate what her husband was suggesting. "Oh, but I am not sure that would be right – not – not the way I am. The band is too energetic."

"You only stand still and sing, for heaven's sake," Gerald persisted, relishing the prospect of showing off to his fellow instrumentalists that he had not only taken possession of this attractive female, but had proved himself virile.

"None of the dresses that I can get into would be at all suitable for singing with the band."

"I'll soon get you another dress – you'll need one, at least, if you're to do a classical concert ever again."

"Of course I shall do more concerts."

Gerald telephoned their band leader later that night. As soon as she saw his expression when he came back into the room Tania asked whatever was wrong.

262

He shook his head, seemed for a few minutes reluctant to explain. Eventually, he turned to her quite fiercely.

"It's all *your* friend's fault, I'm sure. We're not wanted in the band any longer. They've got a new solo trumpet, so I'm told, and they're not doing any more vocal numbers suitable for you."

"Not suitable for me?" Tania was shaken. "But – but I have such a wide range. They know I sing the classics as well as popular music. There are no kinds of music that I could not sing."

Gerald would have argued that point, but this was not the time. He was annoyed, he had enjoyed playing with that band, would miss the conviviality to say nothing of the elation of giving a solo now and again. He could appreciate, though, that Tania needed the band more. Over here, she had made so few friends.

"You believe that Ian was responsible for this, you say? Is that what you were told?" she asked.

"Not in so many words perhaps, but it's obvious, isn't it?"

"On the next occasion when I see Ian Baker I shall tell him how small-minded I consider him."

But Tania was not to see Ian again for a very long time. Only a week later he called at Stonemoor House to say goodbye.

Pamela knew already from Ted Burrows that her brother's forthcoming departure was imminent. She still calculated the wages as well as keeping an eye on the way Canning's was running. She had learned the date when Ian was to leave. The news had taken her over to Halifax that same evening, but Ian himself

263

was out, having a farewell meal with his friends from the band.

Their mother was just as distressed as Pamela expected, though valiantly trying not to let that show, especially in front of Tom, who was seated at the table executing a design for a new magazine to be established by the publishers for which he worked.

"Our Tom's that much in demand, these days," Mildred told her daughter proudly. "He hasn't enough time in the office for all that they want him to do."

"I hope they're paying you well for this overtime!" Pamela exclaimed.

Her young brother looked up with a grin. "Aye, they are an' all. I'm not daft, you know, I don't let enjoying the work make me forget other considerations."

As soon as Mildred confirmed that Ian wasn't in, Pamela took her arm and led her aside to the kitchen. "Knowing you, you'll not want to give Tom the impression that his stopping here isn't enough. But I can see you're upset. Is there owt we can do?"

Mildred shook her head, tears filled her blue eyes, but she clamped her lips together until certain she would not weep.

"It's too late now, I know. But right from the start it'd have been no good talking to him. Even if you'd have handed Canning's over to him – and I can understand he's too young for that – he'd not have stayed over here."

Pamela nodded grimly. "That was the impression I got. And we all know why. If only Tania had been more patient, ready to wait a few years, none of this would have happened."

264

"Aye – well . . . She can't have had much of a life back in Russia, with her father so unhappy about the way the country was run. Then she lost her mother so tragically, poor lass. You can't blame her for reaching out for a better life." Mildred paused, looked questioningly at her daughter. "She is happy now, isn't she?"

"I suppose so. She will be, any road, once the baby's here. I don't think she's got enough to keep her busy while Gerald's at work. Sounds like his father expects him there till all hours."

"Well, he will, won't he? Stands to reason when he intends him to take over the business one day."

"Are you going to see Ian off, Mum?"

Mildred shook her head again. "He doesn't want me to, doesn't want anybody at the quayside, he says. And I can't say I'm sorry. It'll be enough of a wrench having him go, without seeing him set sail. But he did say he'll have to see you afore he goes."

"He'd better do, an' all, else there'll be bother. But what about you, Mum? You'll be lost with only our Tom at home, and him so quiet."

"I'll manage. I've done a lot of that in my time."

"Well, like a said before, don't forget where we are, and that we'll always be glad to see you. In fact, now our Mihail's becoming quite a handful I wouldn't mind a bit of extra help with him. How would you feel about looking after him now and again for me? He's into everything when I take him to the shop."

"We'll see, love. If you really need me. But I don't want you to go creating jobs for me. I shall be all right."

*   *   *

265

"Mum says she'll be all right," Ian began almost as soon as he arrived at Stonemoor House, revealing where his deepest concern lay. "I wish I didn't feel so guilty about leaving her, but it isn't as if she'll be on her own."

"Do you still blame her for not letting you and Tania marry?"

"Not when I'm being honest wi' myself. I knew I weren't ready for all that responsibility. It's just unfortunate that yon chap *were* ready!"

"Happen a change of scene will turn out to be the best thing for you," Pamela suggested.

"Whether it does or not, it's the only way. I couldn't stand it, Pamela, not seeing her with Gerald, and then with their bairn. Maybe I'm soft or summat, but that's the way it is."

You'll have bairns of your own one day, Pamela thought, but could not say that. Ian had indicated already that as yet he couldn't even think about taking out another girl.

"Andre's tucking Mihail up in his cot. Are you coming up to see them?"

"Of course. Can't leave without seeing the little fellow. And Andre's a grand chap, champion. He'll allus look after you."

Pamela nodded, reflecting that she and Andre looked after each other pretty well. He had endured a bad few months, but he had one firm engagement to play, and there was another in the pipeline.

Andre turned from where he was leaning over the side of the cot, then crossed swiftly to shake Ian by the hand.

"You are about to embark on your new life, I hear.

I hope that you will find as much satisfaction in your chosen country as I have over here."

"Thanks. Well, I can only give it a try. There seems to be lots of opportunities with this groundnut scheme. And if it doesn't work out, it could lead to summat else somewhere."

Pamela noticed the way in which Ian gazed lingeringly at the sleeping child before the three of them went down to the sitting room. He might have been impressing on memory every feature of her son's face, each curl of his gleaming head.

Andre poured drinks for them, and spoke as he never had to Ian before, man to man, as though they could not have been more close had they been brothers. Pamela was glad, she was too full of emotion to say very much, and rather afraid of upsetting the lad by becoming sentimental.

While they sat, talking more generally now, she saw that Ian was staring out of the window as though, there too, he found images that he wished to take with him. Cragg Vale was looking particularly fine, with the greens of the young summer enhanced by an earlier shower, deepening the various shades of the woods, brightening meadows and fields beneath the moors towards which the sun now was sinking.

By the time that Ian said goodbye, she was convinced that his feelings about leaving the West Riding were very mixed. Determined though he was to get right away, home was pulling, he would not readily forget. They hugged and then kissed in a way that for years had seemed far too emotional for a lad and his sister. And her own eyes were not the only ones to wear a gloss of tears.

Andre walked with him to the door, extracting promises that Ian would write. Pamela, too choked to speak, ran upstairs to the nursery.

Listening to Ian driving away, she looked down at Mihail, realizing how precious relationships were, praying that she and this babe of hers would never have to part. I need another child, she thought, or this son of mine will become smothered by this possessive parent.

"How could he do it?" she asked Andre when he appeared in the doorway seeking her. "How can he leave everybody?"

"How could he not?" Andre asked in return. "When you believe you have lost everything, you need to turn your back on fate and go."

They held each other close, both made pensive by the changes that life wrought.

"Do not forget," said Andre at last. "I found great happiness here when I believed already that my life was ended."

"And so did I, you know what I was like after Jim died." How could she have overlooked, even for a short while, how her own devastation had been compensated by the happiness Andre had brought her?

He was gentle with her that night, gentle and loving. Pamela found a new kind of peace in his arms, a peace where she could still see the surrounding difficulties, but acknowledge that they were only the prelude.

This is only the beginning, Tania thought. It was going to get worse before there would be any relief from this pain. And for an hour at least she would be on her own.

The midwife had called, timed these contractions that already seemed to be so violent, and had gone away again. Tania had telephoned Gerald in the factory office as soon as the midwife left, but he had been unable to come home immediately. His father was not in the works today, no one else could be relied upon to solve whatever it was that had gone wrong. He had suggested that she should call his mother.

Tania had rung Pamela instead, she would be on her way just as soon as she had closed the shop and taken Mihail back to Stonemoor House.

"Your father should be home by then to look after him. He's been out all day rehearsing."

Tania had smiled to herself, despite another onslaught of pain. It seemed ironical that when she needed someone to be *here* everyone was more occupied than they had been for some time. She would be so thankful when her stepmother finally arrived.

Close to tears, Tania greeted her on the doorstep. "I have been so frightened, so certain that the baby would come while I was alone. And I do not know what to do."

"What did the midwife say, love?" Pamela enquired, ushering her indoors and then up to the first floor living room.

"That it most likely will not be here before morning. But I cannot believe that. You did not take very long when Mihail was born, did you?"

"Not long, no, not really. But that was exceptional for a first. Most folk go a lot longer."

They discussed how frequently the pains were arriving, and at what time the midwife was due to return.

"She said that she will call here repeatedly until she is sure it is really on its way. But how will she *know* – how will anyone know?"

Pamela grinned. "I'm not sure I'm the best person to answer that. Don't forget I went off to my mum's instead of making straight for the hospital. Of course, Mihail was early . . ."

Tania nodded, pressed a hand to her aching back, and sighed. She thought of Mildred Baker, and recognized very clearly that if she had been married to Ian she would have welcomed Mildred's motherly presence at this moment.

"You are not at all like your mother, are you?"

Pamela was surprised. "Why do you say that?"

"I was – well, wishing that she was here."

"Meaning I'm not competent – not for dealing with owt like this?"

"Sorry. That must have sounded dreadful. No, forget what I said, please. I only thought—"

"That my mother would have been better. More experienced, certainly. Although she soon won't necessarily always be. You see, Tania, I'm expecting again. You're the first I've told. Even your father doesn't know yet."

Her stepdaughter smiled. "Then I am pleased that you have told me. It makes me feel, as I sometimes felt before you married, that we might have been sisters." She grew silent for a while, then spoke again, haltingly. "Since you have confided in me, you – you are making me to wish – that – well, that I had talked to you."

270

"Talked? When, love, what about?"

Tania's shrug was awkward. "Oh – personal things. Like – like, when should Gerald . . . Would it hurt the baby if he – if he made me . . .?"

"Made love to you, you mean? Do you know, I can't be sure – I'll find out for you." Pamela could only recall how tender Andre had been, so gentle. Had there been any months before Mihail was born when they had refrained from lovemaking? She grinned. "I shall need to know myself, shan't I? And before *you* have another baby—"

"Another? Today, I do not think that I ever will." And, alongside yearning to have the baby here, she was looking forward to the next few weeks when she would have good reason for fending Gerald off. He was so strong that she always felt overpowered, so fiercely demanding that she feared she could never please him enough.

"You've plenty of time, any road," Pamela was saying calmly. "Not like me, I didn't want to be an old mother to either of my children."

"You plan no more than two then?" Tania asked before groaning as pain again stabbed through her.

The midwife arrived ten minutes later, and mistook Pamela for Tania's mother. "Or is it mother-in-law?" the woman enquired, while Pamela thought that she must be looking old!

"Mother," Tania asserted, smiling at Pamela, and leaving no room for a correction to be made.

Old-looking or not, Pamela reflected, Tania evidently prefers me to Thelma Thomas. On this occasion. She was surprised, only last Christmas Tania had been enraptured by everything about

271

the Thomas family. Today, she wondered uneasily if even Gerald himself could be beginning to pall. She certainly hoped not, with an infant on its way into the world the girl was going to be shackled to him for many a year.

This time, the midwife decided to remain, and Pamela was not sorry to have an expert to hand. She herself had only the one experience of childbirth as a guide, and with going to hospital had been taken over from the moment of her arrival there.

"You must come along as well, Mother," the woman insisted when she judged the time was right for Tania to go up to the bedroom. "She will need some encouragement from someone who's been through it all."

Pamela was glad to be of use. She had been perturbed a short while ago when Gerald had arrived home from the factory, only to go straight out again after giving Tania the briefest of kisses. Pamela had been in the kitchen finding a bucket and cloth. Tania was distressed already, quite alarmed by the sudden rush of water down her legs, and would have benefited from any reassurance her husband might provide.

Gerald's excuse was that he was going to fetch his mother, but Pamela had read in his voice the need for an abrupt retreat. Luckily, Tania now seemed to be unperturbed by his absence.

Perhaps on account of the girl's young and supple body, her labour was blessedly straightforward, and not unduly prolonged. The midwife, strong arms bared below a roll of sleeves, watched from the foot of the bed, alternately commanding and cajoling until the crown of a moist little head appeared.

272

Between soothing her stepdaughter's cries and offering her hand to be gripped, Pamela was so fascinated that the actual birth seemed to pass very swiftly. All at once the baby's shoulders were eased out, then almost immediately the infant cried, and it was there before them, wrinkled and bloodstained, but unmistakably human.

"A little lass," the midwife announced, already wrapping the baby in a soft towel. "You've got a lovely girl, Mrs Thomas."

"I shall call her Pamela," said Tania as the baby was placed in her arms. "Because you were here for me today. Pamela Anichka."

While Tania and the midwife were preoccupied with the child, Pamela turned away and went to look out of the window. She was overwhelmed. Throughout the long months since she had first met Andre's daughter she had struggled to make a success of her relationship with the girl. This – this acknowledgement of her part in Tania's life was beyond anything that she could have dreamed. She could not wait to go home to Stonemoor House and tell Andre.

Since the birth of their own son was only a little over a year ago, Pamela and Andre both found that the new addition to the family made them more aware of their own good fortune. Seeing Mihail growing and developing had interested them, of course; now they recognized afresh how privileged they were to have been given charge of his young life.

As soon as Pamela had got over the excitement of Tania naming the baby after her, she had told

Andre that by the following year they themselves would have another child.

"I hope it's a girl," she admitted when he had hugged her in delight. "But a second Mihail will be just as acceptable. Especially if the lads were to grow up like their father!"

She was so fortunate to have a husband like Andre who, no matter what difficulties they faced, always remained kindness personified.

I wish I believed Tania was as lucky regarding her husband, Pamela thought, and wondered why she felt so uneasy about Gerald. He had arrived with his mother in tow shortly before she herself had left Tania, and no man could have seemed more pleased that his wife had been delivered safely of her infant. It is time that I stopped worrying about the pair and let them get on with it, Pamela told herself. Tania has proved she knows where to turn if she needs a bit of help, but her real need could be to stand on her own two feet.

Pamela would have been appalled, however, if she could have seen how soon Gerald expected his wife literally to do just that. Only days after her confinement Tania was being implored to get out of that bed. The trouble arose from her reluctance to have Thelma Thomas stay in that little house with them.

Despite Gerald's entreaties, Tania had protested that she hated having anyone there. In fact, what she really hated was allowing her mother-in-law the opportunity for discovering the shortcomings in the housekeeping arrangements. Lying in that third floor bedroom she had listened for hours as

Thelma Thomas went about the place, cleaning and polishing, and going through cupboards whenever she must make a meal. She will find out that I am no good at being a wife, Tania thought and, being unable to explain this to Gerald, had succeeded in giving him the impression that she had begun to loathe her mother-in-law.

When he was persuaded to drive his mother back to her own home, Gerald became filled with a sudden apprehension which was not at all the feeling that a new father should experience. By the time that he returned to his wife his dread of coping with this new situation had generated in him a quite reckless reaction.

Deprived of his mother's care, the house would soon become even more neglected than it normally appeared. He was not accustomed to such surroundings, and he certainly did not mean to deal with the chores himself after a hard day's work. This miserable rented house was getting him down. He had fully intended originally that they should be in their own place before the baby was born. He could have explained to no one his reasons for delaying the process of finding somewhere.

His failure to act somehow was related to this strange feeling he had – the feeling that their situation did not justify greater expenditure. His disinclination to move perturbed him. He'd pictured having a garden where his son could play, he knew the kind of life a lad needed. Little girls were very much a mystery to him.

This house though, was all too real, and Tania must be made to see that she should at least co-operate and keep it decent. She was not ill, indeed she had grown quite animated after a couple of days in which to recover from the actual birth.

Gerald began that evening. "I suggest that while you're on your feet to go to the bathroom you might tidy the place, get rid of one layer of dust. That baby powder fills the air to choking point."

Tania was too taken aback to do more than stare at her husband, but while in the bathroom she concluded that she had married a thoughtless boor, totally lacking in understanding. She hadn't really expected any man to be particularly considerate – after all, in Russia many women were obliged to do harder, more physical work than their menfolk. But she was not in Russia now, and she did not intend this Englishman to issue instructions as though she were a maidservant.

Once back in bed, she found her gaze being drawn towards the dressing table and its coating of dust. Her glance strayed to the patterned linoleum also, and the bedside rug, where another scattering of baby powder had settled, even more obtrusively. Irked though she was by these beginnings of neglect, Tania resolved to do nothing about them. She leaned sideways towards the cot and gazed at her sleeping daughter. Men could not be expected to appreciate all that a woman had to endure. That was a fact of nature, but now she had the one thing that could make her forget the many factors in life which she found upsetting.

"Your daddy must clean it up if it worries him," she asserted aloud. "You and I have waited a long, long time to be together, we are going to enjoy each other."

Enjoying the baby continued to be Tania's motivation for weeks after she was up and about again. Gerald could spend as long as he wished away at the factory now. It mattered not at all to her that the infant was too young to respond with anything more than her ever-hungry mouth. She herself had all the company she desired, tending the baby's needs provided all the satisfaction she needed.

Chapter Fourteen

Pamela was astonished when Tania said she did not wish to attend her father's performance. It was to be such a very special event, a sacred concert by a major British orchestra to be held in the glorious surroundings of York Minster.

Mildred had volunteered to come to Stonemoor House for the whole day to look after Mihail, and Pamela had arranged for her infant namesake to be included in her mother's care. She had been pleased that Mildred was looking forward to seeing Tania's baby, and they had laughed together as they thanked heaven that Mihail alone had reached the age of pulling himself up by the furniture to explore everything. A fact that made keeping an eye on him exhausting enough.

Tania's refusal to go with them worried Pamela, so much so that she asked over the 'phone if she was unwell.

"Not in the least, thank you," came the swift reply. "I just prefer to stay here and look after my own baby."

Pamela noticed that her stepdaughter's accent was more pronounced, something which often indicated that she was disturbed. But this did not mean that she would let concern for Tania spoil her enjoyment of that concert.

Andre had been rehearsing for weeks, filling the house with his eloquent violin when he wasn't actually attending practice sessions with the orchestra. The event was already attracting a fair amount of publicity, and his participation seemed about to set the seal on the general acceptance that those who had supposed he could have been a Communist spy had totally misjudged him.

We shall celebrate as we never have before, Pamela decided, relishing the fact that they both had something to rejoice about. The publication in further magazines of Andre's story had brought better fortune to her own antiques business. In recent weeks she had been revisited by the man who had been her first client, and he had purchased one very costly longcase clock and had left her a list of further requirements.

"Locate those on my behalf and I'll be glad to pay you a good commission," he had confirmed.

Fortunately for her, he was a man with a wide circle of acquaintances. Word of mouth proving yet again to be the best of advertisements, Pamela was delighted to find a succession of new customers arriving at her door. Several were interested in the furniture that had started off her business, and she soon was glad to report to old Mrs Fawcett's relative that the sale of his aunt's things was almost completed. He had never complained about the length of time that she was taking, nor had he shown any sign of being dissatisfied with her efforts on his behalf, but Pamela was thankful nevertheless to have the weight of that particular task removed from her mind.

She also was looking forward to having the necessary shop space for items which she herself judged to be worthy of investment. Attending auctions and sales became infinitely more satisfying now that she had some justification for making purchases. Another facet of her work, perhaps even more rewarding, was the increasing confirmation that she had been thorough in absorbing knowledge about this new business of hers. The period when she had lacked customers had brought its own dividends by providing sufficient time for reading up on her subject.

Andre was more philosophical than she had expected when Pamela told him that Tania would not be going to York Minster. Instead of frowning as anticipated, he merely shrugged.

"I suspect that she is finding that baby quite fascinating. Knowing Tania, I think that she also is unable to believe anyone else capable of caring for her."

He had received quite a shock when driving over to inspect his first grandchild. Tania had seemed so totally absorbed in the baby, something that he had not expected before a few months had elapsed and the infant became more animated. She will be a better mother than I gave her credit, he had decided, feeling content that he need worry about his daughter no longer.

Andre reminded Pamela of this and referred again to his delight on learning that Tania had named the infant after her. "We have received ample evidence recently that you and I may feel satisfied that our

280

treatment of Tania has, after all, produced good results."

Clutching her daughter to her breast, Tania clamped her teeth over her bottom lip, determined not to weep. It might not be all that long ago in reality, but it felt such an age already since she had seen her father, since she had seen either of them. And there was young Mihail as well – her little half-brother would have grown so much that she would hardly recognize him by the time she next saw him.

Pamela Anichka was feeding greedily, and she could only feel glad. The bond between them seemed strengthened each time that the baby began to nuzzle her breast. No one in the world knew how desperately she needed this proof that she was wanted. And wanted with such a touching sense of dependence. So many human emotions seemed tainted with cruel self-seeking that her own most earnest desire now was to protect this child from life's savagery.

Eyelids flickering occasionally, tiny hands stirring, but otherwise moving only her lips, her baby aroused Tania's yearning to preserve that innocence. To ensure that this daughter of hers should experience none of life's fiercer moments. Moments which she herself would never now forget.

Gazing at Pamela Anichka, she could not understand how in the world Gerald could feel disappointed. His words had been a tremendous shock, his attitude so old-fashioned that she could not credit that this go-ahead businessman uttered them. But that was only the beginning of everything going wrong.

It had been less than a week after the birth. She

herself had finally acquiesced to his constant remarks about the state of the house and had spent several hours cleaning the place. She had cooked a meal to please him, and had been feeling that her own satisfaction about all that she had achieved was a fair reward.

Moving around the house, unsatisfactory though it still remained, had been better than lying in that room. Although sore, she was quite well enough to be out of bed. And it was good to see the little one in other rooms, to feel that she belonged in the whole of their life. A part of everything they did here.

Gerald had taken the work she had done for granted, which was no great surprise and even made Tania feel that his confidence in her ability might have grown to the stage where he could do so. But then he had ruined everything. And just when she had been trying to explain more fully her own contentment.

Instead of agreeing with her that their baby was utterly enchanting, he had frowned. "I'd have preferred a son, naturally. Don't expect me to enthuse, I'm a man's man – always have been. I'm never going to dote on a daughter."

When her own eyes had registered how deeply he appalled her, Gerald had only laughed.

"Do not fret, Tania, I shall enjoy creating a boy."

His assault on her had begun that very night, regardless of her protestations that it was much, much too soon. Even when she had bled profusely after Gerald entered her, he had been concerned only to insist that she must change the bed linen immediately.

After that night he claimed that she had grown hard and unloving. Tania quelled her impulse to demand what he expected. To ask how she could love someone who had shaken her by behaving so brutally. She was frightened, and until she had thought this through, she must try not to provoke him any further. The horrible way in which he had forced himself upon her had shocked her into realizing that there could be other cruel facets of Gerald's nature.

For baby Pamela's sake, Tania was prepared to endure a great deal. She must be careful not to antagonize him completely, she needed her husband's support more than ever since the child's arrival. She just wished that there was one person who could help and advise her.

On the first occasion when Andre called to see her and the baby, Tania had been tempted to confide in him. Somehow, though, Andre had made that impossible. From the moment that he came into the house, he had seemed determined to emphasize how fortunate she was to have a good husband who would always provide well for her and their daughter. Andre had spoken of his certainty that Gerald would soon purchase a home far more comfortable than this present one. Parents generally provided a clear indication of how their offspring would develop, he had said, and were not Thelma and Barry Thomas quite excellent people?

They are, thought Tania afterwards. They had been welcoming when she was introduced to them, and could not have done more for her. She could hardly credit that their son was proving so unkind. Perhaps it is this horrid little house, she reflected.

Perhaps living here makes Gerald so *different*. She had been surprised by the difficulties of adjusting to married life, could it be that Gerald was finding it even harder to adapt to all this?

Her stepmother and Mihail had accompanied Andre on his next visit, and when Gerald arrived home whilst they were still there he'd played with the boy for several minutes. Tania saw the delighted smile exchanged between her father and his wife, and wondered if her developing mistrust of her husband could be unwarranted. Their own baby was too small yet to be responsive, perhaps all Gerald needed was time? Time in which to adapt to marriage as well as fatherhood.

Almost as swiftly as that thought, however, came the reminder that Gerald had wanted a son. Was his recent behaviour meant to drive the point home to her? They both were acutely aware that she was trying to avoid his insistent lovemaking. As she herself grew stronger with each day that passed, so did her distaste for her husband. She was beginning to be afraid that she would never want Gerald near her, but if she denied him a son they could not be happy together.

Andre had picked up Mihail to carry him to the car that day, and Pamela was saying goodbye to the new parents when she recalled something and smiled at Tania.

"I saw my mum at the weekend, she told me to give you her love."

Tania smiled back. "That is nice. And how is she?"

"Oh, not so bad, you know. A lot better since she

had a postcard from our Ian." Pamela paused the instant that she recognized from her stepdaughter's blank expression that she had known nothing about Ian's departure. "He – he wrote from somewhere *en route*. He's gone abroad for a bit, you see."

Pamela felt shattered by her own words. How could she have imparted the news so carelessly? She ought to remain for a while and comfort the girl, but with Gerald standing there she could hardly do so. She hugged Tania, instead, and resolved to telephone during the following day just to check that she was all right.

"You didn't know, did you?" said Gerald as soon as the door had closed and the car had moved off. "And you needn't pretend Ian Baker means nothing to you, I saw the look in your eyes!"

Tania swallowed and gave her attention to the baby who was stirring in her sleep. It was nearly feeding time, and she could not be more thankful. She needed desperately to get away from Gerald, to think quietly before willing herself, as she must, to try to dismiss how much she was longing for Ian.

The nursery was cool now that the afternoon sun had moved away. She sat by the window, holding Pamela Anichka in her arms and yearning to feel that she belonged somewhere. Hearing her father drive off, she had experienced a massive ache to be returning to Stonemoor House with them. The days here already seemed so fraught, and the nights worse still while she lay beside Gerald praying that he would be too tired to need her. And now Ian had gone. She could not believe that there would no longer be any point in fantasizing about seeing him again. He would not simply arrive at Stonemoor House on an occasion when she was there. He would not relent and urge her to return to sing with the band. *She might never see him again.*

The baby began yelling and Tania automatically unfastened her blouse and offered a breast. She was hardly aware of what she was doing as the tears she had restrained for so long coursed down her face. She felt desolate now, marooned here with a husband she could no longer like, much less love.

The door creaked open behind her, making her jump. She heard Gerald's impatient sigh a few inches behind her head, and felt the hair at her nape rising in alarm while she controlled a shudder.

"So, that's where you are. You stalked off as if – oh, never mind. Hurry that along, will you?" he added sharply.

"How can I? She has got to be fed, poor mite."

"And what of my needs? You'd evidently been too busy fussing over your father and his wife to even think that you should have had a meal ready when I came in."

"I will prepare something as soon as Pamela Anichka has had sufficient— "

"No," Gerald contradicted. "On second thoughts, that can wait."

"Well – why do you not read the newspaper or something?" Tania said, her accent thickening as she grew even more uneasy.

"No. You need reminding what this is all about. Don't think I haven't noticed you're crying for another man! I don't deserve any of this, Tania. We married to give that child a name, don't forget. We're neither of us happy about this place, but I am determined to make the best of living here."

"I do try, Gerald, I have from the beginning."

"Prove it then, let's have a little co-operation for once."

He had walked around her chair to stand looking down at her. Tania refused to meet his gaze. She smiled at the baby instead as she transferred her from one side to the other.

Bending towards them, Gerald cupped the vacant breast, teased the nipple between finger and thumb.

"That hurts."

"Only because you're resisting me. You'd better learn that it's useless hankering after Ian Baker. I'm the one you married. You're mine, Tania, and it's high time you began behaving that way."

Gerald stood over her until the baby was fed and winded, then he hustled Tania across to the cot. "Put her down to sleep now, I've waited long enough."

Tania hesitated only until she was certain her infant was contented, then hurried ahead of Gerald out of the room. Expecting to be hauled along towards the bedroom, she was shaken when he seized hold of her arm while they were still on the landing.

"If you keep me on tenterhooks like this, you must expect no refinements," he said tersely, and flung her round until her back hit the wall with a slap.

He was pressing at her instantly, pushing up her skirt then starting on his own buttons.

Tania cursed him in Russian. "You are a brute!" she yelled, writhing to free herself. "I shall not be treated in this way."

"You can't stop me now, I've waited too long. I didn't get married to spend half my time frustrated."

"I shall not—" Tania began.

Gerald's hand interrupted, slamming down across her mouth so sharply that she tasted blood from her lips. She struck out with her foot and felt him flinch when her shoe connected with his shin. His hand came at her face again, this time as a fist, stinging where the blow landed on her cheek.

"Let that be a lesson to you," Gerald cried between clenched teeth. "You are my wife, you'll not get away with avoiding me."

But she was about to avoid him now. In striking her, he had released the pressure exerted by his body. Tania turned, ran back to the nursery, and slammed the door on him.

"I'll break the damned thing down before you'll beat me!" he shouted from out on the landing.

Leaning against its panels, Tania quivered, she could feel her pulse thundering in her ears, vibrating within her chest. Disturbed, Pamela Anichka began to cry.

"It is all right, my sweet," Tania gasped, inhaling urgently. "I am here, little one."

The baby continued to cry, sounding inconsolable now. Please stop, please, please . . . Tania willed her. If that crying continued she would be unable to resist the impulse to go to her. Beyond the wooden door she heard her husband lunging with a shoulder against its timber.

If he does break that down he will be even more angry, she thought. And there was no way that she would be strong enough to keep him out.

288

Her baby was screaming now, there was no alternative to picking her up. Tania ran towards the cot.

Gerald was in the room by the time she turned with Pamela Anichka in her arms.

"You will not touch me now, I shall not let you harm her."

"How could you even think that I would," Gerald responded, icily calm now. "Any more than I'd want to hurt you, if you would only be reasonable. All I ask of you is a little understanding. I'm a full-blooded man, for God's sake. I need you."

He let it go at that, but was waiting downstairs when Tania eventually settled the baby for the night.

"We must talk," he announced, while Tania went about the kitchen putting together a meal for him. This was one duty she would perform while racking her brain for a solution to the difficulty surrounding the other.

"Our marriage is not going to work while you remain in this obstructive frame of mind," Gerald went on. "You'll be out in the street if you continue like this, without a home for you and the baby. All I'm asking is a normal married life, Tania."

"I would not call your rough treatment normal," she protested, and was surprised by the steadiness of her own voice.

"Only because I want you so much that you drive me crazy – want you, and need to have a *son*."

He sounded quite abject now, so earnest about wanting a boy that she began to wonder if her own behaviour towards him could have contributed to the cruelty between them.

"I only need to wait for a little while, our baby is so

289

very tiny. Perhaps in another few weeks . . ." Tania said tentatively. Gerald was older than she was, far more clever, she needed time in which to work out how to deal with him.

"That sounds fair," he admitted. "Provided that you keep your word, and remain aware that you can't expect to deny me until such time as you agree to having another child."

Worn down by him, Tania said no more. While Gerald was at work she would have ample opportunity for planning ahead. There must be some means you could employ to avoid another pregnancy. This one baby, dearly though she loved her, had become a shackle to prevent her escaping him. If Gerald gave her a second child she certainly would be condemned to enduring his treatment for ever.

Tania's immediate misfortune was having underestimated her husband's determination. Only two days afterwards he arrived home from the factory at the end of hours spent coping with his father's rage. The race to produce new materials for the clothing industry had been going quite promisingly for the family firm. Experimentation had resulted in fabrics that seemed about to revolutionize the entire business. Only today, however, news had broken that one competitor, too large for them to beat, was way ahead.

On that November Thursday in 1950 ICI had announced the construction of another factory – for production of their new fabric 'Terylene'. His father had railed against everyone on their site, but Gerald had borne the brunt of his dismay. At one time Gerald would have turned to Tania for comfort, but he knew in his heart that was something she could not be expected to deliver.

In some men, the day's trauma might have reduced the libido, in Gerald it generated the need to assert that he still possessed some power. For the first time ever, his future in the family company was insecure. His father had hinted at bringing in someone to develop its potential. If they lacked the capital to compete with industrial giants, they must invest in skills to produce materials way ahead of them. "You're incapable of that," he'd been told, and had been left with the feeling that he was contributing too little. If only he had a son he could insist that the boy was their investment in the future. Barry Thomas set great store by family. But a daughter was useless.

Gerald approached Tania as soon as they had finished their evening meal. She was not exactly unprepared, she had anticipated that he would insist on making these demands before the week was out. After much thought she had decided that continuing to deny him would be pointless. He was, and always would be, the stronger. From experience, she had learned he would exert force if necessary. Her only solution was to allow him to take her, and involving as little force as possible.

Her acquiescence seemed initially to be all that he required. Gerald sated himself shortly after he had talked her into going to their room. The moment that his breathing slowed as he slept beside her, Tania got up and went quietly towards the bathroom. The door had never locked properly since the day they had moved in, but tonight she gave that no thought.

Gerald was asleep and she relished the prospect of cleansing herself of all trace of him.

The door crashed open as she was about to step into the bath. Gerald tore along to seize her by the arms. He was shaking her fiercely before she could even gather her wits and fend him off.

"No!" he shouted. "No, no, no! That's not what this is about. You shall not rid yourself of our son."

"Gerald, please – I am only taking a bath." Tania tried to reason with him.

But reason had no part in his thinking that night. He continued shaking her and shouting. "I'll not leave this business unfinished. I'll not be satisfied until we have a boy."

She sensed him glancing towards the bath, but his mind was in overdrive and before she understood his intention Gerald had lifted her bodily and placed her in the water.

He followed at once, clutching for her breasts as she slithered beneath him. Afraid now that she could even drown, Tania struggled.

"Stop that!" he commanded, and seized her chin, intent on kissing her.

Tania turned her head away and in so doing enraged him. Grappling to take a firm hold on her slippery shoulders, Gerald tried to make her face him.

"No!" Tania shouted back, twisting her head away.

He gave her a shove and she felt the bridge of her nose slam against one of the taps.

Even Gerald was shaken by the speed with which the bruising appeared around both of her eyes. Before they went to bed for the night he was contrite, but he also was too late. Tania had known too many insecurities in her life to be reassured by a few words from the man whose inhumanity had shattered her.

"You will not ill-treat me ever again!" she declared, but even days afterwards had not the slightest idea how she might prevent him from doing just that.

Even without her excited anticipation of Andre's performance in the concert there, Pamela would have loved York Minster. She had not visited the city since she was a girl, and recognized now that at the time she had been too young to fully appreciate the Minster's atmosphere. Before the orchestra's final rehearsal they had wandered through the interior, letting the quiet of centuries seep into them.

Lights were being turned on to counteract the fading rays of a weak November sun. First the area around the altar and then the choir stalls were illuminated, drawing their attention towards the focus of the sacred building.

I do wish Tania had come, Pamela thought, and decided that when she and Andre returned here to explore York more thoroughly, they must bring his daughter with them. Her own mother had been happy enough to take charge of Mihail, and actually had been sorry that she would not be seeing Tania's baby that day.

The concert was taking place where the nave and transept converged, and when Andre left her to join the other musicians Pamela experienced a strange sensation. Walking away down the aisle as the Minster was cleared for the final run-through, she glanced back over her shoulder. For one moment before Andre reached his fellow instrumentalists, he looked small and isolated amid the grandeur of the building. But she sensed more strongly than ever since first meeting him, that Andre was not alone, that he never would be. He had spoken little of his faith, had rarely indicated what his true beliefs were, yet now she felt as certain as anyone could be that this husband of hers was a part of what this Minster stood for.

A shiver of recognition stirred the hairs at the nape of her neck, somehow calming all old anxieties while it excited with promises for their future. Stonemoor might be the house where they lived and created their family, but *here* they had come home.

This feeling of belonging persisted even while she investigated the narrow streets, raw with cold now that dusk was settling over the city. And the serenity increased when she finally entered the Minster again, and took her seat for the start of the performance.

As always, Pamela felt stirred when that initial hush overtook the audience. But today her intense anticipation was for more than a few hours of pleasing music. The overture now was the prelude to their personal fresh beginning, and she realized that she and Andre were to be united as never before in a life that was taking on a new sense of direction. The moment when Andre appeared for his first solo she smiled, more certain than he himself would be that the sounds his Stradivari created would be exquisite.

His first piece was well received: beside the pro-longed applause Pamela heard appreciative remarks from the seats around her. By the time her husband came forward to perform again, she knew that he had won over everyone present. This seemed to be confirmed when in the final surge of clapping, members of the orchestra joined the audience.

I do believe we might have survived that awful time when people were beginning to be afraid that, Andre could have come to England as a spy, Pamela reflected, and wished yet again that Tania was with them.

"I wish I had tried harder to persuade her," she admitted to Andre when she saw how elated he was at the end of the performance. "She seems to be on her own such a lot, with Gerald busy at the factory."

Andre smiled. "We must have a word with your mother, she appeared quite happy to look after both babies, and until Mihail is much older he is not going to enjoy outings like this, is he?"

Pamela grinned. "Well, I certainly don't relish the prospect of taking him out for a whole day, much less Tania's tiny daughter."

"Or our own second baby when that is here," her husband reminded her. "By the time the weather for long outings is with us again, we shall have another small person to consider."

As they drove back to the West Riding Pamela was still feeling contented. Andre seemed destined to have his skill acknowledged to the full. She herself had found interesting work in her antiques business, and it seemed as though her mother might be compensating for Ian's absence by becoming more deeply involved with the Malinowskis.

"I'm glad I've caught you in, love!" Mildred exclaimed, and then she looked again at the girl who had opened the door to her. "Eh, Tania love, whatever have you done to yourself? Did you have a nasty fall?"

"Er – yes, that was it, a fall," Tania responded hastily, then glanced about to either side as if afraid of what her neighbours might see. "I am sorry – please, you must come inside. I was just so surprised to see you here."

"I could tell that!" Mildred exclaimed. "Is it all right if I bring the pushchair inside?"

"Of course. I think perhaps that you should, we are too near the road here to risk leaving things outdoors." Tania went down on one knee immediately, to release the straps holding Mihail into his seat.

His firm young arms had outstretched towards her as soon as she appeared at the door, heartening her with the knowledge that her half-brother loved her unreservedly.

"Pamela Anichka is sleeping, I may spoil Mihail a little before she wakes. And now you must come upstairs to my living room."

When Mildred was seated in one of the armchairs, Tania smiled at her again. "I am so pleased that you are here. I have had no visitors since my father and Pamela came here last."

"Well, it was such a nice day for the time of year, and I didn't quite know what to do with his lordship here, not in somebody else's house. Pamela's made it that nice at Stonemoor that I'm a bit scared of owt getting spoiled."

Tania nodded. "But I am sure that they will be used to mishaps now that Mihail is becoming so adventurous."

"So I thought, why not take him for a nice bus ride?"

Tania struggled to gather her wits and find something to say. She had only just returned to the house. Unable to endure another minute she had set out with the baby in her arms, walking uphill until they were far above the dark stone terraces. Tramping onwards, she had reached the moors where she had stood looking all about her, thrilled and rather intimidated by the splendour of the range of hills where she had gazed into the far distance. Strangely, the space had bestowed a new sense of hope, it might have been that the landscape which seemed to stretch before her for ever, were reminding her of the infinite possibilities remaining in her life, of the fact that hope still endured, limitless.

Although Tania had come back here with no concrete idea of how she might remove herself from this disastrous present life, she had felt reassured that its traumas need not be endured for the rest of her days. Some mysterious force abiding in these Yorkshire hills had brought her more faith in her own ability to survive.

And now here was her old friend Mildred – being given tea and cake and then introduced to the new baby as she awakened and was brought down from the nursery. They were talking, almost as freely as in the past, whilst keeping an eye on Mihail, now tottering around to explore the room.

"Where did you fall then?" Mildred asked at last, unable to quiet her intuition that there was more than she had been told, behind the black eyes and swollen nose of the girl sitting across from her. And wasn't that a bruise on Tania's cheek as well?

"In the bath, I was very careless, I think. I hit my nose on one of the taps." But her attempt to laugh sounded false even to herself.

Mildred, who had seen the bathroom, struggled to picture how that might have occurred. "How on earth did you manage that, love?"

Instead of the rueful explanation she anticipated from Tania, she received a strangulated gulp, and a surge of tears.

"Eh, whatever's to do, Tania love?" she asked, and rushed to sit on her chair arm. "Everything's all right, isn't it?" she persisted, sensing suddenly that a great deal was amiss.

"I was going to tell no one," Tania blurted out. "It is I who got myself into this situation. This is all going wrong so soon, I was thinking that I have not made enough effort. And for the baby's sake, I have got to make sure we stay in a home— "

"Go on – tell me all about it."

"At first – at first, Gerald was very demanding. Do you know what I am saying? And then he began to be very angry if at any time I – well, denied him. I know he has these rights, but I think he has become unreasonable."

"And he hits you?" Mildred was appalled. The husband she had lost all those years ago had been gentle, both of the sons she had raised had been taught that kindness was not unmanly.

"Once only, or perhaps twice. This was a sort of accident. I did hit my face against the bath taps."

"Because he pushed you, is that what you're

saying?" Mildred Baker might be getting old, but she was not a blind fool.

"Not exactly, not so cold-bloodedly as that sounds. It was not . . . how do you say – premeditated?"

"But if he was in a temper that could be even more dangerous."

Mildred's enquiries drew out more instances of Gerald's brutality towards his wife, and encouraged her to ask one final question.

"Do you love him, Tania? Is that why you've stayed here, do you really love him?"

The girl considered for several minutes before replying. If she admitted the truth to Pamela's mother, they all would be told. They would insist that she must not remain with Gerald. They would be on her side. She was not so alone as she had supposed. And remaining here was not the only means of having a home. Suddenly, she knew that overriding everything that she would feel amid such an upheaval, would be immense relief.

"No, I do not love Gerald. I do not believe now that I ever loved him. I wanted to belong with someone, to have a home that was mine." She was weeping again, hardly coherent. "And he did not even wish to have the house that I liked."

Mildred helped Tania to pack clothes for herself and the baby, then got both Mihail and Pamela Anichka into their outdoor things ready for facing the November day. She checked the timetable in her bag, and had the four of them standing at the bus stop with five minutes to spare.

Tania waited up for her father and Pamela that night. Thankful though she was to have Mildred organize her into leaving Gerald, she was determined to explain everything herself.

Explanations certainly were expected the moment that they came in to be confronted with Tania's bruised face.

"Oh, my sweet!" Andre exclaimed, rushing to hold her and to examine the damage. "You have had a terrible accident."

"I have come home," Tania said. "The baby and I have come home. Gerald and I do not get on, we never have, not really."

"Has he done this?" Andre demanded, his voice incredulous.

"No. Yes. It was not that he hit me, not then, but we – had a kind of struggle."

"I will kill him! I will— "

"Andre," Pamela interrupted gently. "We must listen first, decide what must be done. And more violence will not help Tania."

"All the same . . ." Andre sighed, shrugged. "Tell me . . . tell me all of it."

"Presently. All I need to know is that we may stay here."

"Of course you must," said Pamela, recalling how uneasy she had felt at times concerning Tania.

"I cannot ever go back," her stepdaughter said. "Will you help me to learn what must be done to obtain a divorce?"

"We shall make quite certain that such a wretched marriage is ended," Andre confirmed, holding Tania to him. "It could take years, but we will ensure that you are free of him."

Hearing him, Pamela silently thanked the destiny

300

that had brought her this husband who seemed able instinctively to know what to do, and what to say. Divorce for Tania would not be easy when she had only remained with Gerald for these few short months. At this moment, though, the girl needed comfort rather than harsh facts.

Andre was right in believing that freeing his daughter of Gerald Thomas could take years. But at least that would allow Tania time for growing up, and for accepting these recent traumas.

I shall be glad when this wretched business is sorted, thought Pamela, and then a curious peace enveloped her. It was the same feeling that she had experienced in York Minster. A new certainty. There would be problems, so long as anyone lived problems remained. But the future was theirs. Mihail would, as always, give interest and direction to their lives, as would his tiny niece now sleeping upstairs. And there would be Mihail's brother or sister, as well. Stonemoor House would be a different place in a few years' time. And whatever happened they all would somehow be given the strength to persevere.

Chapter fifteen

The children were playing on the lawn which Andre had created for them at the back of their home, well away from the drive and the road beyond. Mihail, now almost four years old was in command, as usual, ordering the two girls to follow as he climbed the slope towards Stonemoor House.

"He thinks he is Edmund Hillary – look!" Andre exclaimed, placing an arm about his wife and drawing her against his side. His son had listened intently that morning while he explained that Everest had been conquered.

"Which one's Sherpa Tensing, do you suppose?" Pamela asked, smiling.

"Pamela Anichka, I think. I am afraid that Mihail still considers our Sonia too little for a major role."

The children were almost out of sight now, so close to the house that their heads were below the level of the window, but they could see the wooden stake with a grubby handkerchief representing Mihail's flag on the mountain's summit.

"No, do it properly," their son's voice drifted up to them. "Salute, now. Like this . . ."

Sonia had dropped her mother's old shopping bag half-way up the slope. It didn't even look like

302

something that a man who climbed mountains would carry, Daddy had shown her the pictures. And it smelled horrible, of cabbages and things.

"My turn, me be the Tween now!" she cried. She wanted to have a crown, and to wear the curtain that Pamela Anichka had trailed behind her. It was soft and you could stroke it, like Fluffy, her rabbit.

"It's not your turn," Mihail contradicted. He didn't want go back to the other game, Everest was more exciting than coronations.

"Well, *you* can't be her," Pamela Anichka pointed out. "The Queen's a lady."

"Me – it's me," Sonia persisted.

"We could let her," Pamela Anichka suggested. "You be the bishop again."

"*Arch*bishop," Mihail insisted, not to have his authority undervalued. "Well, just for five minutes then," he conceded, in a tone that reminded his listening parents how readily children pick up phrases.

"We'll be good at this when we've seen it all on television," said Pamela Anichka. She was old for her years, liked to get things right, and hadn't yet perfected her own playing of the Queen.

"Won't it hurt?" asked Sonia, her eagerness to take the role diminishing as she recalled Pamela Anichka's wince when Mihail had slammed the round baking tin 'crown' onto her head.

"You don't have to do it," Mihail reminded her. Acting out a ceremony when the reality might become boring anyway had palled. All he wanted was to watch the procession on that tiny screen. Daddy had told him there would be carriages, and lots of horses.

"Raining!" Sonia exclaimed, holding chubby hands

303

over her head as if to prevent the drops from soaking her blonde curls.

"Race you to the house . . ." Mihail loved racing. The two little girls were hopeless at running.

They were told always to use the back door, especially on days like this when showers had made the garden muddy, but the front door was nearer. He was approaching the drive when he saw the man striding uphill from the road.

"It's Uncle Tom!" he called back to the others. But then he checked, stood quite still and stared towards the visitor. "No, it isn't . . ." His voice trailed off because he did not understand.

The girls had caught him up. Sonia thrust one sticky hand into his and three fingers of the other into her mouth. They tasted of that horrid, dusty shopping bag.

"Don't," said Mihail, very much the older brother trying to help cure a babyish habit.

"Who's that?" Pamela Anichka asked.

"Just – somebody," said Mihail airily. "He might be coming because we've got a television." Grandma had been here since early that morning.

"Mihail? It is Mihail, isn't it?" the man said, nearing the trio.

The boy nodded energetically. "'Course. Who are you?"

"You wouldn't remember."

"I might. I'm four now. Well, nearly— "

"And these two?" the man persisted.

Mihail jiggled his sister's arm in the attempt to make her move. "My little sister – Sonia. She won't be three for ages."

Pamela Anichka, who tended to be wary of men, was lingering almost out of sight behind Mihail's back. But then the rain started falling more heavily, and Mihail hustled them towards the front steps.

As soon as the man saw Pamela Anichka he knew. Introductions were superfluous. He prayed that the child's mother would be here also. The lad had stood on tiptoe to press the bell. Andre opened the door and began chiding the youngsters for using the front entrance. And then he looked beyond them.

"Ian!" he exclaimed, and smiled. "Pamela," he called over his shoulder. "Come and see who is here . . ."

In the bedroom, which even on a dull day like this still appeared bright, Tania heard her father. Heat flared upwards from her breast to the crown of her head, and drained from her to produce a sudden shiver while her heartbeat thundered in her ears.

I cannot go down, she thought, and knew immediately that she could not do otherwise. She reached the bannister rail and felt its wood beneath her clutching fingers, while she watched her old friend Mildred greeting the man they both had loved throughout his long absence.

It was Pamela's turn next, bringing tears to Tania's eyes as she hugged Ian as though she had feared they might never again see him.

When Ian looked up it was so like that first time, that Tania heard her own gasp over the excited chatter in the hall. Even his expression seemed the same, that strange wonder, and a sense of recognition that always had owed nothing to previous acquaintance.

On legs barely able to support her, she began

descending the staircase towards him. No one but Ian had turned. Without exception they talked on, marvelling at his sudden return.

Somehow, though, when she reached the last step, the group parted to allow him through. And the children, even her own chatterbox of a daughter, grew silent.

"Hello."

"Hello."

They echoed each other's words, their smiles hesitant, but what harm was there in awkwardness now that his hands grasped hers. And then she was in his arms.

"Mummy?" Pamela Anichka had been perplexed for too long. Small feet came padding along towards her, a hand tugged at her skirt.

"This is Pamela Anichka," she said, lifting her daughter high in her arms. "We both live at Stonemoor, have done for a few years." There must be no room for confusion now, no more wasted opportunities.

Ian cleared his throat. "I could see who she was." Thank God the child did not resemble *that chap*.

Pamela had noticed how shaken Mildred appeared and went to place an arm about her. Shocks, even wonderful ones like this, could take their toll on ageing mothers.

"You could have let us know you were coming, Ian. Don't get me wrong, you're very welcome— "

"I should leave it, Pamela." That was Andre interrupting, more in command of emotions than anyone, and the ideal host. "I am so delighted that you are here, Ian. And today – when we all are gathered at Stonemoor. We must offer you a drink . . ."

Chairs were set out in readiness for watching the Coronation ceremony. The most comfortable armchair was proffered. Ian chose a sofa with Tania between himself and her daughter.

"No Tom?" he asked when Andre had gone to the drinks tray and Pamela was dashing out to heat up the kettle.

"At his fiancée's," Mildred told him, her own sudden sharpness surprising her. She had tried not to favour Tom in her affection these past few years, but Tom had always stayed at home, and next year would marry a Halifax girl.

"Good for him," said Ian smoothly.

Tania shuddered. It had not struck her until this moment that Ian could be married. He had been away so long and, since the groundnut scheme came to nothing over two years ago, had lost touch even with his own family. I can't bear this, she thought, but nor could she begin asking questions. Mildred and Pamela did not ask him, they either knew what his situation was, or considered it unimportant. But she needed to know, she needed that quite desperately.

Even the return of someone absent for years did not entirely distract them from events in London.

"You don't mind, do you?" Pamela asked her brother, going to switch on the set. "It is such an occasion, and we've been priming the kids so they'll view it all with a bit of understanding."

Ian grinned. "OK with me. Matter of fact, it was all the lead up to this that set me thinking. Time I came home."

"Where were you, though?" his mother demanded.

But the tiny screen was showing the London streets, rain drenched but lined with millions of loyal citizens. Ian indicated the scene before them. "Later – I'll tell you all about it."

Nothing had been the same since the day that man had come to Stonemoor House. His Uncle Ian. Mihail hadn't liked it when the grown-ups began talking. That had been as soon as they switched off the television when the Coronation was over. For a few minutes everybody was speaking at once, like when you were excited. But soon they were shouting.

His big sister had started it. He had felt frightened because Tania was a grown-up and they told you off for yelling at people. The man said something to her and she snapped back at him. "It was your fault in the first place. You ought to have known your own mind."

Daddy had interrupted then, sounding stern. "Be fair, Tania, you were the one who would listen to no one. All you wanted was a means of escape. You could not get away from here quickly enough. And to this day I do not know why!"

"It was because of Mihail, wasn't it, Tania?" Mummy's voice was softer than anyone's. She wasn't cross, she was sad. But not as sad as Mihail himself. They were blaming him. And he would never, never have made Tania go away.

Even now, ages and ages afterwards, he could feel that tight lump in his chest when he thought about Tania. He loved her so much, she had such pretty hair, and she sang songs to him at bedtime.

A sister, even an old one like Tania, sometimes was better than a mother or father. When Mummy told him off for being naughty Tania cuddled him better. Or *used* to cuddle, he added silently, remembering that he was the eldest among the small people at Stonemoor, and should not behave like a baby. And yesterday Daddy had explained that Tania would not always be here, she would live in another house, with Pamela Anichka and Uncle Ian.

He was going to be a pageboy, one day, and both girls bridesmaids, but he would not like it after the wedding. Sonia cried a lot when Pamela Anichka kept saying that she was going away. Sonia was such a baby, games with her would always be boring.

"We shall need your help," Mummy had told him. "You're such a big boy now that you will have to look after Sonia for me when I'm busy. You're good at thinking of things to do with her . . ." Mummy had been cross when he had made sick noises, and had only laughed when he'd shaken his head. But she didn't understand, no one did, he couldn't play with such a little girl, not all the time.

Although gazing out of the window from where he was standing on the windowseat, Mihail knew that somebody was watching him. He did not want to turn his head and look, but even he himself knew that curiosity would force him to do so.

It was Tania. Tania with her smile, and outstretched arms which locked around him when she sat at his side and gathered him to her.

"Why do you not like me any longer, little one?"

Mihail wished he *could* be little again – the littlest

one of all. Sometimes he hated being big. 'Specially when he was unhappy.

"What have I said, what have I done?" Tania persisted.

"Is it true?" he asked in a tiny voice. "What Mummy said – is it true?"

"Is what true, Mihail? You're talking in riddles— "

"I'm not, I'm not." Riddles made you laugh. And he would not laugh again, ever. "What she said when the man – when Uncle Ian came."

Tania did not question him again, she did not need to. She had been appalled that her stepmother had identified the truth, so carelessly and aloud, in front of the children. She herself had rushed the three of them from the room, but Mihail's eyes had told then that it was too late.

"I have always loved you, Mihail," she insisted, hugging him so tightly that he could hardly breathe. "And I always will. But I was a silly girl in those days. I could not see that mothers and fathers can have lots of children and still have enough love to make each one know they are special. You will not make that mistake, will you? Promise?"

"Promise," Mihail said obligingly, but without understanding.

"Oh, dear." Seeing his puzzled frown, Tania sighed, smoothed his curly hair. "Are there no times when Sonia is upset or unwell, and everyone here seems too busy to care about you?"

"I can play by myself. I did before Sonia was big enough. I have lived here a lot longer than her."

His half-sister smiled. "But I was too old for playing

when you were a baby. I had no friends, had not been in England very long."

"But you belong here . . ." This big sister of his had been at Stonemoor for always and always. Hadn't she?

Being here had not been the same as belonging. "I thought that I could make it all come right, that I could make a home where I would have babies that belonged to me. You see, as soon as I saw you I did want a baby just like you."

"Then why did you only get a girl?"

Tania's laugh was like her singing, it made him smile. And she hugged him close once more, before placing him firmly on the floor.

"I will tell you that another day, I think!" she exclaimed. "You ask too many questions."

"But you don't tell me the answers. Grown-ups never do!"

"We don't know all the answers, Mihail."

He smiled at her. She liked him, she had said. And she liked Stonemoor House. Daddy had said that one day it would belong to him, because he was the oldest son. When he was older still – not next year when he started going to school, older than that – he would ask Tania and Uncle Ian and Pamela Anichka to come and stay here. They might come at Christmas.

"Yes, Christmas," he said aloud.

"Never mind Christmas!" his mother exclaimed from the door. "It's bedtime. And you've still not had your bath."

And when I'm older, Mihail thought, I shall have a bath when *I* want. Or even have no baths at all.

He giggled to himself then turned to smile rather grandly at his mother.

"I was making plans," he confided, "for Stonemoor House."

She turned to smile at Tania, and winked.

After Mihail had been hauled off towards the bathroom, Tania lingered, gazing out towards the mauve-tinged summit of the moors. She would be sorry to leave Stonemoor House. Even marriage to Ian would not quite remove the affection she felt for her home. But she would be at peace living with him, just as she would be content anywhere, now. She had stopped struggling, had paused for long enough to allow her dreams to begin to develop into reality.

No one had known that Ian would come back. Even his mother had been unable to do more than trust that the long period out of touch with them all would help him come to terms with the past, only then could he be drawn back towards his roots. Even the anguish she herself had endured had all been a part of the plan. Someone once, it might have been long ago in Russia, had likened life to the wrong side of a piece of embroidery. It had taken her years to learn to look, and to wait, until all the threads began to form a picture.

312